Before becoming a writer, RON BUTLIN was a pop-song lyricist, a footman, barnacle-scraper on the Thames and a male model. Widely translated, his work has twice been awarded a 'Best Foreign Novel' prize. His previous novel, *Ghost Moon*, was nominated for the international IMPAC Dublin Literary Award 2016. He lives in Edinburgh with his wife, the writer Regi Claire.

D1458978

ALSO BY RON BUTLIN

NOVELS
*Ghost Moon*
*The Sound of My Voice*
*Night Visits*
*Belonging*

SHORT STORIES
*The Tilting Room*
*Vivaldi and the Number 3*
*No More Angels*

POETRY
*The Wonnerfuu Warld o John Milton*
*Stretto*
*Creatures Tamed by Cruelty*
*The Exquisite Instrument*
*Ragtime in Unfamiliar Bars*
*Histories of Desire*
*Without a Backward Glance*
*The Magicians of Edinburgh*
*The Magicians of Scotland*

DRAMA AND OPERA
*The Music Box*
*Blending In*
*We've Been Had*
*Sweet Dreams*
*Good Angel / Bad Angel*
*Markheim*
*Faraway Pictures*
*The Perfect Woman*
*The Money Man*
*Wedlock*

FOR YOUNGER READERS
*Here Come the Trolls!*
*Steve & FranDan Take on the World*

RON BUTLIN

# BILLIONAIRES' BANQUET

LONDON

PUBLISHED BY SALT PUBLISHING 2017

2 4 6 8 10 9 7 5 3 1

First published in Great Britain in 2017 by
Salt Publishing Ltd
International House, 24 Holborn Viaduct, London EC1A 2BN United Kingdom

www.saltpublishing.com

Salt Publishing Limited Reg. No. 5293401

A CIP catalogue record for this book is available from the British Library

ISBN 978 1 78463 100 0 (Paperback edition)
ISBN 978 1 78463 101 7 (Electronic edition)

Typeset in Neacademia by Salt Publishing

Printed and bound in Great Britain by Clays Ltd, St Ives plc

Salt Publishing Limited is committed to responsible forest management.
This book is made from Forest Stewardship Council™ certified paper.

*To Malcolm and Béatrice McCallum for their
unfailing friendship and support; for Anthony Pilley
and everyone who stayed at Barclay Towers or picnicked
on its roof; and for Regi, who picnics with me now.*

# BILLIONAIRES' BANQUET

# *Prologue*

B ARCLAY TOWERS WAS a split-level flat, four storeys above the Edinburgh streets. Four wearying flights of hard stone steps. The tenement was well over a hundred years old and when northerly gales swept down from the Arctic, its floor timbers shook, its large windowpanes billowed in and out like sails and, like a crows' nest lashed to the tallest mast, the whole top floor shuddered in the storm. That was in winter. Come summer the flat entered calmer waters.

For once, it was a hot evening and the window had been propped open. Five of them were crammed around the kitchen table in the alcove where the maid would have slept a century earlier. No maids these days, and so they'd helped themselves. When the Cat finally arrived, the special Midsummer's Eve spaghetti banquet was already over. She sat down. A candle was lit for atmosphere. Time for confessions, time to kill each other—

*What's the biggest lie you've ever told?*

*Your biggest regret?*

*Who would you most like to sleep with that you haven't already?*

Hume soon brought the search for after-dinner truth to a standstill. Said he'd been waiting for the right moment

3

and could wait no longer. Jumped to his feet. 'Back in a sec.' Rushed out into the hall . . .

'Where do you think you're—?' the Cat called after him.

. . . and returned a few seconds later, wine bottle in one hand and flourishing the latest edition of *Thought* in the other: 'Howzat!' He held the journal open at a double-page spread: *The Appearance of Reality and the Reality of Appearance, Dr S. Hume, Edinburgh.* 'Snappy title, eh!' He uncorked the celebratory Don Cortez. 'This'll get me a job. A real one, a paying one. Mrs. Thatcher claps her eyes on it she'll make me her chief advisor!'

Midway through taking his bow Hume winked, and killed the Electric Boy. Then with a quick one-two, killed St Francis and the Coconut. *Bam-bam-bam*, he was on a roll. Job well done, he left them to enjoy life for a few seconds longer.

Because those were the rules.

St Francis was the first to peg out, giving his best theatrical groan before slumping facedown on the table. Officially dead. Head on the tomato- and pasta-flecked pine, the once-upon-a-time junior priest counted out the regulation *one . . . two . . . three . . .* Then sat up again, officially resurrected. At once, he glanced towards the door. Glanced at it urgently. Gripping the table more firmly than he'd probably gripped any priest-school altar rail, he took a deep breath. Cleared his throat, stood up. 'Goodnight, everyone.'

Just then the Coconut rolled her eyes and uttered a lady-like shriek that turned into a contented sigh as she collapsed into the Electric Boy's waiting arms. Having given up the ghost, she gazed upwards expectantly. The kiss of life?

As for the Electric Boy himself – first to be killed, but still in the land of the living? Did their landlord consider himself one of the immortals? Hume took aim and killed him all over again. Direct hit.

Next, he turned his attention to the evening's first-time visitor - a friend of someone who'd been invited but couldn't make it. The instant black-haired, dark-eyed DD had come swaying in through the kitchen door with her midsummer smile and bottle of Blue Nun, Hume had locked on target. He'd launched into his well-practised routine of witty one-liners hinting at his more serious side, his hidden depths . . . and at bed.

Their glances met . . . and was that a *for-your-eyes-only* smile she'd just given him as he delivered the killer blow?

Back to the Electric Boy. Not still with us? Fucking McLazarus. Third time lucky. That was him eliminated, finished off, taken out. Dead, and no excuses.

Which left only the Cat, the last on Hume's hit-list. Taking aim and—

But she'd turned away to call after the no-longer priest: 'You'd better not keep me awake again half the night, Francis.'

'She speaks, she speaks!' cried the Electric Boy, who didn't need drink or drugs as he'd come into the world fully wired, and was so deep-down drowned in love with the Coconut that he'd clearly forgotten how to die. So Hume killed him again.

Then leaning across the table in one smooth unbroken movement, he was about to catch the Cat's eye when—

. . . she stabbed *him*. A vicious bee-sting of a wink. Venomous.

Killing *him*? But *he's* the—

She was pissed off.

Totally.

Because he'd been treating the lovely DD to some hospitable flirtation? But he and the Cat had their *arrangement*, didn't they? They were both free. Friends who frolicked and fucked, that was all. Not lovers. No love equals no jealousy. Has to.

Tonight, though, nothing could faze him. He'd be turning thirty next month and here, and not a moment too soon, was his first-time publication, the perfect alibi for his entire life to date. It vindicated six years' selfless dedication, commitment and round-the-clock study. Validation, if any were required, for the one-night stands he'd needed to get himself through. Forget trying to sublimate sex into ever-greater heights of analytical thought – he'd managed a month's consciousness-raising celibacy at one point, and nearly gone blind. But from now on, let the good times roll. No more signing on, no more on-the-side, cash-in-hand cramming ENGLISH FOR EVERYONE into roomfuls of foreign students. No more having to sleep in a cupboard. And so – Mr. Magnanimous – he raised his glass to toast the Cat as the evening's *femme fatale*.

It was then that new girl DD announced a MIDSUMMER MADNESS disco was being held on the outskirts of town, and did anyone fancy coming along?

Hume did, in spades.

The Electric Boy declined, which surprised no one as he almost never left the flat. *Ditto* the Coconut, whose recent skull-shaver of a haircut – intended to keep any stray strands out of open wounds and give the emergency room drunks that much less to grab hold of or be sick over – had gained her a new name, and *love*. After gazing deep into each other's eyes in a moment's wordless communion, the two of them disappeared to the attic upstairs. The Cat said thanks, but she wasn't up to it. Still wiped out after her finals. Needed an early night.

Hume gave DD his best puppy-dog look, a puppy-dog eager for walkies. Just them then.

'It's on the edge of town,' she pointed out, 'but we've still time to get a bus.'

The puppy-dog all but rolled over.

Straining on an invisible leash, he glanced back before leaving the kitchen to offer the Cat a half-apology/half-promise: 'See you.'

'Sure.' She winked, getting him right between the eyes – a friendly wink this time, more or less. 'Have fun.'

Out in the hall, Hume opened the door of the understairs cupboard: 'Just a mo, DD. I'll get my jacket.' He clicked on the light.

She all but gasped. Surprise? Shock? Pity? 'This is where you . . . live?'

Side by side, the two of them stood in the doorway and contemplated the low stepped-ceiling effect created by the underside curve of the staircase rising to the attic flat above, the books piled uneasily beneath the line of shirts, jerseys and jeans hanging on their nails. His narrow mattress covered the entire floor with only an inch or two to spare. It was a snug, windowless, Occam's Razor of a fit, but the perfect accommodation for his low-rent, low-maintenance life. A life that was about to change forever.

'Moved in here on the very day Margaret Thatcher moved into Downing Street. Got everything I need.'

'And what's *that*? Modern sculpture?' She pointed to a hefty piece of sheet-metal that hung along the back wall, free to swing loosely in its iron frame. It might have been ideal as an extremely large dinner-gong intended for an extremely large mansion, but not for a cupboard.

'Ah, yes. That's the Electric Boy's.' Hume moved into tour-guide mode. 'You'd think something that size would make my room smaller, wouldn't you? The paradox is – that *with* it, my room can become even bigger! Close your eyes.'

'What?'

He lowered his hand in front of her face as if pulling down an invisible veil. 'Close your eyes. Sometimes, DD, the world is *so* much vaster than it appears.' Bending down to avoid the low ceiling, he stood on his mattress. 'Infinitely vaster, in fact. Think Doctor Who's *Tardis* to the power 100.'

He reached across and gave the dinner gong a firm thump with his fist. CLANG-CLANG-CLANG-CLANG-CLANG-CLANG-CLANG-clang-clang-clang . . . the one note seemed to fill the cupboard's interior a thousand times over, suggesting the ever-greater reaches of boundless space lying far beyond.

'Fantastic, eh? Great for those thoughtful moments when—'

'When you're feeling a bit cramped?'

'That too,' he conceded. 'It's a homemade echo chamber, wired to the recording studio upstairs. Gives me an occasional glimpse of infinity, you might say.'

Also, the smaller the room the more likely was the occupant to score. No need to mention that, of course. But it was true. Like the first time he'd met the Cat in the university library. Him straying from the Logic & Epistemology section along a narrow corridor of stacked shelves to track down an essay by Poincaré on scientific method, and her coming from the opposite direction in search of a commentary on Russell's *Principia Mathematica*. Cartoon-like they'd backed into each other.

After mutual apologies, a quick chat about Poincaré and

Russell followed by coffee in the library's basement cafeteria, he'd invited her back. And fucked her. That was the great thing about his cupboard – no room in it to do anything else. Once the Cat herself moved into the flat, things had become even easier. Separate rooms, but spontaneous, no-strings siestas any time of the day or night. Their arrangement.

He unhooked his jacket from its nail.

'That's me and my glad rags, DD – let's go!'

As he clattered down the stairs to the promised disco and a let's-hope night of passion with DD, the apprentice philosopher felt a momentary twinge of guilt. *Unease*, rather, he quickly corrected himself. He'd gone off and left the Cat behind, alone in the flat – St Francis didn't count – in effect, abandoning her. Was she feeling sad, neglected? Lying slumped forward on the pine table as if she too had just been winked at and killed?

No, not the Cat.

And, anyway, he reminded himself, Wittgenstein had quite emphatically maintained that no one could experience another person's feelings, another person's pain. Close scrutiny of his unease would show only that he *cared* for her, which he did. Okay then . . . it followed that his sense of unease was not guilt, but genuine caring. He was feeling sorry for her at having to miss out on the disco. That was all. She'd been too exhausted to come out to play. She'd even said so herself.

So, no problem.

Besides, the two of them had their arrangement, didn't they?

He and DD had now reached the bottom of the stairs. 'Some Midsummer Madness, ma'am?' He held the street door open for her. 'Let's see how really mad we can be!'

# PART ONE

R UNNING STRAIGHT AHEAD from the Barclay
Towers' front door was a corridor – on the right the
internal staircase that led up to the Electric Boy's recording
studio in the attic, Hume's cupboard came next and finally
the communal kitchen. On the left were bedrooms one, two
and three – for the Coconut, the Cat and St Francis. The
corridor ended at a frosted glass door – a small bathroom. All
the rooms could be slept in; if the sleeper was well padded
and under five foot four, the bath was reckoned to be very
comfortable.

St Francis had the grandest room of all – a nearly intact
cornice, a black marble fireplace, brass light-switches and polished floorboards. Whenever his bed was near enough the bay
window, he'd prop himself up on one elbow to gaze out across
the city rooftops or stare down at the busy main street and
the tree-lined walks of Bruntsfield Links.

'Stunning view you've got!' Hume had commented as he'd
helped him get moved in that first day, rejoicing, as a true
philosopher should, at his fellow-man's good fortune. To the
windowless cupboard-dweller, of course, *any* view would have
been stunning.

St Francis had glanced quickly round. Would Hume mind
lending a hand?

- bed over to the other wall
- desk and chair next to the bed

- wardrobe to stand opposite the fireplace
- and so on

Twenty minutes' push and pull later, the new layout was in place.

Or was it?

Having lost God, St Francis no longer took anything for granted, not even the furniture: 'Still doesn't feel *quite* . . .' Could Hume lend a hand, again? Please?

The movables were once more Laurel-and-Hardied to and fro across the room. 'Yes, I think that looks just about . . .'

Only to pause, glance round, then ask a moment later if Hume would mind lending a . . . ?

But Hume had run out of hands.

From the day he moved in, the former priest had kept his furniture on the move. By Midsummer's Eve his elegant wooden floor had come to look like an ice rink scored by the blades of a thousand skaters.

It was after he had been killed off and was resting head-down on the kitchen table that St Francis had glimpsed the perfect layout of furniture for his bedsit room – everything exactly as it should be, as it had to be. Next moment, his part in the Midsummer Eve's celebrations finished, he'd hurried back to his room and got straight to work.

The bed was dragged across the floor. The brick-and-plank bookcase was reassembled, relocated and rebuilt.

Status check?

*Looking good!*

Next, the bane of his existence – that two-door, double-coffin-effect tombstone of varnished gloom, his wardrobe. Victorian, cumbersome and too top-heavy for its own good.

He hugged the monstrosity as best he could in a fingertip embrace. Two half-steps, half-staggers later his fingers began to slip. He hugged it tighter. Another half-step, half-stagger backwards and—

CRASH!

He got out of the way just in time.

Quarter of an hour later, the job was done.

The room felt good, he felt good.

Good? Hell, he felt great! Then, precisely as in Brother Michael's catechism class when everyone had been told to sit in silent contemplation of the wonder and perfection of God, he relaxed in his armchair the better to gaze around at all he had accomplished.

It was almost with reluctance that he eventually reached for his *Mammoth Book of Crossword Puzzles*.

From time to time during the next couple of hours he indulged himself with an occasional appreciative gaze around the room. Then it was back to Puzzle Number 25.

Puzzle Number 25 completed, he moved on to Number 26.

And got stuck. Seriously stuck.

He needed to *focus*, needed to concentrate. Again he glanced up—

His desk! What on earth had he been thinking? Next to that monstrous dark roar of a wardrobe, the poor thing was down on all-fours, almost cowering . . .

St Francis was so near tears he gritted his teeth. Clenched, swallowed. Month after month spent moving the same pieces of furniture around the same room, and he had achieved *nothing*. Absolutely nothing.

Once again his room's disintegration, its imminent collapse, felt as close as ever. He sensed the long night stretch out before him like an unspoken threat and, beyond it, all the nights to come . . .

# 2

MIDSUMMER MADNESS WAS being held in a dead-end housing estate, an overspill reservation for the unwaged and unwanted at the edge of town. Probably there had once been plans to turn the abandoned church into a community centre, arts venue or the like. Probably the money had run out. It usually did. Which left the derelict shell standing isolated in a part-demolished nowhere land, adrift on a sea of waste-ground mud. This far from the main road, however, it was the ideal location for something late and loud.

Hume, DD and the others they'd run into *en route* arrived shortly before midnight. They picked their way across churned-up mud littered with charred timber, rubble, plastic bags and pools of rainwater. As though being shown their way out of the wilderness, they were guided by the noise ahead and the flicker of strobe lights that came through the few stained glass windows not yet bricked up.

'Kirk Alloway aa in a bleeze!' misquoted someone.

'A real Tam O' Shanter Night Out!' answered the surrounding darkness.

Inside, the stone pillars and flagstones shook. The bass pounded the floor beneath them, they could *feel* it – 500 watt satanic music booming up from the Underworld. The air was rank with plaster dust, the stench of drains, sweat and dope. Mostly dope. The last of the ecclesiastical furniture and fittings – old pews, lengths of padded seating, the hymn board, rolls of rotted carpet – had been ripped out and heaped against the stone walls to clear some floor space for dancing. Having set up his turntables where the altar would have been, the DJ was flanked by two bathtub-sized speakers aimed directly at the congregation and loud enough to blast them all into Kingdom Come. Filled to the brim with blessed-again water, the font kept the beer cans chilled. The pulpit was still *in situ*, hovering ten foot or so in mid-air and reached by a narrow curve of staircase.

*Romantic potential* if ever he saw it. Hume led DD up the shaky wooden steps. At the top he stood aside, bowed to mime helping a lady into her carriage. He lowered the minister's small hinged seat and then, in the absence of a holy cushion, rolled up his jacket to provide for his ladyship's ease and comfort. The perfect gentleman.

They were able, just and no more, to peer over the carved lectern where the bible would have rested and watch the dancers cavorting below, crammed, sweating and mostly stoned. The pulpit shuddered to the bass beat.

Alone at last. Hume produced a can of McEwan's Export. It spurted open. Just in time he jerked it to one side to protect her ladyship's evening dress.

'Scottish Champagne, tinned.' Courteously, he wiped the lid before offering it.

'Your good health, sir,' DD toasted him.

As they passed the single can between them, Hume talked, shouted. Yelled. The music had been cranked up even louder. He discoursed at full volume on the revelries below – from the elevation of their pulpit they could observe how the dismantling of organised religion revealed what lay suppressed within us all, the elemental energies seeking expression . . .

His philosophy paper, he went on to scream at her, was perfectly timed for the new era, it was a radical polemic that gave good old-fashioned values a good old-fashioned kicking. Taking Bradley's iconic essay 'My Station and Its Duties' as a starting point, it presented a profound re-evaluation of the politics of individual responsibility that Mrs. Thatcher would . . . and so on, and so on.

His lady companion hardly heard a word but nodded politely every so often, drank her share when it was offered, and occasionally made comments that he didn't quite hear. They drank to his catchphrase: 'A modern ethics for modern times'.

Beer finished, he scrunched up the empty can and tossed it down to the *hoi-polloi* below. Bending nearer to bellow into her ear how beautiful she looked, he calculated that this was the moment to make his move. He had intended to conclude the compliment with a kiss . . .

. . . when all at once his eye started winking and winking and winking like he was playing the murder game again, and couldn't seem to stop.

Who could he have been pretending to kill just then in that romantic retreat of a pulpit, in that wrecked church? Not DD, surely? Was it a *tic* of conscience re his cavalier abandoning of the Cat? An emergency light pulsing on and off, warning him that—?

Something of his distress must have shown for, after a moment's hesitation, DD reached up and touched the side of his face, lightly, as if unsure she should. Her touch was calming, soothing. Under her fingers the jumping nerve eased gradually, and relaxed. When it finally settled, she withdrew her hand. Then, awkwardly almost, she leant towards him and kissed the hurt place better. Their first kiss. A healing one. Hers.

I T WAS AFTER eleven, the eve of the longest day of the year was drawing to a close and daylight fading to a final pale sheen. The Cat gazed out at the topmost branches of the nearby trees – clear-cut silhouettes, tangled bluish-black against the approach of darkness. She was tired. She wanted to go to bed, but remained there at her bedroom window tapping her fingers lightly on the glass. Hume was welcome to his disco. She needed sleep, sleep and more sleep.

For several minutes she stood watching the red tail lights of the traffic make their way up the left-hand side of Bruntsfield Place and the white front-lights come down the right. Most taxis returning to town had their orange FOR HIRE signs switched on. With a fingertip overlaying one of them, she tracked the taxi's descent for as long as she could before it vanished from sight towards Tollcross. Then she tracked a second, a third. When no more appeared, she found herself, instead, pressing briefly on the pane to extinguish the glow of a sodium streetlight. Then, as if to turn it back on, she removed her finger, restoring its brightness. And moved on to the next. Turning them off, turning them on . . . *Dab* . . . *dab* . . . *dab* on the glass – such a familiar gesture . . .

So, so familiar . . . It reminded her of . . . ?

Reminded her of . . . ?

Then she had it. Reminded her of when as a little girl she'd dabbed her tiny wet-paint fingertips onto a sheet of paper to form the separate faces of a dice and see all its six sides at the same time – just like when she and her twin sister Kirsty stood in front of the mirror, one facing and one with her back turned to it, so they could see all of themselves at once. *Dab . . .* for one. Then *dab . . . dab* next to it, to make two. *Dab . . . dab . . . dab* in a slant to form three; a square of dabs making four, same again with a dab in the centre to make five. Amazingly, six could be two things at once – either two columns of three, or three horizontal lines of two. A magic number, someone told her.

$1+2+3=6$ and $1\times2\times3=6$. Magic.

The more she'd learned about numbers, the more she came to feel their magic – negative numbers, unreal numbers, imaginary numbers, irrational numbers, transcendental numbers. Zero. Infinity. Most exciting of all was the isolated splendour of primes, their elemental mystery. Appearing always unpredictably and out of nowhere, they were like so many meteors fallen from the skies. They were not of this world.

The boys at school had seemed very much like primes – most were low order, of course, basic 3s, 5s and 7s, puzzling as all boys were, but nothing special.

From the day that Kirsty died the Cat had felt a responsibility to live and achieve for them both. She worked twice as hard in class and in the playground played for two. In time, this came to mean having to kiss and, eventually, fuck for two. Kevin, in the unknowable realm of faraway sixth year and whom she imagined as the intriguing and sexy prime number 179, she chose to be her fifteenth birthday present to herself. Letting him fuck her was like discovering the first in a new number series.

That girl DD and her disco . . . and Hume. Who cared?

But smearing her fingerprints on the window pane wasn't quite what she'd had planned for the evening . . .

It had been late when she'd left the University Library to set off home across The Meadows. The pitch-and-putt course had been deserted except for a couple of old men playing in the dusk. She'd stopped for a moment to share in the pleasure of their final game—

That was when, standing there in the near-empty park, she'd glanced up at the darkening sky and been suddenly overwhelmed by a sense of the absolute *certainty* of every single thing around her. It came out of nowhere. It blew her mind, utterly. The structure of every tree, every leaf, every blade of grass, the dynamic tension concealed in every drop of water vapour making up the scattered clouds, everything in the world, herself included, had felt *perfectly* integrated and in place. For one brief moment the individual atoms of the entire universe became a massed chorus crying out YES! in affirmation of existence.

How wonderful and how *obvious!*

She'd almost yelled back 'YES! YES! YES!' in reply.

Having hurried the last hundred yards or so home, she'd pushed open the street door, taken the stairs two at a time, ready to grab Hume the instant she was inside the flat. Ready to fuck his lights out – a fuck to celebrate the entire universe.

Only to find visitors. Visitors and cold spaghetti.

Through the window she could see the cosmic wheel had turned a few inches since that glorious moment in the Meadows. A few inches, a few million light-years. Orion, the Plough . . . She bit her lip remembering the great Cosmic Rush that had coursed through her.

And now?

She waited. Waited.

And nothing.

The wrong time? The wrong place? The wrong universe? The wrong *her*? Certainly felt like it sometimes.

Time for bed. She really wanted to sleep, but knew she wouldn't. Too wired up. What she needed was a bedtime story, something to soothe her, absorb her, something to drowse her until she slipped into dreamland. A few relaxing pages on the life and times of Nicolas Causanus might just do the trick. Although the sixteenth-century bishop had begun with the notion of God considered as the Infinite Being, his meditations had opened the way for Leibnitz and differential calculus. Fascinating work. Yes, Nicolas of Cusa was the man for tonight! She'd let him do the work while she turned the pages. After four years of pure mathematics she was tired of having to think for herself.

The girl who'd called herself DD (and what sort of name was that?) had straight black hair, very like hers, but shorter. Not bad looking in a clean-cut, determined sort of way. If Hume made it back from MIDSUMMER MADNESS alone, he was going to get dragged from his cupboard. If he was knackered, they could have fun unknackering him. Maybe throw in a few lesbian fantasies involving the clean-cut DD – that sort of pillow-talk never failed.

But in the meantime?

She reached over to give Nelson a scratch behind the ear. Woolly and one-eyed, Nelson was her closest companion. The lifesize wooden sheep, a jumble sale bargain, had been love at first sight – the nearest she'd come to it, anyway. He'd clearly been in the wars, poor soul, him and his one remaining eye. Loyal, trustworthy and a good listener with no desire to offer advice or share his problems, he was a vast improvement on most human beings. A modest green tuft of rug to stand on and the occasional pat was all he required. His kindly single-eyed gaze beamed benevolently on everyone alike. She gave him a wink, a friendly one, and reached for *Mathematics: A Historical Perspective*.

Okay then. Causanus. Her eyes glided over the first paragraph . . .

Maybe she'd get Hume to tie her up? Or, for a change, tie him up? Perhaps a spot of role-play - teacher and pupil, master and slave? Nelson could always be relied on to turn a blind eye.

Hume was primal, truly *primal* in every sense, pure *ego* held together by selfishness and lust. None of the usual body/mind dilemmas with him, no fragmenting into good bits, bad bits and lost bits. Not so much handsome as relentlessly keen. Emotionally a complete dud. Which suited her.

Back to Causanus. One page nearer to infinity and—

Their very first get-together in his minimalist cupboard had said it all. Less a no-frills fuck than a full-on mutual assault, and with no post-coital awkwardness afterwards.

'That was really good, Cat. Thank you.'

She'd laughed. 'Needed it, did you?'

'Doesn't everyone?'

At last, she'd thought, a truly eligible prime, solid to the core. Strangely, it had made her feel secure. Usually she felt secure only by herself.

They got together whenever the mood took them. They never went out as a couple and were free to see other people whenever they fancied. No deception, no jealousy, no feeling trapped - she'd felt better than she had in years. Even better when she'd moved into the room directly opposite his cupboard. No need for phone calls or letters – a glance across the kitchen table was enough, or a light tap on the door. Occasionally not even that. Pre-breakfast she'd sometimes woken to find him already climbing into her bed, or *vice versa*. Movable feast, movable fuck. Stability of a sort. Her work had taken on an intensity that was truly exhilarating. Just like when she'd looked up into the sky above Bruntsfield earlier, she'd come to *sense* almost physically the ebb and flow of mathematical forces, allowing her to solve problem after problem with an elegance that delighted her tutors.

An hour later, she looked up from her book. Had she managed to get herself so absorbed in Causanus that she'd not heard Hume return? It wasn't so *very* late. He might have come back by now. It was possible.

Maybe she should go and check?

# 4

HUME AND DD stumbled out of the derelict church into the early morning light, their ears numb. They had hugged and kissed away the hours on their high-above-it-all pulpit and now were brought back to earth, picking their way across the muddy waste ground. The opportunity to help his lady step over an oil-slicked puddle gave the gentleman the perfect excuse to take her hand, and keep it. Arms around each other, they passed through a gap in the protective hoarding that enclosed the demolition site.

No hanging around, not here. Keep moving. After taking a quick recce in every direction to make sure there were no late-night teenagers still out and about, no skinheads on the prowl for something, or *someone*, to do – Hume hurried them along a street of mostly boarded-up windows and the occasional burnt-out top floor. They moved rapidly past front gardens converted to dumping grounds for broken-down beds, abandoned cookers, rain-sodden carpets and sidestepped a gutted mattress that had been left to rot on the pavement. Stripped of its doors and wheels, a car rusted at the street corner. Total silence – no dawn chorus apart from the occasional screech and scuffle of seagulls among lidless bins.

Keep moving, keep moving. Street after deserted street was taken almost at a run until they reached the relative safety of the main road and its early morning traffic. Finally Hume slowed down and turned to ask her real name.

'DD, like I said.' She was a little out of breath.

'Is that short for something?'

She whispered into his ear, shyly and so low he could hardly hear: 'Diana *the Damned!*' Then, before he could ask her to repeat what she'd said, she ran off in the direction of town, her high heels clacking.

The Council estate now a good half-hour behind them, Hume was growing seriously impressed. With DD leading the way, they had entered a part of Edinburgh where the socio-economic grades seemed to ratchet up at every corner. C2, C1, B. Here the newly risen sun warmed litter-free streets and hedges, its fresh new-day colours soaked into well-groomed lawns, neat flowerbeds and rockeries. The houses had front porches, extensions, conservatories like shrunk-down glass palaces. There were cars, garages. From the trees and gabled rooftops, early morning birds celebrated another day of peace and plenty.

As they advanced deeper into the Grange, with its sandstone walls, wrought iron gates, gravel drives, greenery and the occasional secluded mansion, Hume reflected on Seneca. Few philosophers had been particularly well-off, but at one point Seneca was reputedly the richest man in Ancient Rome, only just in time having the good sense to hand over his latest and grandest palace to emperor-pupil Nero whose jealousy was beginning to look murderous. Taking Seneca as a model, it could surely be argued that the search for wisdom and the pursuit of wealth need not be mutually exclusive. Indeed, it might be possible to maintain that—

'Nearly there!' DD called out. They were now in Dick Place.

To date, apprentice philosopher Hume had scorned luxury with its trappings of arrogance and privilege. But now, surrounded by the kind of affluence and solid success that can only be expressed upmarket property, he couldn't keep a certain awe out of his voice:

'You live around *here*?'

'Oh, yes.'

'Really?'

She turned to him. 'Do I look as if I don't?'

'No, no . . . Not at all.' Back-pedalling the tone of surprise, he switched to mock-charm: 'For such grace and beauty as yours, anything less than a turreted, three-storey Victorian townhouse would be . . .'

'You can come in, if you want.' She'd stopped outside a varnished wooden door set in the high sandstone wall that bordered the pavement. She unlocked it.

A moment later, they were standing on a stone-paved path. Two lines of low trees arched above them – a guard of honour that all but blotted out the light.

The gate was relocked. Then DD was beside him again.

'It's only a small place really,' she said.

'Oh.' Hume nodded.

*Only a small place* was precisely how Seneca was reported to have described his dangerously magnificent palace. The very rich love to play these games of self-deprecation, making their wealth seem of little consequence, thus glorifying it and themselves even more. Hoping to stay alive a little longer, Seneca had, of course, been desperate to be taken at his word.

Further down the path, the trees gave way to a modest parkland of lawn, bushes, more trees, flowerbeds; trellised greenery adorned the distant wall. From the back, the townhouse looked even more impressive: full-length windows, ornamental stonework, some stained glass, a couple of balconies. The roof had a shooting-gallery of decorative urns set along its edge, plus a gargoyle at each corner and more chimneys than he'd ever seen on one building before.

They passed under a second archway to arrive at lawn number two – houses like this didn't have *drying-greens*. More flowerbeds, more bushes, a weeping willow that trailed its branches in the waters of an ornamental stone pool where a life-sized stone nymph bathed. A half-dozen or so golden-brown fish swam around her base.

'They're koi.'

Hume began working on the punchline of a possible joke about how they wouldn't look quite so coy if . . . when DD added:

'Cost over fifty pounds apiece, some of them.'

No joke then.

'My rent is to feed them twice a day.'

The small wooden summerhouse was painted yellow, with one door, one window, slatted shutters and a metal pipe sticking out of its green-felted roof for a chimney. A Marie Antoinette-style imitation shepherd's bothy? It really *was* small.

'Is this where you live?'

'For the moment. Usually I just play here.' She went up the two wooden steps to the door.

Play? Marie Antoinette and her rustic fantasies was maybe not such a bad guess – some kind of full-sized doll's house for adults and their adult games? Sounded promising. He followed her in.

The single room contained an easy-chair, a bed, a small

table, a few shelves. A wood-burning stove stood in one corner. Most of the floor space was taken up by a piano, a baby-grand.

'It's Mrs. Chisholm's piano. She lives in the main house. Dora is elderly and doesn't play much now though we sometimes go through some duets. She's a really good player. This was her practice room.'

Hume crossed to the window – the archways of flowers, the weeping willow, the nymph carrying an earthenware pot on her shoulders, tilted in readiness to pour herself a shower. Would there be a timer-switch set to send water splashing and bubbling over the mossy green nakedness of her stone breasts, before it trickled down to refresh the koi carp swimming below? First light had now finished colouring in the whole garden. The birds were building up to full chorus . . .

A perfect morning for the perfect summer's day to come. Midsummer's Day . . . So far the entire night with DD had been perfect, too. From the moment he'd first seen her come into the Barclay Towers kitchen, then the Madness disco, the pulpit, walking her home through the empty streets.

Time to move into romantic mode. That was what he was here for, wasn't it? Romance.

*Romance?* Like the master and slave games he and the Cat had been getting into recently? Ordering her to lie back and lift up her skirt; and then, as he took her, she'd sometimes stage a slaves' revolt and spit in his face, before begging him to fuck her as hard as he could. Good fun at the time, but with the inevitable aftertaste of disgust. Not that that lasted, of course – it never did – and soon enough the two of them would be at it all over again. Lust-and-disgust, lust-and-disgust . . .

Was that what he wanted here?

Of course not.

He wanted to take DD in his arms and kiss her. He wanted her to become the woman he'd always longed for, the woman he'd been hoping for all his life. The queen of his heart, the princess of his dreams.

They'd kiss. Their lips, their tongues would touch . . .

His hand would begin undoing the buttons on her blouse . . .

He'd lead her over to the bed where—

But then afterwards? Sneak a look at his watch to see if the buses were running yet?

Was that what he wanted? Was that what he really—?

## 5

THE CAT PUT Causanus aside, got up and crossed to the door. Very slowly turning the handle, she pulled it open a few inches. She stepped into the corridor.

Not a sound from Hume's cupboard.

From St Francis's room came the muffled *rumble-grumble* of cushioned furniture being dragged across bare floorboards.

Holding her breath, she put her ear against the cupboard door.

Was that whispering she could hear? There was no light showing in the gap around the door frame. She pictured the two of them snuggled together in the dark, talking. Which, considering what she knew of Hume's post-coital charms, meant they hadn't yet got round to sex.

Or maybe the whispering was all her imagination? Should she ease the door open, just the very tiniest, littlest crack?

Not a good idea.

She tip-toed back to her room, back to Causanus. Next sentence, next paragraph.

Another paragraph.

Of course Hume was free to do whatever he liked, with whomever he liked. Just as she was.

But still.

It was after three when she went out into the corridor again to check on him.

Still nothing.

She strained and strained to listen . . .

Finally she opened his door.

Nothing. No one.

Having been to the toilet, she returned to her room and changed into her night things ready for bed. That was the plan. Instead, she sat down in her chair. Not reading anymore, not thinking even. Sitting. Feeling calm, quite calm. Wasn't she?

After a while she began to get chilled. She'd go to bed soon. The trees were starting to take on the faintest hint of colour, the sky shifting from a faint pearl-sheen emptiness through to the very palest blue. No traffic apart from the occasional taxi or early morning delivery van. Dead, dead silence.

This same time last weekend she'd been lying in a man's arms, thinking about Gödel's Theory of Unprovability. They'd met at a party near Cameron Toll, gone back to his bedsit on Dalkeith Road, some coffee, some chat, then bed. Quick fuck, then Gödel Gödel Gödel. Walking home through Marchmont an hour later she'd turned into Spottiswoode Road, and for a split-second been dazzled by a sudden streak of early morning sunlight reflected from a top-storey window. All at once and for no reason she'd found found herself thinking of Kirsty . . . but almost immediately begun wondering if there were equations to describe the tensions she could see in the glass, tensions that would allow a sheet of fragile transparency to curve itself so gracefully in its frame and yet not shatter? Might a part-differential equation be sufficient to describe the rate of change in its—?

Then she'd laughed to herself. The middle of the night and here she was, fascinated by a window pane? She'd turned away to carry on home. And that's when she'd felt its broken shards inside her.

She could feel them now, cutting into her.

She remained in her chair, Nelson at her side, her fingers gripping then letting go the knotted tufts of his stuck-on wool. Gripping . . . letting go . . .

That glass with its sudden arc of reflected light. Kirsty.

She remembered the two of them standing side by side at the top of the staircase. Kirsty telling her she could fly: *Why go down slow, clumpity-clumpity-clump?*

Kirsty shifting her weight from foot to foot as though to better concentrate her centre of gravity. Kirsty taking her hand, raising both their arms. The two of them on their tiptoes like high-board divers, holding their position until they'd gained perfect balance, total poise. *One . . . two . . . three . . .* they'd pushed off to soar effortlessly up into the air, their perfect arc of flight that—

Was that a door opening?

But it was only St Francis. She heard him go into the kitchen, fill the kettle and rinse out the teapot, all the while humming to himself as the water came to the boil.

From far below down in the street came the screech of brakes as a taxi stopped outside. Hume had come home in a *taxi?* No chance. Maybe the girl DD was rich?

Then the cab door was slammed shut. The taxi started up again and, after doing what sounded like a U-turn, the driver headed back into town.

She waited, hoping to hear the street door bang shut, the steady thud of a man's footsteps coming upstairs. She waited . . . waited.

No banging door. No footsteps. Not a sound. No one had come in, no one had been returning home. Not to this stair.

She heard St Francis retire to his room.

How long before she pulled the downie from her bed and wrapped it around herself, how long before she lay down on the floor as she'd done night after night all those years ago, in tears and hugging herself for comfort?

A few minutes later she stood up and pulled on her dressing gown.

## 6

S T FRANCIS WAS feeling pretty tired. Repositioning his desk had been more laborious than he had anticipated, but the resultant fallout elsewhere in the room proved minimal. A few ornaments switched around, his armchair relocated, his Descartes poster rehung and that was that. He sat and completed crossword Number 26.

The new layout of furniture seemed to be holding up. Could he have finally cracked it – as casually as that?

A well-deserved cup of tea, then bed.

Tea brewed and brought back through. Returning to the room after a period of absence, no matter how short, always occasioned deep anxiety. The Heisenberg Uncertainty Principle. To leave the room and re-enter violated the unique relation between the observed and the observer. Sometimes with distressing results.

But not this time. No. Quite definitely – and surprisingly – all was well! He'd gone out, and he'd come back . . . and nothing had changed.

The layout was holding.

But for how long?

The threat of disintegration . . . and with disintegration would come despair.

It was when they'd been walking out of the chapel together one day that his class teacher, Brother Michael, had explained to him why despair was a sin. 'Young Francis . . . ,' the priest had placed a friendly hand upon his curly head, '. . . despair is a denial of God.' As usual, St Francis had swiftly ducked away from the Brotherly attention and the words of comfort and guidance.

Now that he no longer *believed*, of course, St Francis was free to wallow in a sea of despair. If he wanted, he could let himself sink effortlessly, fathom by drowning fathom, ease himself down to the ocean floor, to rock bottom. At rock bottom he could surely rest, surely find peace.

Brother Michael had been forever flashing his beatific smile, forever laying a too-friendly hand upon the junior priests' heads, putting a too-supportive arm around their young shoulders and offering words of comfort and guidance. That aside, confessing to him had become a glorious game for the whole class – forget owning up to the trivialities of missing early mass, telling lies or petty stealing. Offer him, instead, anything that involved sinful thoughts, wet dreams and the like, and Brother Michael was soon heavy-breathing, turned within seconds into a hot and panting priest – but safely kept behind the slatted grille of his dark confessional. The tackier the confession the more entertaining and extractor-fan loud became the breathing.

St Francis took another sip of tea. Easy enough to mock that sorry excuse of a lay priest getting stoked up in the half-darkness of his lonely wooden cubicle, but what about himself? Night after night alone in *his* solitary room?

Came the day when the first junior sinner had no sooner gone into confession than he came rushing straight back out: 'It's Brother *William*! Brother *William*!'

Game Over. No one messed with Brother William. His tonsure, robe and rosary might fool God Almighty Himself

– but not the boys. Brother William was Bad News.

Just then St Francis heard a knock on his bedroom door. Probably Hume wanting a late-night chat.

'Come in.'

But it wasn't Hume.

## 7

D'S FIRST 'COMING alive' as she called it, had happened when she was four. She'd been about to dash pell-mell down the corridor and out the back door to play in the garden . . . when she found herself brought to a sudden stop. Just like in a game of 'statues', she'd remained *frozen*. She wanted to quit her room, longed desperately to be out in the sunshine running across the wet grass in her bare feet. But . . . she couldn't. She had no idea why – she just *couldn't*. Instead, rooted to the spot, she was held there, her body tensing tighter and tighter, her heartbeat slowing and the same words repeating over and over inside her: *I won't go, I won't go.*

Next, a most amazing thing happened. Everything around her – the flower pattern on her bedroom wall, the pink of her bedspread, the wild-eyed energy of the white horses galloping through the surf of their painted beach – everything suddenly became *intense*. The room with herself at its very centre was charged with an almost unbearable sense of anticipation. A kind of pre-storm, electric stillness that—

Then, with an abrupt rush, she'd come alive for the first time. Like a dam bursting, it felt. Utterly, utterly glorious. She'd cried out with relief, jumped into the air, run round and round the room like a dog in a craziness of sheer exhilaration.

That summer, she taught herself to slow down her heartbeat. She learned to concentrate. She practised. Standing legs apart, feet pressed down on the floor, she'd take a deep breath, tense every muscle of her body until it locked rigid, clench her fists so tight her fingernails cut into her flesh . . . and stay like that. Forever, it seemed. As her heart gradually slowed . . . and then stopped. And time itself stopped. Then, when she could bear it no longer, she'd all at once let go - her heart would kick-start itself and begin beating again. The glorious relief! The joy!

These were the good days. On bad days she lived as if she were held on the palm of someone's hand, a hand she feared might close around her at any moment, and crush her.

A year or so later she heard for the first time about the torments of hell. It was then that she adapted the nickname her parents had given her and which was intended to stand for Darling Daughter and Darling Diana - re-christening herself Diana the Damned. Her secret name expressed how she sometimes felt. As she grew older, it became like a secret part of her, a part she could trust.

Immediately she and Hume were inside the summerhouse, DD slipped off her shoes and sat down to rub the soles of her feet. It had been a long trek home. She glanced over at Hume standing at the window. She'd never told anyone her secret name before. Why this evening and why *him*, Mr. Glib, of all people? What had made her whisper it to him like that, then go running off down the street? *If he runs after me*, she'd bargained with herself, *I'll let him sleep with me*.

So, was that what was going to happen now? Perhaps, but not any time soon by the look of things. Ever since he'd come in, Hume had been staring out the window, with his back to her. Not saying a word.

Shy? Not him.

Screwing up his courage to make his move? Perhaps. But she'd not figured him as a slow starter.

Surely not still thinking about his essay . . . ?

She went across and touched him lightly on the arm. 'Admiring my garden? Great for sitting in.'

'Oh?'

Stuck for words, or meaning *she* had a sunlit garden while he only had a cupboard? She'd try again.

'Really nice first thing in the morning, don't you think?'

'Hmmm.'

'You *don't* think?'

What the hell had he come back with her for if he was just going to stand and stare out of the window? Now he'd seen how she lived, he didn't fancy her anymore? She blundered on: 'Not that it matters. You don't need to *think* here. This summerhouse is a no-thinking zone.'

'Oh.'

'Ever tried not-thinking?'

'Eh?'

'Think about it.'

Which, thank goodness, made him laugh. Not a hearty guffaw, a split-your-sides laugh, more of a micro-chuckle. But it was a start.

'Fancy trying it?'

He turned to face her. 'Trying what?'

For the first time since they'd met, he seemed uncertain. So far it had been mostly *his* jokes, *his* philosophy-flirtation banter, keeping himself firmly on solid ground, *his* solid ground. Coming here seemed to have brought things to a halt. Was it her? One last try.

She met his gaze. 'Not-thinking, of course.'

41

Again, that uncertainty. His gaze slipped briefly out of focus, then he seemed to recover. As if something had clicked back into place and everything was once more on track, he smiled at her:

'Like this?' Next moment he was reaching forward to take her in his arms. So very smooth. So very predictable, and now so very mis-timed.

She stepped away. 'No.'

'I don't understand.'

'That's a good start.'

Another micro-chuckle of uncertainty.

She didn't like taking the lead. It wasn't *her*. She felt clumsy. Best to start again, get herself back on solid ground. She led him over to the bed. 'Now, you lie down here.'

'All alone?'

'Go on, stretch right out. Make yourself comfortable.' If nothing else, she had certainly regained his attention. 'Feels good?'

'Yes. But if you were to lie here beside—'

'Just relax. Enjoy it. And no thinking, remember.'

'Remember? But the very concept of memory implies—'

'Shh! No thinking, I said.'

Which made him grin. Progress.

She sat down at the piano. 'Do you like Mozart?'

He shrugged. 'Always sounds like eighteenth-century *muzak*. Too pretty and neat, too many powdered wigs and buckles.'

'Oh?' So much for the greatest composer ever. 'How about this, then?' She'd give him one of the *nocturnes* she'd had to learn recently, something in the minor with maximum expression and feeling.

As she played, Chopin's restrained and dark-shifting bass chords overlaid with a melody of heart-breaking longing provided her with the perfect soundtrack for a review of the evening so far. Leaving her fingers to follow their well-practised route among the keys, she let herself drift back through scene after scene: coming to the flat, meeting Hume, the disco, the abandoned church, walking home together through the deserted streets . . . The man was all intelligence and charm – *surface* charm. What lay beneath would be far more interesting, it had to be. Like most men, of course, he couldn't see beyond his own cleverness, his own glibness, and had succeeded in totally charming himself. It would be hard work to dig beneath, getting down to what really mattered. Plenty of time, though.

She glanced across to see how His Glibness was enjoying Chopin.

With his eyes closed, it seemed.

*Cloth-eared twat.*

She was about to shock him awake with some jagged Bartòk when that familiar part-ecstatic, part-terrifying *rush* swept over her. Her heartbeat was slowing . . .

She stopped playing. Her hands remained raised above the keyboard . . .

Everything in the summerhouse was suddenly so *vivid* – the spread of black and white keys under her hands, the sheen of early morning sunlight spilling across the polished surface of her piano and flooding into the shadows on Hume's face . . .

When she came alive again, all that remained were the nail marks on her palms like faint stigmata.

43

## 8

S T FRANCIS WAS so surprised when his unexpected visitor walked in that he jumped to his feet, and then just stood there. Couldn't speak. Couldn't move even. Simply stood and stared.

The Cat's long black hair was unbrushed, her face pale and without make-up, arms loose at her sides, cream-coloured dressing gown over a white nightdress, bare feet. A dishevelled-looking Sleeping Beauty. He couldn't believe it – the Cat had knocked on his door in the middle of the night? The Cat was wanting to see *him*?

'Can I come in for a short while, Francis?' She wasn't smiling or being the least flirtatious. 'I really need to be . . . with someone.'

'Of course. Of course. You're welcome.' He watched her cross to the chair at his desk. She turned it round to face him, and sat down.

'Just to sit a little, if that's all right. Carry on with your crossword. I'll be quiet. Won't disturb you.'

'There's still tea in the pot, if you fancy some. Really no trouble.' It would be a pleasure, he wanted to add. Also, if she had a mug of tea she'd maybe stay longer.

She shook her head and said nothing.

'Cat . . . ?'

She didn't look up.

'Has something happened? Anything wrong? Is there anything I can do?'

Still she didn't look up.

'Just let me know if there's . . .'

'Yes. Now I'm here I'll be fine.'

He reached for his pen and crossword. The Cat *here*, in his room. A miracle almost. Sitting with her hands on her lap, hair down in front of her face.

A miracle, like that day in the catechism class when kindly Brother Michael had held up his hand to stop one of the junior priests midway through reciting his *Credo*. To announce the impossible.

The snowstorm of the night before had still been blizzarding heavily enough that morning to bring the city to a near-stand-still. Cars moved in a single-line crawl, buses were running late. All during the first class, stragglers had come in with sodden clothes and excuses, and been good-naturedly nodded to their seats. There was an air of festivity, of lawlessness almost. Coats and scarves steamed on radiators that rattled and gurgled to push out maximum heat. Snow-brightness filled the classroom windows. Outside, the winter day seemed to glow.

Then had come the impossible. The miraculous.

'Why don't you boys go out and play in the snow?' The lay Brother had smiled at them. Such an inviting smile.

What? The entire room gasped. Playing in the snow was utterly, totally and strictly forbidden. Completely and abso-lutely. Always.

'Yes, boys. I'm sure you'll enjoy yourselves.'

Had the world become flat overnight? Had the Pope issued a new edict permitting joy and anarchy?

'Can we throw snowballs, sir?'

'Of course, Francis.' Such an indulgent tone of voice. 'How can anyone play in the snow without throwing snowballs?'

From GENTLE KINDNESS, its everyday expression in stationary mode, as it were, Brother Michael's benevolent smile accelerated through POSITIVE CARING to GLEEFUL ENTHUSIASM. The class were baffled, incredulous.

'Are you saying we're to go and play outside *now*, sir?'

'Of course, of course! No time to waste. Get out there, boys!' Next moment, he was holding open the classroom door. 'Have fun!'

St Francis glanced up from his crossword. The Cat was sitting exactly as before – half-turned towards him, dressing gown folded over her knees, hands still on her lap. She seemed to be biting her lips. Nervous? Uncertain? He asked again, 'Is anything wrong?'

Without looking up she answered, 'Please, Francis, just carry on with your crossword. You don't have to entertain me. Really.'

He nodded and went back back to his crossword, filling in several clues with random letters . . .

As he squeezed the snow between his hands to make his first snowball that morning, he'd glanced up and caught sight of Brother Michael gazing down at them from the classroom, his beatific smile firmly in place. The saintly man then made a snowball-throwing gesture . . .

Within seconds the boys were tearing around in circles, pushing each other into the snow, rushing up and down the front steps, taking cover behind railings and ornamental urns only to bob up again and let fly. And all the time yelling, screaming, shrieking and snowball-pelting . . .

Until . . .

'STOP THIS AT ONCE!' And again: 'STOP THIS, I SAY!'

Brother William! Standing at the top of the short flight of steps. Glaring down at them. He was furious.

They halted in mid-throw, mid-yell. The snowballs dropped from their hands onto the churned-up snow. No one moved.

'INSIDE, THE LOT OF YOU! NOW!'

Punishment awaited them and they knew it. Brother William. His red-faced, spittle-flying anger. His double-fisted rage. They stumbled up the snow-trampled steps.

As he'd edged through the doorway, Francis had tried to protest that Brother Michael said they could go out and play in the snow. Brother Michael had said they could throw—

'DON'T LIE TO ME, BOY!' The accompanying blow sent Francis staggering into the doorpost.

Inside the front hall they were made to stand in a long line, every boy now chilled to the bone.

'HOLD. OUT. YOUR. HANDS.'

With measured tread, Brother William worked his way down the line, belting each boy in turn, two full-strength strokes. *Thwack! Thwack!*

Kindly Brother Michael followed a step or so behind, smiling his ever-beatific smile.

The Cat had just asked him something.

'Pardon?'

'You don't mind me being here, do you, Francis?' Hardly above a whisper. So hesitant. Seeking his reassurance. The Cat?

'Of course not. You're really welcome. Are you sure there's nothing I can do for–'

'No. Thank you.'

Not knowing what else to say, he randomly lettered in another clue. Then another.

*Thwack-thwack!*

Each *thwack* of Brother William's leather tawse had been succeeded by an even more intense version of Brother Michael's beatific smile. It flitted across the lay priest's smooth face like a shaft of purest sunlight.

But why wasn't Brother Michael speaking up, protesting?

Francis was next.

'Out with your hand, boy.'

*Thwack-thwack! Thwack-thwack!*

'And again. For lying.'

THWACK! THWACK!

Skin, nerve and bone dissolved until only raw flesh remained. Flesh that started to burn and burn and burn.

Too young and too unknowing on that day of miracles, and drawn, bewildered, into the confusions of the adult world for the first time. But he'd got it a few years later, got what had really been going on. *Bastards. Perverted bastards, the pair of them.*

The Cat had just cleared her throat: 'You trained to be a priest, didn't you?'

He looked up. 'Not exactly. I – I sort of stopped before really getting started.'

'But you did train a bit? Took part in services, in prayers, in masses and things?'

Sometimes the Cat could be a bit of a tease with the way she dressed and acted, a real flirt. Not with him, of course. Never even a hint of it. No doubt she could recognise a life-long virgin when she saw one. For once, though, she was paying him close attention, very serious close attention. He felt flattered. Overwhelmed slightly.

'I took part in services, yes. As an altar boy.'

'Sort of an apprentice?'

An apprentice to Our Brother of the Beatific Smile who got his rocks off watching little boys being beaten?

'Well, sort of, I suppose.'

'Good.'

To his complete surprise, she came across and knelt down at his feet.

She mumbled, 'Did you hear confessions?'

*Never*, was the true answer.

She bowed her head. Her long hair fell forward as if its jet-black glossiness were about to pool itself on his lap.

'Confessions?'

His solitary room, his confessional. Then he understood. Her visiting him like this in the middle of the night had to be some kind of game. A version of the confession game they played round the kitchen table, only a more private version. More adult. Hume wasn't available tonight and so the Cat was making do with him? OK, he'd follow her lead. Her seriousness, her pretend shyness and lack of flirtation were probably all part of the rules. He nodded, 'Oh yes. Sometimes I heard confessions.'

'That's what I hoped.' She raised her head. 'It was Kirsty who made up Angels and Devils.'

St Francis: 'Pardon? Who's Kirsty?'

'My twin sister. She was the first angel.' She lowered her head again.

He could hardly see her face for the downward sweep of hair falling like a veil across her eyes.

'Angel? I don't understand.'

'What do you have to say to get things started? *I confess* or—?'

To steady herself, she'd let her fingertips rest lightly on his knees. Her nails were painted a soft pink.

'You say: "Forgive me, Father, for I have sinned."'

He placed his left hand on her shoulder, then, almost trembling, leant forward and breathed in the scent of her hair. Like apples. So very, very feminine.

She fumbled for his hand. 'Forgive me, Father for I have sinned.'

He didn't get the twin-sister bit, but maybe that was some kind of secret darker self needing to be discovered and set free, and that's what she meant by Angels and Devils. He began stroking her hair. Very, very lightly.

'Yes, my child.'

'We were six years old. Kirsty had climbed up onto the sofa back and stood there, her toes gripping the folds of the throw-over. I crawled under the hearth rug where I was a devil trapped in darkness, and when I peeked out I saw her stretching out her arms as wide as she could, ready to make her angel-of-mercy flight down to hell to save me. The brightness from the wall-lamp made her curls glow reddish-blonde, like a halo almost.

'She called out *"Father, Son and Holy Ghost!"* which we decided was a more Angels-and-Devils version of *Ready, Steady, Go!* Then she jumped. We rolled about, laughing and shouting, and getting all tangled in the rug. When we agreed I'd been saved, it was my turn to be the angel. That was the game.'

She paused. Several very long seconds passed. St Francis continued to stroke her hair.

'You're doing very well, my child,' he whispered. Too right she was. He had started getting hard.

'Then one time, when it was my turn again to be a devil, I waited under the rug while Angel Kirsty balanced herself on tiptoe on the sofa, ready to leap into the air . . .'

How thick and soft the Cat's hair was. Brother Michael sitting in the shuttered darkness of his confessional and Brother William battering the hell out of them – really, who cared?

'*Father-Son-and-Holy* . . . Except that this time, to make the game go even better, I . . .' An even longer pause.

'Yes, my child?' Should he kiss her hand?

'. . . I reached out and gave the sofa a . . . a secret shake . . . to help the angel on her way . . .'

St Francis breathed in deeply. The scent of the Cat's skin, her perfume. Her skin's warmth. He let his fingers trail through the softness of her hair.

'Father, I can't go on like this. Not anymore. I need . . . I need someone to . . .'

This was surely his cue. He pressed his lips to the top of her head.

The Cat continued: '. . . cried every night . . . really bad nights . . . lay where her bed had stood . . . wrapped myself in my quilt . . . pretending . . . her arms around me . . . hoping to . . . to wake up and find her . . . still alive.'

St Francis was no longer listening. He was rock-hard.

Quickly, he moved into full priest-mode babbling about love and redemption, the purity of confession. Telling her she would be made innocent once more.

For a moment she seemed to have gone limp. He tilted her face up towards his and was bending nearer to—

'You bastard!'

The Cat had jerked herself back out of his reach. She was

glaring at him. 'You fucking bastard, Francis. You creep. I came in here for . . . and all you can . . . You FUCKING, FUCKING BASTARD!' There were traces of tears on her cheeks.

'But . . . but, Cat, I don't . . . I don't understand . . . I thought you wanted . . .' He watched her scramble to her feet, pull her dressing-gown tight about her.

Next moment, she was stumbling out the door.

For several minutes he sat in his chair without moving. First light was already slanting into his room through a gap in the curtains. He stared down at the unexpected shaft of sunlight lying at his feet . . .

Then he leant forward, dipped his finger into the brightness as into the shallowest stream. It was the merest trickle, but one whose course he was quite unable to alter.

## 9

THE CAT WOKE up late the next morning, feeling even shittier than she had the night before. Hume and St Francis - fucking clowns, the pair of them. The one following his prick everywhere it went, spattering sperm over any woman stupid enough to get within range; and the other a religious fuck-up, dry-humping furniture around the room for his nightly thrills.

She hated them, hated them both. Really fucking *hated* them.

Noon had been and gone. The sun had long ago cooked her to stifling sweat-heat. She threw off the covers. Nelson was peering over at her from his patch of green. Though he himself had clearly been up and about for hours, his fluffy body-language held no hint of censure - he seemed to be grinning, rather, giving her a kindly nod and a benevolent blink of his one glass eye.

Feeling a few degrees cooler, she rolled over and turned her back on the sun. She was determined to doze off again, to sleep her way through the rest of the day and the night to come.

If only.

A few minutes later she dragged herself out of bed.

'Being nothing but wood and wool has its advantages, eh Nelson!'

Out in the hall, Hume's door stood wide open, his cupboard still empty. No Hume, no dark-haired stranger.

Coming back from the toilet, she found the Coconut waiting at the bottom of the internal stairs.

'It's a lovely day. A lovely Midsummer's Day. Fancy coming to celebrate? Tea and hash cake on the roof; we'll be starting soon.' She added that the Cat could turn up whenever, and Hume and St Francis too, if they were around. Perfect roof-picnic weather, quite windless, and they'd be there for hours. 'Please say you'll come, Cat. Tell everyone!' gushed the girl-in-love. She glowed. She was radiant. Her *Is everything all right?* was followed by a quick hug before she rushed back upstairs.

The Cat stood in the empty hall. Still in her dressing gown at nearly one in the afternoon, did she look so *very* miserable? So clearly in need of that friendly hug?

Probably.

Other people's happiness was tiring. She returned to her room, slid open the top window to let in some air, pulled the curtains shut and climbed back under the sheet. A soothing near-darkness. With any luck she'd sleep right through the rooftop picnic.

For the next half-hour she tossed and she turned. Finally she sat up.

Forget that sad pair of clowns – who needed them? One click of her fingers – and they were gone! Forget last weekend's pointless post-party fuck. Another click of her fingers – and it was gone, too, along with all the other post-party fucks she'd lived through and forgotten. One final finger click – and goodbye to self-pity! Gone, and good riddance.

Today was Midsummer's Day, the fulcrum of the year.

She'd be given her degree in a few weeks. A First for sure, everyone told her. A new start.

Okay then! Time to get started on her new start!

Out of bed. Quick shower. Brush her teeth, brush her hair. Back to her room to get dressed. Brand-new clothes for a brand-new girl. That was her, after all, Miss Brand-New M.A. (Hons).

Wasn't she?

On with her t-shirt. Her latest. Red with *Riemann Rules* written across the chest. She'd inked the letters herself in a moment of post-finals' euphoria, even managing to hint at a few non-Euclidean surfaces by letting some of the curves traced out by her pen follow her own. Sexy, and multidimensional – the perfect definition of pure mathematics. At the very least, it was a conversation piece. On the back she'd settled for a tasteful scattering of prime numbers loosely framing a mathematical quote from the great man – the *zeta function*, his proposition which so successfully determined the distribution of primes, and yet had resisted definitive proof for over a century. Enigmatic? Inspiring? Well, it inspired her, which surely counted for something.

She was giving her hair one last brush in front of the mirror when she found herself bending forward, breathing out slowly to make the glass mist over. What did the afterlife hold for brand-new her? The Afterlife – another game that she and Kirsty had made up. Taking turns, they'd breathe on their bedroom mirror then stare into the clouded glass, pretending it was a gypsy-teller's crystal ball. As the condensation faded, they'd hope to catch a glimpse of the man they would fall in love with and marry, to see the grown woman they'd one day become, and maybe even be shown the house where they'd set up home. The Afterlife lasted only for the length of time it took for their breath to dissolve, of course, its ghosted outlines becoming fainter and fainter as it faded, leaving behind the ever-unformed and unseen future.

But not today. The glass cleared almost immediately, and if her future had been revealed, she'd missed it.

She was suddenly in tears. Not much, but enough. Love? Standing there at the mirror, she knew less about love now than she did when she was a six-year-old playing with a pretend crystal ball. Even sex, which at least had the *potential* of intimacy, had been reduced to mutual masturbation with Hume or else to one-night stands with no more significance than choosing where to cross the street and hardly lasted much longer than her childhood breath dissolving on glass . . .

Angrily she wiped her eyes clear. Fuck's sake, what was the matter with her?

All done, all finished.

She pressed her forehead against the mirror. Forget The Afterlife – she'd settle for getting through the next couple of hours.

Her lipsticked party smile in place, she heard lover boy come through the front door whistling his triumphant return. Actually whistling, the fuckwit.

She went out into the hall to greet him, give him a BIG smile:

'Have fun, did you?'

'Yeah. She's a nice girl.'

'Seeing her again?'

'Maybe, you know how it is.'

'How is it?'

Just then she heard the Coconut shout down from the top

of the stairs that they'd better get a move on if they wanted some cake.

'Come on, Hume. Party time!'

'Where are we off to?'

She shoved him towards the carpeted stairs that led up to the Electric Boy's attic flat. 'The fun's just about to begin.'

The entrance to the roof was in a storage room, a dumping ground for old recording equipment. Empty spools, half-dismantled tape decks and speaker casings were stacked along the walls, draped in dangling tangles of recording tape and electric cable. More empty spools and cassettes littered the floor. There was a smell of damp and a vague hint of mushrooms, and only the sunlight coming through the open hatchway, a rectangle of clearest sky-blue, looked fresh and unused – the gateway leading to an afternoon of hash cake and other people's happiness.

For easier roof access a homemade ladder had been nailed to the wall. The loose rungs hammered onto the shuddering plasterboard felt unsafe enough in themselves, but the Cat knew that worse was to come. She'd been to picnics on the roof before – the flat section was a windswept plateau of patched felting across which loose cables from the TV aerials trailed in all directions. Most dangerous of all – there were no railings guarding the five-storey drop to the street below.

She clambered up into the full glare of the June sun.

As always, the view was spectacular. So high above the streets and houses, she could see the whole of Edinburgh spread out below: the tenement roofs and church spires, the office blocks, the Castle, Arthur's Seat; in the distance were the Pentland Hills, the Firth of Forth glinting in the sun and the cat's cradle of red girders that was the Forth Rail Bridge. Directly above, as if torn from an advert for the Seychelles and Sellotaped invisibly into place, was a cloudless azure sky. A perfect summer's day.

'Hi there, you two!' called out the hostess. 'You're just in time.'

The Coconut was there with the Electric Boy, plus a few Mohicans, Heavy Metal Men and their groupies, including school-leaver Josie. Spread on the flat section of roof was a large Sunday-school picnic kind of tartan rug covered with plates of food and bottles of wine. Salami and cheese, rolls, a dish of butter already melting in the heat, some pickles, and homemade hash-cake. The Cat's breakfast.

Treading carefully, she and Hume circled the group; only a few feet away, the forty-five degree slope of slates rushed unfenced to the roof's edge.

'The sky's near-perfection of blue,' began Hume once they were safely seated on a couple of cushions and with their backs against a chimneystack, 'suggests innocence, the colour of a new-born baby's eyes, the human soul in all its pre-lapsarian purity. In fact, Plato says that the soul remembers . . .'

The Cat was saved by the Coconut coming over to give her a slice of cake and a glass of wine. She smiled. '*Bon appétit!*'

'*Bon amour!*' the Cat replied, giving a friendly thumbs up.

Josie got to her feet, probably about to go into the strip-tease routine she always did when she was stoned. She took a deep drag of her joint, then called out: 'Cabaret time!'

The Cat looked on as the teenager performed an inviting bump-and-grind to a chorus of 'Hey, Big Spender!' from the Mohicans and Heavy Metal Men. With everyone watching her and clapping in time, she wiggled and giggled herself once round the edge of the tartan rug. High-kicking and hip-thrusting, she was less than a yard from the plateau's rim – had she no fear? At her age she probably believed she was immortal and the world had been created for her entertainment alone. Getting stoned and getting laid – it was all one big laugh. Laughter without end. Amen. Still too young to take life, or death, personally. Returning centre-stage she addressed her audience, demanding to know who was ready to see some of the sights of Edinburgh.

Hume had caught the Cat's eye, and winked. Had they actually been playing the murder game, his wink would have killed her. For the moment, she would ignore it.

The Coconut had once asked her if she fucked so free-and-easy because she had no respect for men, or because she had no respect for herself? The question had brought her up short and made her think. Well, at least until the next fuck.

But from now on she wanted things to be different.

The dope-chorus belted out 'Big Spender' grand style while Josie slipped off her purple top, button by teasing button. When the Coconut grinned over, the Cat grinned back like a good girl. A grown-up girl. A girl with self-respect. A woman.

Hume had winked again, and abruptly turned away to claim an eyeful of the entertainment on offer. The Cat ignored this second invitation to go into her death throes. The would-be stripper even had Kirsty's rusty-blonde hair. Her slow-motion slither-and-tease out of the cheap silk blouse finally over, Josie was now completely topless except for a string of coloured wooden beads that looped down over her breasts. Slowly her gaze swept across the audience and then, letting the tip of her tongue slide along her lips, she took hold of the hem of her shiny pink-red skirt and yelled out loud enough to be heard above the 'Big Spender' chorus:

'WHO'D LIKE TO SEE SOME MORE?'

While half-listening to Hume's mock-serious commentary on how this groupie stripping herself naked was, in fact, a genuine *tableau-vivant*, a flesh-and-blood metaphor-in-action of Man's deepest longing to return to a state of Innocence and Grace, the Cat decided she'd play the game. She'd die. For the fun of it, if nothing else.

The scene, according to Hume, was a kind of Morality Play in Reverse which would restore the roof and everyone on it to the Garden of Eden. With a wink he tried to kill her again.

To the Cat at that moment, a couple of minutes' R.I.P. suggested a well-timed break, a welcome pause from living. Given the splendid, open-air rooftop setting with its near-Bayreuth scale of city backdrop – vast skyscape above, hills and sea in the distance – not to mention the competition from nubile Josie, she was determined to take centre-stage and make her death as dramatic as possible. She'd put her heart and soul into it. Some staggering about, some screams, maybe even a few last words.

A teasing glimpse of black-lace underwear brought the 'Big Spender' chorus line to a wolf-whistling, catcalling frenzy.

She'd certainly have to pull out all the stops. Time for a final pre-performance hit from the joint before passing it along.

Josie had unzipped her skirt, and let it drop. She was barefoot, curling her toes around the heap of cast-off silk to keep her balance. Standing at her full height, raising her hands high into the air. Her reddish-blonde hair caught the radiance of midsummer light, and became haloed. She was rising up on her tip-toes. Rising higher and higher.

*Father, Son and Holy . . .*

At once, the Cat was on her feet. And before she knew it, she was rushing across the roof towards the young girl. Her arms outstretched in front of her to—

# PART TWO

# I

LIKE SHE'D BEEN travelling in the wrong direction for longer than she could remember . . . and travelling was all she could ever do until things stopped for good. Or bad. A few nights in a wrecked portacabin; someone's garage with a piece of loose cardboard jammed in the broken window; a builder's skip. Stopping places. Coming back to find the portacabin gone, the garage window fixed, the skip collected.

For her, Edinburgh was really a thousand islands – sandstone cliffs, shopfronts, superstores, minimarkets and tenements – and around each one of them, around the smallest spit of land even, was a cement beach where she could sit with her blanket and plastic cup out in front of her, washed up on the shore of that never-ending surge of sea. Days were the traffic's ebb and flow, pedestrians, shop lights. When night came, when everything was closed and shutting her out, she was the reflection that looked back at her from dark windows.

Today she was outside Discount Furniture – outside a softness of chairs, a comfort of sofas and beds.

There was only her, only the plate-glass. See-through, see nothing. Break the window to break into – what?

The future?

Most times she was too exhausted to get to her feet, to heave herself up from the cement beach. Easier to keep her eyes closed, to let herself be carried backwards and forwards by invisible tides: so many days, so many nights . . . And before the days and nights? Before she'd started wandering up and down the edge of the sea, wandering the shore of these never-ending tides? Before she'd started travelling in the wrong, to the wrong? Before she'd—?

A handful of loose change rattling into her cup . . .

Bringing the city to a standstill, making the sea pause. Inviting her to speak . . .

. . . but she couldn't. She couldn't. Not a word. Too exhausted to say thank you.

The tide roaring around her once again.

So she sat and breathed, turning the air into mist, clouding her stretch of pavement, covering her blanket and her cup, covering herself. Hiding herself. The people trampling past, the way they looked at her . . . Yes, she was hidden, invisible.

But she had a name. Megan. *That* came from somewhere, from someone. Someone chose her name even if they didn't choose her. But she didn't choose to be her. Didn't choose when day came, when night came. Struggling to keep on her feet, struggling to go this way, that way.

Right direction? Wrong direction? The direction she was facing.

Till here. Till this stretch of pavement. Till now.

Yes, a name. Megan. Hers.

## 2

WHILE THE OTHERS tried to comfort the naked girl who now sat shivering wrapped in the picnic rug, Hume and the Electric Boy went as far down the slates and as close to the edge of the roof as they dared. Clutching the side of a chimney stack, they leant over and looked straight down to the dizzying street below. The same as usual. The same line of shops, the same stone tenements directly opposite. The same traffic heading to and from the city centre, the same pedestrians. Everything the same as usual, as normal.

A five-storey drop – and everything was normal?

Gradually calming down, Josie managed to sob out that she'd seen the Cat get to her feet, but then, at the very last minute, she had turned away to birl herself round again.

'. . . and when I looked back she – she'd vanished.'

'Cat! Cat! CAT!' Calling out her name, Hume and the Electric Boy covered as best they could every dangerous inch, clambering down into the gulleys where the roof dipped, crawling on their hands and knees along the slopes. So did the Mohicans and the Heavy Metal Men. They peered down from every side. If she'd fallen to the street there would surely have been the sound of sirens by now, there would have been an ambulance. Police even. Could she be playing hide-and-seek among the chimney stacks? There was nowhere else, unless she'd vanished. Literally.

Could she have tripped and fallen through the open

trapdoor, with no one seeing her? Hume squinted down into the dimness – no one there.

But surely she'd have screamed?

Or could she have done it deliberately? While everyone else was distracted by Josie, had she simply upped and gone without a word? It hardly seemed likely, but . . . ? Otherwise, she'd still be on the roof. Which she wasn't.

Hume helter-skeltered down the ladder and out the attic room, through the Electric Boy's flat and down the internal stairs, calling her name.

No Cat. Her room looked the same as usual, probably just as she had left it earlier. Difficult to tell.

He'd only winked at her. It was a game, that was all. He couldn't have *killed* her. Vanishing like this, she'd need to have been vapourised, for fuck's sake.

He went right through the flat, pushing his way into every room, waking up St Francis. Checking the kitchen, the bathroom, the Coconut's room. Last of all, he looked into his cupboard.

Was it his fault? She'd gone because he'd spent the night with DD? Couldn't be. No. They had their arrangement. Whoever you want when you want, and no strings attached. He'd stuck to it. She'd not gone away because of him. Wouldn't have, couldn't have . . . NO!

The Electric Boy's echo chamber hung in front of him, its discoloured alloy a confused violence of swirling dark reds, greens and blues.

Next thing, he slammed the palm of his hand hard against it, making the sheet metal jangle in its frame. NO!

Slammed it with his clenched fist – BOOM!

Hammered it with both fists – BOOM-BOOM!

The pain in his fists, sweat running down his face—
BOOM-BOOM! / BOOM-BOOM! / BOOM-BOOM!
BOOM-BOOM! / BOOM-BOOM! BOOM-BOOM! BOOM-
BOOM! BOOM-BOOM-BOOM-BOOM-BOOM-BOOM-BOOM-
BOOM . . .

. . . until the reverberations ebbed away, leaving behind only the indifference of his books lined up on their shelf, his clothes hanging on their nails.

Leaving his knuckles skinned and bleeding . . .

When everyone was sitting round the kitchen table that evening, St Francis told them that the Cat had looked in on him briefly during the night. She'd seemed very upset about something, but hadn't explained.

They went over the possibilities again, and again. Too stoned or too distracted by Josie, no one had been looking at the Cat. While everyone had been watching the striptease, she must have simply gone off. Through the trapdoor, down the tenement stairs, out the street door and away. For whatever reason. Quite simply, she'd wanted to disappear, had seen the opportunity and taken it. People did sometimes. She'd been working too hard. She'd looked exhausted, depressed. Should they tell the police? Shouldn't they have told them already? They agreed to give her a few more days. She'd turn up. Had the Riemann formula on her t-shirt become a spell for invisibility? joked Hume.

No one laughed.

The Coconut and the Electric Boy were the first to break things up, retiring upstairs to their recording studio/love nest. Which left St Francis and Hume. Starting off with the Cat's vanishing act, they quickly moved on to discuss the epistemological and ontological implications of perceived disappearance, the notion of absence, the concepts of being and non-being. Then they went to bed.

A few days later, Hume was surprised to discover his knuckles had almost healed – and that it was another morning, another day.

Mrs. Williams, the Cat's mother, came to collect her daughter's belongings. Came and left in less than ten minutes.

Hume followed her into the Cat's room. 'So Catherine's all right then? We'd no idea what happened to her, we've been so worried and—'

'You're the one called Hume, are you?' She made the question sound like an accusation.

No cup of tea wanted. No conversation either. Mrs. Williams packed up some photographs, jewellery, clothes and a few books. 'You can take the rest to a charity shop. Here's her door key.'

A plastic bag in each hand, Mrs. Williams led the way downstairs in silence. Hume followed behind, carrying two cardboard boxes.

Christ, it hadn't been his idea to go up onto the roof, he wanted to tell her. He wasn't responsible. What else was there to say? Explain that he and the Cat were never really boyfriend and girlfriend *per se*, tell her about their friends-who-fucked arrangement? Instead, he said that her daughter was a lovely girl, very popular, a brilliant student, a hard worker. She was sorely missed by everyone and he was sure they would all send her their greetings. Without a word, the woman put everything in the boot of her car and drove off.

## 3

WHEN ST FRANCIS stopped his furniture-moving, everyone assumed it was out of respect for the Cat. But it wasn't.

Having left Hume after their discussion on the night of the Cat's disappearance, St Francis returned to his room and immediately fell on his knees. The words came easily. Words like guilt, penance, contrition. So many words, so much shame and disgust. Their weight crushing him.

Then came the tears. He didn't wipe them away. Not because they were a symbol of repentance, an offering to God who sees everything. Because they weren't. They were his, not God's, and he needed them. Needed to feel them burning him, branding him. The Cat had turned to him in trouble and distress; she had trusted him. And in return he had . . .

He now understood why some of the saints had demanded to be scourged and, when that wasn't enough, they'd taken the whip in their own hands and scourged themselves till the blood flowed. Flowed freely as his tears.

When God had been on his side, things were bearable. Exit God – and St Francis was totally alone. Just him and a roomful of dead furniture. He stayed on his knees for as long as he could bear, then remained there even longer.

Finally he arose. Without undressing he lay on his bed and pulled the top blanket over him.

In the weeks following Midsummer's Eve he rapidly slipped into a complete day-for-night cycle, not going to bed until long after the sun had risen, and not getting up until early evening. Move the furniture? – he hardly had the strength to move himself.

Then late one night, something happened, something quite wonderful. Traffic had more or less stopped running; the street was utterly quiet. His room also. He felt too tired to heave himself out of his chair and get ready for bed. Even the thought of the effort involved exhausted him – washing, cleaning his teeth, taking off his shoes, his clothes, putting on his pyjamas, climbing in under the blankets. Instead, he found himself gazing round his room. The same walls. The same scarred floorboards, the same furniture. Then all at once and for the first time in weeks, in months, he saw his furniture needed to be moved. Not only *needed*, but was desperate, crying out for it. He could almost hear it pleading with him to get off his ass and start moving things.

His bed . . . his bookcase . . .

But no, he couldn't. Not anymore. That all-too-familiar bone-bone-weariness . . .

As usual, he hadn't got round to closing his curtains. Across the triptych of panes that made up the bay window, his whole room could be seen, fragmented and yet perfect in every detail – reading light, the top of the bookcase, the near edge of the wardrobe, his desk.

So what? Christ, was this what he'd come to – his bits of furniture were getting too much for him, so he'd started looking at their reflections instead? Not much better than being trapped in Plato's cave, and believing the shadows on the wall were real. Once he reached that stage, he wouldn't even bother getting out of bed. No point. He'd just lie there, staring up at the window pane and—

Then it came to him. One of Man's great leaps forward, the vision that had got human understanding up and running nearly two-and-a-half thousand years ago. Not Plato's cave, but his—

Of course!

Within seconds St Francis was charged with energy.

He leapt from his seat. He needed a couple of sheets of A4. Stiff card would be even better, more durable. Quick. Quick. He needed a pen, something to lean on.

Scissors. Ruler.

Next moment he was down on his knees. But not out of shame and self-abasement, not this time, and began measuring sections of the floor, taking notes as he went.

The lightest pencil mark on the top of the skirting board, then slide the ruler along another foot - pity he hadn't a measuring tape - which made the wall 20ft 2ins. The door was next - 2ft 9ins. He worked his way around irregularities like the fireplace, and estimated the angles at the base of the bay window.

Plato's Realm of Perfect Forms! What a great idea! This would solve everything. Thank you, Socrates. Thank you, Plato. This early theory of knowledge stated that every object in the physical universe - the chairs, tables, waste bins and so forth - was merely an imperfect example of some perfect Chair, Table, Waste Bin or whatever, whose ideal *form* was at once unique and timeless, and existed in a Realm of Perfect Forms. It was as if the world of everyday physical objects were nothing more than a warehouse of factory rejects and seconds.

Having completed all the necessary measurements, he stood up. His knees were killing him, but it was all in a good cause. No, in a *great* cause. Life-changing. A quick glance round the room to check nothing had been missed out. No? Okay, now for the deskwork.

Using the length of the longest wall as a base, he calculated a scale that would allow his room to be fitted onto a sheet of cardboard. Next, he took his LP of *Gregorian Chants Vol 1* – brought from priest school and for which he had ever since been meaning to purchase a record player – and snipped off the back cover. On the blank inner side he began tracing out in pencil a plan of his room. Not so easy. Twenty minutes and three botched attempts later, he inked it in.

'That's the Realm done. Now for the Perfect Forms,' he grinned to himself.

Down on his knees again, this time to measure and note down the base of each item of moveable furniture: Bookcase – rectangular, 3ft 4ins × 10ins . . . Waste bin – circular, 8ins diameter . . .

In less than half-an-hour he'd established the dimensions of his bed, desk, chair, couch, bookcase, armchair, wardrobe, waste-bin and rug and traced their outlines onto the remaining inner side of his *Gregorian Chants Vol 1* cover. Carefully, he cut them out. Painstakingly. The nail scissors were curved, which was custom-made for trimming the circular base of his wastepaper basket but otherwise a bit of a handicap. The resultant Perfect Forms, representing his furniture, were then laid out on the desk, next to the room plan, ready to be positioned and repositioned at will.

He had not been so excited for weeks, for months . . .

No more need for the labour and stress of furniture-moving. His search for the ideal layout had been raised to a higher plane – that of pure concept – and could thus be conducted from the comfort of his armchair. Relaxed and totally at ease, he balanced the cover sleeve of *Gregorian Chants Vol 2* on his lap and reached for the plan of his room. Finally, precisely in accordance with its current location, he positioned each item of cut-out furniture. Now for the big test – he picked up his Perfect Wardrobe and slid it back and forth across his Perfect Room.

Excellent! Wonderful! Complete success! He could now move his furniture around at will, wherever he wanted and whenever the mood took him. He could even have fun with it – for example, did he fancy the wardrobe standing in the fireplace? No problem. A second later – there it was! He could build a mini Tower of Babel, stacking one piece of furniture on top of another until they reached the ceiling!

Seriously though . . . From now on, whenever he felt his room clamouring to be re-arranged, all he need do was make himself a cup of tea, sit down, and begin soundlessly gliding his cut-out furniture across the surface of his cut-out room.

He sighed with content, then picked up the wardrobe once more and slid it over to the wall opposite the window. Holding the desk between his fingers, he tried it next to the fireplace, moved it to just inside the door, into curve of the bay window itself . . .

## 4

AFTER THE CAT had left and the Coconut had moved in more or less permanently upstairs with the Electric Boy, Barclay Towers quickly degenerated into an all-male domain. Within a few weeks it had become a bleak and comfortless place of Pot Noodles, beer cans, unwashed dishes, sticky linoleum, shared towels and rancid sheets.

The morning after the only night DD ever slept there, Hume found himself looking with fresh eyes at his compact, snug, little retreat. Seneca had his palaces, okay, lucky him. Diogenes might have lived in a barrel, but at least it came with plenty of sun and a Mediterranean climate. But an understairs cupboard in central Scotland? When it was time for him to be slotted into his coffin, he'd hardly notice the difference.

His philosophy paper was going to change all that, of course.

Of course it was.

Come September he was still living in the cupboard.

On the first day of October, while the rain hammered down morning and afternoon in the wind-battered streets, Hume kept warm and dry labouring at the chalk-face of the crammer. Being paid cash-in-hand supplemented his Supplementary Benefit. 'We value our students', proclaimed the ENGLISH FOR EVERYONE brochure, and so did he. Indeed, to motivate himself at the start of every session, he let his eyes wander over the roomful of French/Spanis/Swiss/German/Italian students arranged in rows, reminding himself they weighed in at approximately 17 pence per capita, per hour. It also made him a kinder and more patient teacher.

But from today, this was all going to change.

Last class finished, he decided to treat himself: he'd take a bus for once, and get home sooner.

Sitting in the upper-deck front seat, he looked down at the wet street with its even wetter pedestrians being blown round corners, battling with umbrellas, sheltering in doorways – but saw nobody, nothing. For him, there was no wind, no rain, no city centre at all. Instead, there was a lectureship at Edinburgh University that further along Princes Street became a professorship at Oxford. By Woolworth's at the top of Lothian Road, this turned into a specially created Chair at Berkeley, UCLA. Between times, he was appointed to head a government think-tank, host a TV show and, as they turned right at the Tollcross clock, discovered he was under consideration by the Nobel Prize committee. He was still drafting his acceptance speech when he got off the bus. The Barclay Towers stairs were taken at a run, every step bringing him closer to the letter that was going to change his life.

Key in the door.

No post on the mat. On the kitchen table, maybe?

He had a very late lunch of tea, toast, Cup-a-Soup (minestrone) and disappointment. Afterwards he remained at the kitchen table staring at the pine-panelled walls and lowered ceiling. The room felt like a sauna, Scottish style. Unheated.

Now what? A lie-down in his windowless cupboard? Go

for a self-righteous stroll in the downpour? He did have some books needing returned to—

But of course! His subscriber's copy of the autumn edition of *Thought* might not have reached him yet, but the *library* copies would have been dispatched earlier. Public library, university library. Next moment, the original typescript of his essay stuffed in his pocket for easy reference, he was clattering out the door and down the stairs at mega-warp speed.

The first few times he'd taken the tenement stairs after the Cat's disappearance, he'd found himself counting out the brass studs set every few feet into the wooden banisters in an attempt to stop himself feeling guilty. Now, three-and-a-half months later, he counted them only on bad days. But today as he hot-footed himself down, he touched each one of them lightly, for luck. Today was going to be a Good Day. A Great Day. Like every single day in his life from now on. The soon-to-be professor at UCLA went out into the street humming 'California Dreaming'.

Perhaps *Thought* would feature a lengthy rebuttal from a distinguished professor? His was a ground-breaking essay, after all, radical stuff. The journal was read worldwide. There might even be a vigorous forum-type discussion. He wanted coverage. He wanted columns and lots of them. The start of a controversy, of notoriety. *Professional* notoriety. It would be his ticket for a seat on the academic gravy train. He certainly needed it. Earnings-wise, 'The Appearance of Reality and the Reality of Appearance' hadn't so far been worth the postage stamp. His DHSS goodwill would soon be running out.

A grim autumn afternoon, Scottish-grim. Darkness falling. Grey sky and sagging clouds. Heavy, heavy rain. A cutting eastly wind. A rawness in the air, a chillness that threatened sleet. Dirty rainwater was puddled in the dips and cracks of the uneven pavement; oily-looking sludge oozed blackly up from between the loose-fitting slabs. Scrunched-up chip papers and pizza cartons blew the length of the street.

He pulled his coat tighter around him and splashed past the small grocer's, the Taj Mahal carry-out at the corner, then turned into the main street. Shops, shops, and more shops – fruit shop, charity shop, bread shop, vacuum-and-washing-machine shop, another charity shop; past the garage with its forecourt banner snapping in the wind and the blue plastic bags of coal stacked and gleaming wet against the wall; past the bookie's where the owner stood, legs wide apart in the shelter of his doorway, puffing away at an end-of-day cigar while he stared out at yet another Scottish October. Then the Auld Toll pub, the butcher's, the Yangtse Goodwill, the Co-op, Bennett's Bar, the King's Theatre.

To Hume, all shops, restaurants, garages, pubs and theatres were no more than the ongoing blur he coasted past every day. They weren't even on his radar. Most people check they have enough money on them before leaving home, Hume usually checked to be sure he had none. It gave him a sense of freedom, of detachment and independence.

Then, for the first time, he saw a beggar on the streets of Tollcross.

When her student grant ran out, DD had begun teaching little angels the piano at £1 per little head per half-hour. They kept her in food, clothes, bus money and cigarettes, and the koi paid her rent. Survival, but only just.

Her one night spent in Hume's cupboard had been one night too many. The next morning, half-standing and half-crouched down because of the low ceiling, she'd teetered from side to side trying to maintain her balance as she struggled to get dressed. She managed to be crisp and to the point:

'This how all philosophers live?'

'Only the Scottish ones,' had been the witty comeback.

She hadn't laughed.

She loved waking up to see her summerhouse. She loved to wake and see strips of shuttered light spread fan-like across the floor and the room wondrously sun-filled. Yes, she loved her summerhouse – in the *summer*. Now autumn had arrived, the mornings were chill. The first day of October and she could see her breath – how soon before she'd find ice on the inside of the windows? In this glorified wooden shed, Scottish winter would be Scottish Arctic.

Then it began to rain. Again.

There were two little angels that afternoon. £2 to the good. Having shown the last one and its mother off the premises, she lit a cigarette she didn't really want and smoked it in the summerhouse doorway. She did her best for the little angels – listening to them, encouraging them, being nice to them. She liked them. It was their mothers who were the problem. Pushy, patronising, ambitious or indifferent – it all came to the same, the women were *there*. They made suggestions; they bossed her. She tried her best to be nice to them, too. Hard work. Insincerity was exhausting.

Heavy rain fell in sheets across the drowned garden. Cue Debussy's 'Jardins sous la pluie', if she could be bothered. The light was on in Dora's sitting room, in Dora's warm and dry sitting room. Again she read the note the old lady had slid under her door during the last lesson: it seemed that Kyle of the Wandering Hands had phoned to suggest 'an informal get-together over some late-afternoon tea and biscuits' for a 'friendly chat about her future'. Ever discreet, Dora had added an exclamation mark in brackets. The two of them had discussed her tutor before. Mr. Raymond Kyle. Rumour had it that when it came to female students, passing or failing an exam was in his hands. Quite literally.

Having ignored a similar invitation to let him fuck her back in June, she had been failed. A refusal second time round would probably mean her getting failed for good and all. Four years wasted. She had re-sat her performer's certificate the previous week and the results were due out any day now.

Cigarette finished, she stubbed it out on the doorstep. To be fucked or not to be fucked, that was the question. No sense in asking Hume unless she fancied hearing Plato's or Kant's thoughts on the matter – she never heard him mention any women philosophers. And anyway, what would she tell him afterwards? Least said . . .

She'd said no to Dora's offer of a tactics discussion in June. This time she'd get some frank advice on what best to wear, and take it from there.

Her shoulder bag packed with the necessaries for her 'friendly chat', she set off to Kyle's lair. Despite the rain she decided to walk – not only the best way to think things through, but she could turn back at any moment. Also, as Dora had suggested, letting him wait would probably make him that bit easier to deal with.

Doucest Morningside was a good part of town, a very *nice* part of town. Today it was also a very wet part of town, the heavy rain streamed along the Kinnemount Road pavements and gutters, and whirlpooled down the Kinnemount Road drains. Wanting to look her best for the 'friendly chat' ahead, she stepped carefully to keep her high heels and tights as splash-free as possible. Such solid, respectable sandstone houses on either side. Such trim-and-tidy flowerbeds and lawns.

Nice street, nice houses. Nice tutor.

Having found Kyle's nice house, she went up a front path of jigsaw-neat paving stones. In the bay window of the house next door, an elderly lady sat knitting. DD gave her a cheerful wave and a big smile. The old lady beamed and waved back. A good omen, and she was going to need it. But maybe everything would be fine, a friendly chat and nothing more?

Who was she kidding?

Her ring at the bell was answered almost immediately.

※

The beggar was huddled under the tarpaulin awning next to the entrance to the Co-op, trying to keep out the rain. Slumped forward, head down and miserable-looking. Shoulders covered by a torn, mud-spattered blanket, chilled-looking hands clutching each other.

Hume had seen street beggars the last time he'd visited London; he'd been told of teenagers down there living in cardboard boxes. He'd been bewildered. Mrs. Thatcher's new policies were creating new wealth and opportunities, offering everyone the chance to set their own goals and to succeed. But here was someone begging in Edinburgh now . . . and not one of the straggle-bearded, meths-battered down-and-outs that staggered from dosshouse to dosshouse in the Grassmarket. This was a genuine beggar, possibly in danger of starving to death on streets he walked along nearly every day. A young beggar at that. Younger than him even. He was truly shocked.

Though frantic to get his hands on a copy of *Thought*, he was deeply saddened to see someone who'd become one of the all-too-visible wounds of society. Also, on a personal level, it was a warning – if philosophy didn't start earning its keep, he might find himself setting up his own begging bowl in competition.

For the time being, however, his sense of natural benevolence – as described by his namesake, David Hume – urged him to offer support and comfort. A show of sympathy at the very least. But was the concept of beggary really so straightforward, were its implications so self-evident? Even the most superficial analysis threw up some very basic questions.

For example, if he were to give this beggar a handful of loose change – assuming he actually had any, which of course he hadn't – would that *really* help them? In his groundbreaking essay, such behaviour had been categorised as 'indulging in false compassion', and the conclusion was irrefutable. Such acts of spontaneous charity achieved nothing except to keep the unfortunate beggar in a state of permanent beggary. This was the only possible inference that could be drawn, he had argued, either empirically or *a priori*. Such acts of casual benevolence were irresponsible at best and, in the long term, positively harmful. They created dependence and, as a consequence, limited the beggar's freedom. A more constructive and morally responsible approach would be to give the beggar sufficient money *in a lump sum* to lift him out of beggary altogether, or else to give nothing at all. No other response was either reasonable, or desirable. Indeed, the latter could perhaps be considered the more advisable course of action as it created an opportunity to promote the beggar's self-reliance, and, in the long term, his self-empowerment. That said, Hume was still deeply moved to find a fellow human being in such a sorry state and, though pressed for time himself, felt compelled to spare this unfortunate a few minutes and a few encouraging words.

He approached the huddled figure: 'I'm truly sorry to see you like this. How come you have to . . . ?'

Shock number two came when the beggar looked up.

It was a young *girl*. He had naturally assumed . . .

Filthy-looking, her blondish hair a tangle of grime and hardened mud, she had painful-looking scratches on her face and the backs of her hands were ridged with hardened blood. There was a livid bruise where her right eye should have been.

'What?'

'I said, how come you have to sit here and—?'

'Had a good look? Feel better, do you?' She glared up at him.

Ignoring the driving rain, he switched to benevolence-mode: 'Please accept my sincere apologies, I wasn't intending any—'

'No? There's places where people have to pay to stare the way you're staring. Like I'm in the zoo or something.'

'The zoo? No, no. I'm trying to find out—'

'20p'll make it all right.'

'Actually, I don't have any money on me.'

'Oh, don't you, *actually?*' She shrugged. 'Then fuck off.'

She dropped her eyes and slumped forward head down

once more. 'Make it 50 pence next time you're passing. Call it interest.'

At the corner of Gilmore Place, Hume glanced back. The beggar girl gave him the fingers. So much for his taking the time and trouble to show compassion.

Checking that his essay was still safe and dry in his inside pocket, he crossed the street. There was a spring in his step as he strode through the deluge towards George IV Bridge, towards the new issue of *Thought*, towards the academic gravy train he could see waiting ahead, waiting for him to climb aboard.

⌘

'Enter, please, Diana. So very good of you to come, and on such a day, too.' DD's wet coat and brolly were taken from her and hung on a peg where they immediately began dripping onto the Morningside parquet.

She was shown down a corridor and ushered into a large study that overlooked the back garden. In addition to a cabinet of neatly arranged books and music scores, there was a black leather couch, an upright piano, an armchair, a desk and a small plantation of empty music stands over by the window. The walls and carpet were puke-pastel. Then she noticed her exam paper lying face-open on a small coffee table.

'Nasty out there.'

DD watched in alarm as Kyle of the Wandering Hands pulled the curtains firmly shut. It wasn't even dark yet. Refreshments were laid out – not the afternoon tea mentioned in the note, but red wine. A whole bottle already opened and standing casually, as though by accident, next to her essay.

Clearly Kyle was determined that she would pass her exam. So was she, but now she was here could she really . . . ? There was also a dish of biscuits so tiny and delicate-looking they had to be expensive. Very.

For her tutor, the professorial armchair; for her the leather couch. They sat facing each other. Seemed that he'd brought the biscuits back from Italy where he'd recently been researching early eighteenth-century fortepiano construction – 'Cristofori's *clavicembalo col piano e forte* and the like,' he name-dropped as he poured the wine.

'Cheers, Diana! Here's to your success this time round!' His smile was warm, his manner encouraging. Very.

They clinked glasses and drank. They chatted.

'Have a biscuit. Do you know Italy at all, Diana?'

'Wish I did. Sounds like such a wonderful country.'

Kyle beamed at her. 'Yes, you've got it in one, Diana. Wonderful is the word. That special translucent quality of the sunlight. And the language, of course. Its liquid lyricism, as some have called it. Inevitable, really, that it was to become the accepted tongue for opera and that from Monteverdi onwards . . .'

A bottle of red later, Kyle's flow of professorial chit-chat ran out. He opened another, refilled their glasses and came abruptly to the point: 'Well, Diana, it all depends on you now.'

Her heart-rate started doubling. 'I know, Mr. Kyle—'

'*Raymond*, please.'

'Raymond.' She gave him her best eager-student smile. 'I practised as hard as I could and did my best in the examination.'

'Of course you did, Diana. You played really well.' Even

sitting three feet away she could sense an unpleasant warmth coming off him.

'Did I? Did I really, Mr. K – I mean, Raymond?' She paused. 'Good enough to get my diploma?' Her last hope.

'Well now, Diana . . .'

His tone of voice said it all. She took a sip from her nearly brimful glass. Plan B?

She had no Plan C.

At Dora's suggestion she'd opted for no bra and a sleeveless blouse that could be unbuttoned a stage at a time according to circumstances, and so, the top two buttons already loose, she now leant forward to allow Kyle a come-on glimpse of cleavage. Having lingered there for several moments, his gaze soon overheated. Then it was on the move, travelling due south, scorching a path as it went.

After some different try-outs, she and Dora had settled on a denim skirt, medium-length, with a discreet, but startlingly effective side-slit. Aware her tutor's gaze had modulated to *hard stare*, DD crossed her legs, shakily.

Kyle seemed to have forgotten how to speak. Stared even harder. Swallowed.

His eventual, 'As I said, Diana, it all depends on you', came out sounding cracked and husky.

Plan B it was. She took a small sip of wine, replaced her glass and gave him the glance she'd practised in the summerhouse mirror, a glance that was at once half-shy and half-hopeful.

Her best little-girl voice: 'How do you mean . . . Raymond?' DD was aware of the pastel shades around them becoming even paler and fading to near-colourlessness. The room itself had receded to the merest suggestion of a distant backdrop.

Her cleavage, her side-slit skirt, her slightly exposed thigh – these alone now had vibrancy and substance. You have to try and take control, Dora had told her. Do what needs to be done, but once you've started, don't stop. DD's heart-rate quadrupled: 'But, please, Raymond, what more can I *do*?'

Kyle put down his glass. It rattled against the table top. He leant towards her: 'You've always been one of my favourite pupils, Diana. One of my *special* favourites.'

'Really? Have I, really?' She smiled her most wide-eyed smile of mega-innocence, giving it full-wattage: 'Thanks to you, I just *love* classical music. You've taught me everything I know.'

Kyle leant nearer still, his voice trembled: 'And I just love the way you play, Diana. The way you play . . . Mozart . . . and play . . . Mozart . . .'

Then, as though suddenly inspired by his enthusiasm for the late-classical piano repertoire, her tutor spontaneously got up from his seat and came to sit on the couch beside her.

Their knees touched, his body-heat flooding her in wave after clammy wave, he turned towards her: 'I want you to get your performer's diploma, Diana. I really do. You . . . you deserve it. I want to be sure that . . .'

Had all her years of study and practice, all her dedication and hard work really come down to this – a middle-aged man's arm sneaking round her shoulder; the sticky-looking sheen of his overheated, red-boiled face; a spray of nose hairs, sour-wine breath, sweat under a slick of cologne?

'Your diploma . . . I want to be sure, Diana . . . that we do everything within our power to make certain . . . you get it.' He leant nearer.

Clearly he was about to kiss her.

Hume hopped, skipped and jumped his way through the downpour, past the deadbeat-looking DHSS office in Tollcross, down West Bow with its mangled time zones of eighteenth century tenements, twentieth century concrete brutalism and boarded up churches, then into the Grassmarket, past the Women's Hostel, the parliament of dossers in session on a gathering of benches next to the public toilets, and Greyfriar's Men's Hostel. Two late-afternoon drunks came lurching towards him, hauling themselves along the street on an invisible rope, the one in front shouting back every few steps that he wanted left the fuck alone or someone was for a good kicking.

A neat body-swerve, and Hume had left them far behind. Then it was up the curved slope of two-tiered Victoria Terrace and its patisserie-like layers: the street-level shops and doorways that had been topped as an afterthought by ornamental railings, another pavement and another row of tenements. Finally reaching solid ground – George IV Bridge and Edinburgh Central Library.

He pushed through the massive double doors, took the coach-and-horses-wide staircase two steps at a time, pell-melling himself up to the top floor and into the glass cupola and terrace-shelved sanctum of the Reference & Periodicals department.

The new issue of *Thought* had indeed arrived that morning, he was told. It had been processed and catalogued, and just that very minute been placed in the Current Periodicals section which was over by the—

Hume grabbed the journal from the shelf and immediately began scanning every page from first to last and last to first all over again. Twice through *Contents*, then once more. There *had* to be an essay in response to his own. There had to be a mention somewhere, an indication that someone had read his article, that someone had noticed it even. Once more he flicked through the close-typed, double-columned, illustration-free pages. Ransacked them. Ransacked them again. Had his challenge to established *mores* really gone unanswered? Had no salaried professor, no comfortably tenured lecturer, bothered to come up with even the briefest attempt at refutation?

He tried the letters page for fan mail, hate mail, anything.

There was nothing.

Not even a footnote.

When he found himself staring at the back page to read the printer's address and telephone number for the third time, he knew he had to leave.

Fuck. Fuck. FUCK!

Outside, it was still raining. Of course it was.

He reached the Forrest Road Post Office just before it closed and withdrew the balance of his life savings. Next minute he was forcing a path through the closely-planted clumps of dedicated drinkers in Sandy Bell's to get to the toilets at the rear.

A quick rub down with a paper towel, giving his dripping hair a blow-dry at the hot-air machine. He blow-dried his essay too. Its crinkled remains safely buttoned into an inside pocket, he elbowed his way through a cheerful ceilidh of fiddlers and raw-faced singers gathered to lament their lost heritage. He stood at the bar. A few pints later he was joining in the chorus of national grief.

To judge by the pressure of her tutor's lips against hers and the trembling in his hand as he undid the next button on the front of her blouse, DD guessed that the strictly verbal part of Kyle's 'friendly chat about her future' had been concluded. His tongue felt swollen and smeary-warm, a blob of wet fleshiness trying to force her lips apart. A bloated slug. She imagined biting it off, spitting it out onto the carpet.

So, so tempting.

After lingering for a few moments to fondle her breasts en route, Kyle's free hand slid quickly downward till it found the side-slit that gave access to her thighs. The hot fumbling fingers, the damp palms – she pictured them as belonging to some species of sightless rodent, a rodent now seeking to burrow its way up her skirt.

Plan B. She had to. Too late to turn back.

Slowly, ever so slowly, she opened her legs . . .

The rodent seemed to have cockroach-feelers that tested out the path ahead, exploring, straining forward an inch at a time. Always little further . . .

She tensed her body, held her breath. Stilled her heartbeat. If her heart wasn't beating, then somehow *this* wasn't happening . . .

A little further . . . a little further . . .

NOW!

Abruptly, she clamped her legs shut. Tight shut. Then twisted herself round, dragging her tutor-rodent till he was half off the couch and half on the floor.

'What the hell d'you think you're—?' Forced down onto his knees, his hand trapped between her legs, Kyle was held there, unable to move.

DD could feel the ecstasy of total control as her heartbeat

came surging back to its full rhythm, a pounding force, a power that was *her*. She let her voice do all the talking while she herself merely sat back and listened. She was impressed. No little-girl speak any more:

'Here's the deal, *Raymond*. One performer's diploma, *with distinction* – and I say nothing.'

She opened her legs and pushed him so that he tumbled backwards onto the carpet. He scrambled to his feet.

'Your word against mine, and who the fuck'd believe *you*? Respected lecturer against third-rate slut of a low-grade student. You'd end up with no diploma at all.'

'Oh really?' She stood up. 'Then all I need to do is *this*.' Grasping the top of her blouse firmly in both hands, she ripped it wide open.

'Performer's diploma, Raymond, *with distinction*.'

In her exultation she could feel the room re-assembling itself around her, the colours flooding back into the walls and the beige carpet.

Kyle was tucking in his shirt. 'Forget it, you slag. You're finished.'

Then she heard herself say: 'I'm sure that nice elderly lady neighbour of yours will have a phone.' She crossed to the door.

'You wouldn't dare.'

'Watch me.' She marched off down the corridor.

'Diana! Stop!' Kyle hurried after her.

Unsnibbing the Yale lock, she opened the front door. 'Well?'

'Don't go, Diana. It was a misunderstanding, that's all. I never meant anything, not really. You must see that sometimes . . . A man in my position . . .'

'A man with his hand up my skirt, you mean?' She went out onto the front step.

'Not so loud.' He gestured frantically for her to come back inside. 'No. That was all a mistake.'

'You got that right.'

'Please come inside. Please. We can talk.'

'What's there to talk about?'

Having stepped onto the path, she turned to face him. Rain was running down her bare arms. The torn blouse blew open in the wind. No passers-by, thank goodness. A few more steps and even in the darkness she'd be visible to the elderly neighbour next door. If she took those steps there would be no turning back. She would have to follow through – calling out for help, knocking on the old lady's window, looking distressed and in tears. She'd come too far just to . . .

'OK, OK.' Kyle was hissing at her under his breath. 'You win. Now come back inside. Please.'

She paused. Waited.

'OK, I said. I'll do what you want. Only, come inside. Now.'

'With distinction?'

'Yes. Yes.'

Holding the front of her blouse tightly closed, she slipped in past him and hurried back to his study. She felt dizzy.

She sat down. A sip of wine. A big, big victory sip. Then she took a jersey out of her shoulder bag, turned away and pulled it on over the torn blouse. The wine worked wonders, she could feel it surge through her like electricity. No little-girl voice anymore: 'You have some college-headed notepaper?'

Kyle could only nod.

'Get it. I'll dictate.'

Hume was down on his knees in the bathroom, hugging the Barclay Towers porcelain. His Scottish-style purge had started with a couple of high-speed pints of Belhaven's 80/- to get him loosened up before moving on to a steady diet of Black Velvet. The quick-return cider-and-stout mixture had taken him rapidly from fuck-them-all euphoria to misery, then to consolation, and back to misery again, stopping at every station on the way. He was still heaving up when he heard the phone ring through in the kitchen.

Which brought on another heave.

*Brr . . .brr / Brr . . .brr / Brr—*

Someone answered it. An abrupt silence . . . which triggered a further heave.

There was a knock on the bathroom door.

St Francis was calling him: 'Hume, are you okay to come to the phone? It's DD.'

'Tell her . . . Tell her I'll call her back . . . in a few minutes.'

St Francis went away . . . and returned almost immediately: 'She says she's in a phone box. She's just put in more money.'

'I'll be there . . . in a moment.'

One more heave.

Finally he got himself off his knees and onto his feet, leant against the bathroom wall . . . a wall that at once began sliding away from him. A few attempts later, he got a good grip on it, held it steady. Some toilet paper for a dab round his mouth, some more for a wipe round the toilet bowl rim. Quick flush. Steadied the wall again. Found the washbasin. Hand wash. Face-splash. Mouth-rinse. Towel-rub. He was ready.

In the kitchen he found the receiver lying on the table.

'Hello?'
The dial tone.
Back to the bowl.

⚘

'Bastard! That fucking lazy selfish bastard!' DD banged down
the receiver and stormed out of the phone box, slamming the
door behind her. She'd nearly been in tears coming down the
road from Kyle's, she was still shaking. Men! She'd fixed Mr.
Wandering Hands Kyle, fixed him good. Now she'd have to
fix Mr. Philosophy Fuckwit.

All she'd wanted was to invite him to the Taj for a curry
to celebrate her diploma. The useless shit. No counting the
pennies for once, it would have been her treat. But the rotten
bastard hadn't even made the effort to come to the phone. The
rotten bastard preferred his shit-hole of a cupboard, preferred
shit-brained Kant for company.

Well, who cared? Plenty more where he came from, more
and better. There had to be.

Fuck him, and fuck this walking in the rain, too. There was
a bus stop next to the phone box. Her luck was in, and less
than a minute later she was on a 16 headed into town.

⚘

Hume's shower and several restorative mugs of tea were
followed by a slice of thick-cut toast. Pot Noodle was forced
down to consolidate recovery. Every so often he felt the
ghost of his last heave rise within him, but having kept down
several more slices followed by more Pot Noodle he began

feeling normal, near enough. The next time DD rang, he'd be ready.

Rain battered the kitchen window, wind howled down the chimney. He lit two rings on the cooker to get the room temperature up a few degrees. The gas flames flared and dipped in the draughts.

He waited for DD to call back.

He watched some television.

He had more tea and toast. Finished off the loaf.

He turned to Kant, but for once the great man's insights into the Categorical Imperative failed to grip.

⚜

The worse the weather outside, the more welcoming was the Café Royal with its dark polished wood, its brass fittings, mirrors, tiled walls, the central island bar for speedy service, the side tables in their curved lagoon-bay alcoves for those who were in for the long haul. DD was sure her friends Jenny and Carol from college would be here by now. This time of day, they were bound to be.

*Performer's Diploma, with distinction* – she couldn't wait to tell them!

She pushed open the doors into a din of conversation and . . . no one. Twice round the bar, checking all the side tables. Still no one. Here she was with the news bulletin of a lifetime and no one to tell it to except a line of after-work businessmen flexing their macho-postures by drinking standing up.

She took a barstool and ordered herself a whisky, going for a double as it sounded more celebratory. In the mirror behind the bar she could see herself perched clumsily on her stool. A woman sitting alone – she looked awkward, and felt awkward. Like she was gradually freezing up from the inside outwards, to form a protective shell of brittleness. The clatter of glasses, the *skoosh* of the beer taps, people talking, laughing – a very human warmth that seemed less and less able to reach and include her.

She toasted herself in the mirror, toasted her victory over Kyle. The whisky burned . . . then she remembered she didn't really like whisky. Diana Cummings, Diploma in Music, *with distinction*. How could a day that had gone so well end so . . . so much an anti-climax?

She took out a cigarette and lit it, blowing the smoke toward her reflection. Why hadn't that *bastard* picked up the phone? They could be sitting with a biryani each, mango and onion chutney on the side, a stack of poppadoms, pints of lager – no expense spared. They'd toast her success. But would she tell him the actual details of how she'd gained her diploma? Would she tell Jenny and Carol? Well . . . Should she try the philosophy fuckwit again? Give him one last chance? There was a public phone in a hooded booth over by—

'Is this seat taken?'

⁂

Sometimes Megan became so afraid to speak, so afraid that if she opened her mouth – she'd bite. So most times she sat on the pavement and said nothing. Nothing at all.

Like that guy staring down at her a few hours back, saying he was sorry seeing her and how come she had to beg? A real shit question, so she'd answered him shit. She begged because she was a beggar. What had happened to her? Nothing. Everything. What was she doing? She was sitting. She was wet. She was cold.

Wetter now, colder now. Dark streets, dark city.

So she kept trying . . .

Kept trying to lift up her head, trying to raise her eyes.

She could feel all the words trapped inside her. Like wild things tearing this way and that, clawing at her chest to get out, choking her throat to get free. Her mouth sometimes so crammed with words that she couldn't speak, so she spat them out.

Men staring down at her, men wanting to touch her. But she knew about men, knew about being touched.

Wanting only dreams, dreams that were really happening. Waking up was like rubbing grit into her eyes, like cutting her face with glass. How else could she know a dream had stopped?

Wanting dreams that lasted so long they became real. Wanting to hold them, to grab them tight . . . and pull herself, hand-over-hand, out of here. Out of wherever.

If only.

Cement-beach/cement-cold/cement-hardness . . .

⌘

Is this seat taken? The man who'd spoken to her looked older, well into his thirties. Business suit, white shirt, red tie, short fairish hair. Close-shaven. No flirty smile at least, no trying to catch her eye. It was just a question. But was it ever?

'Help yourself.' DD took another drag at her cigarette. Another sip of blended firewater. Bad as the first. Best to ditch the rest and just go home? Or switch to lager and lime instead? And some crisps. Suddenly she was hungry, really, really hungry. All that wine at Kyle's plus the double whisky . . . and she'd had nothing to eat except for those micro Italian biscuits that looked like oversized nail clippings.

'Lucky to find a seat at this time. I was working late.'

The Business Suit was addressing her.

She kept facing straight ahead. 'Oh, right.'

'That's the problem when your company's a one-man band – if *you* don't do it, it never gets done.'

'Hmmm.'

'Ah well, cheers.'

'Cheers,' she echoed automatically. Out of the corner of her eye she saw the Suit raise his glass and take a sip. Shortly after, she was aware of him taking another sip. No more conversation. Good.

That bastard, bastard Hume. What a loser, what a waste of fucking space, what a . . .

Accidentally catching the Suit's eye in the bar mirror, she stared instead into her glass. Down the rest in one, like medicine?

She did so.

'Whisky's better with a little water, brings out the taste more.' The Suit smiled at her in the mirror, then turned to face her: 'Would you like another? You'd be doing me a favour . . . I really do hate sitting and drinking alone.'

*Why don't you stand up then?* She stopped herself just in time from saying it out loud.

What was she being so bitchy for? What she really wanted to say was: *I've just got my music degree. Performer's Diploma, with distinction.* She wanted to tell someone, anyone – even this complete stranger. As for Mr. Philosophy-Fuckwit who wouldn't even get off his arse to . . .

The pub door banged, she glanced across and saw Jenny, Carol and the rest of them coming in. The cavalry, thank Christ.

She stood up. 'Sorry, it's very kind of you, but that's my friends arrived. I'd better go.' She gave him a smile. 'See you.'

Having reached a workable compromise between queasiness, residual drunkenness and still-distant sobriety, Hume felt it was time to review his position, and do something. As there was no phone in DD's summerhouse, he usually left messages with Dora Chisholm. Too late now though. The old lady went to bed early.

And so . . .

He pulled on his partly dried-out coat and his sodden shoes, then set off down the stairs, touching every single brass stud on the way.

Outside, the wind was more cutting and the rain even wetter than before. Suited him – he deserved it. And, given the hour and the stormy conditions, DD would be sure to appreciate the nobility of his intentions. The nobility, the romance.

But he should have brought a brolly. He should have put on a proper waterproof. He should have put on shoes that didn't leak even worse than they did before. Too many *shoulds* and not enough *dids.* Shoulders hunched, he set off across the rain-lashed, wind-battered Bruntsfield Links towards Marchmont and the Grange.

Not another pedestrian in sight. Everyone else had more sense. Even the muggers were probably stopping indoors, keeping dry and warm. Every so often he was splashed by passing cars, vans and taxis. The biggest splashes were from double-deckers.

After twenty minutes' head-butting his way through solid wind, horizontal sleet and driving rain, he stood outside the familiar wooden door. He was more sodden through than ever. Divers emerging from the ocean depths surely felt drier than he did.

In his right fist he clutched a bunch of flowers liberated en route from someone's front garden. Roses? Tulips? Carnations? All he knew was that they were flowers and that they were mostly red. They'd help strike the romantic note.

Or they would have done. Thanks to its passage through the storm, the improvised bouquet now looked bedraggled. It sagged, it drooped. Like himself. Okay, he'd go for the sympathy vote.

There was a bell marked *Chisholm*. He raised his hand to press it, then stopped hmself. Far too late now. The old lady might get alarmed and have a heart attack. At best she'd be furious. Bell ringing was out.

The wooden door was locked and this being upmarket Grange, far too well-constructed. Locked solid.

FUCK!

Give up and go back to the flat? Which meant a long slog home through more rain, more razor-edged winds. Then a four-storey climb, with only his solitary cupboard and hours of bone-aching weariness waiting for him at the top.

What a fucking awful day. What a fucking awful night.

He'd not even thought to bring a pen to write DD a note.

All the fucking way here. Fucking waste of time.

By now, his flowers were mostly petal-free stems. He discarded the completely bald-headed and bundled the rest between the blow-dried opening pages of 'The Appearance of Reality and the Reality of Appearance', which, luckily enough, he'd forgotten to remove from the inside pocket of his coat. This sad bouquet, wrapped in his blighted hopes and dreams, would tell of his desperate journey through the storm to clasp the woman he loved in his arms. This was hardcore romance. From the heart to the heart, as someone once said. A sodden, wretched-looking offering, drenched in tears and rain. Truly heart-breaking.

Toss it over the wall for DD to find in the morning? She'd be deeply moved and immediately rush to Barclay Towers full of love and forgiveness.

Wouldn't she?

Well?

Then again . . .

OK. Noble and romantic gesture – Take Two. He took a quick look up and down the street. No one in sight.

And so . . .

Gripping what was left of the bouquet between his teeth – like a pirate his dagger – he placed his right foot on the gate-handle. Then arm at full stretch, he made a grab for the top of the stone wall. Getting good hold . . . steadying himself . . . Getting balanced. Both hands on top. Heave-heave-heaving himself up.

Seconds later he was sitting on the wet stonework, astride the parapet. Luckily there was no broken glass embedded in it.

He took the flowers back into his hand and dropped down into the darkness.

As she went over to join Carol and Jenny, DD knew she had to get her story straight. With Distinction? They knew and she knew she wasn't that good a pianist. All the performer certificates in the world wouldn't get her a concert, and certainly never a second one unless she did a Kyle on all the reviewers. Though she was bursting to tell the girls the good news, she said nothing. A bit of gossip to start with, a bit of joking from them about the slit skirt – was she on the hunt? How were things with her cupboard man?

Some beer, some crisps. Still she didn't tell them.

Fuck's sake, what she'd done was only right and fair. Back in June she could have been Cristina Ortiz and Martha Argerich rolled into one, and Wandering Hands Kyle wouldn't have awarded her a diploma – not unless she'd spread her legs.

His slug tongue, his slimy body heat . . .

More crisps, more beer. Fact was – she'd been *denied* her certificate back in June. Fact was – she'd deserved it. Earned it for the hours and hours she'd spent in the university practice rooms, hammering away on the old battered uprights. The evenings and weekends in the summerhouse. More studying and more practising. Accompanying the student string players, flautists, singers for their exams, their end-of-term concerts. Fucking Kyle. She'd been treated badly, totally unfairly. No fuck meant no future. What she'd done was to even things up. Restore justice – nothing more, nothing less.

By closing time she still hadn't told them. Didn't matter. They'd find out when the results were published, of course. But she'd done what needed done. No more, no less.

They left the pub and walked together down the short

cobbled lane that ran onto Princes Street. Only when Jenny and Carol were preparing to head off towards Leith Walk, did she almost blurt it out suddenly. She'd been about to speak when—

'Bloody rain, bloody Scotland, eh!' said Jenny.

They said goodbye.

She picked up a celebratory fish supper for the bus home. Only slightly pissed. All along Princes St, up Lothian Road, through Marchmont to the Grange, she kept repeating to herself *Diploma With Distinction, Diploma With Distinction*, and passed from feeling good, feeling so really fucking *good* about what she'd done, to feeling bad, to feeling ashamed, then back to good again. She'd done right/she was a cheat/ done right/was a cheat. Changing from moment to moment.

Her fish supper finished, she screwed up the paper and tossed it under the seat. She was glad she'd told no one. Not boasting made it feel better.

※

Hume's fall was broken by a bush at the side of the path. As best he could in the pitch dark, he headed towards the lawn. Having got through the archway, he heard the sound of rainwater splashing to his left – the koi pond. He gave it a wide berth.

A light went on in an upstairs room of the house. Moments later, the curtains were pulled shut. Mrs. Chisholm going to bed. Had to be. He could have phoned after all. But maybe it was better arriving like this – with a bunch of flowers, an apology and a smile?

He reached the summerhouse. No lights. No closed

shutters either. He peered in and saw . . . nothing. No DD, that was for sure. Not unless she was already fast asleep.

He rapped on the window. A trickle of rainwater ran down the back of his neck. It was ice-cold, and exceptionally wet. He started shivering.

He rapped again.

No response.

Now what?

Maybe, at that very moment, DD was sitting in the dry and pine-warm Barclay Towers kitchen, sharing a pot of tea with St Francis? She might be. It was a possibility. A one-percent possibility.

And as for waiting here? She might not come back for hours. If at all.

Then again, she might turn up at any moment. He could wait for a bit, get his breath back, think through exactly what he was going to say.

Then again, she might not come back alone.

He paused to let that particular passing thought do its worst. Then pass on.

So, what was he going to do? Stay on her doorstep until he caught pneumonia? Trudge back through the downpour in the hope that she really was waiting for him at Barclay Towers? Some hope.

Yes, going round in circles and getting nowhere, to end up drenched to the skin – him and the fucking koi had a lot in common.

Right.

As firmly as he could, he wedged what was left of his sad-looking apology of a bouquet behind the door handle of the summerhouse. Now for the long squelch home.

On the move now, street into street, Tollcross into Fountainbridge, on the move for skips in side streets, for sheds with busted locks, for somewhere to stretch out, somewhere to sleep safe . . . past the warm brewery . . . into Morrison Street . . .

Whenever someone asked, she told them she came from a nowhere village out in the country, or from a new-town housing scheme, Livingston, Glenrothes, from a small town like Peebles, Kelso. Sometimes she came from a city. Edinburgh. Dundee. Glasgow. Somewhere. Anywhere.

The countryside, the small town, the city – she made them all up. Leastways, she seemed to. Once she'd started saying that kind of stuff, it started coming true. Like it had really happened.

Maybe it had.

All she could say . . . was *all* that she was. There was nothing else. Only like now, her reflection in Woolworth's window. Saying: *there*, that's me. Megan. That was all she knew. No letters, no photos. Everything stolen that night in the hostel. Never went there again.

That bruise healing around her eye . . . She must have got hit. Must've been a real bastard that did it. When she said what happened, what she said came true. Like she remembered it.

. . . up Lothian Road past the Tollcross clock going towards the Meadows . . . into Tarvit Street . . . back into Tollcross . . .

Wandering for somewhere to rest, somewhere to lie down, wanting to dream so much that she was shaking with the effort not to. Becoming the dream and nothing but – a dream among the buses and lorries and cars, the vomit and dogshit.

Bruntsfield Links. The empty street, doors shut, curtains pulled. The winter-locked bowling green. Railings with broken spikes that no one mends and no one clambers over. Except her. Spreading her plastic sheet on the ground and closing her eyes.

Darkness, like someone's kindness covering her – their hands steadying her, keeping her from shaking more, their gentleness holding the dream, helping it sink back inside her.

⁂

The following morning, Hume was woken by DD phoning to announce she'd been awarded her Music Diploma.

He congratulated her. Heartily.

*With distinction*, she added.

He congratulated her a second time.

His valiant-struggle-through-the-storm floral offering received less than a passing mention before she started on about 'his windowless little life'. DD was clearly still very pissed off and told him that now she'd achieved her diploma, she expected him to get off his arse and achieve something likewise.

He explained about going to the Central Library and the disappointing response to his essay, i.e. none at all.

Her 'very sorry to hear it' sounded genuine, but was far too brief. In her next breath she invoked Mrs. Thatcher and the entrepreneurial spirit, telling him he had to start taking some responsibility for the way he lived. Social Security was only for wasters, no-hopers, scroungers and deadbeats – it was pocket money. He should grow up.

He congratulated her a third time.

There was a long pause, during which no further observations came from DD.

To his surprise, Hume then heard himself say that it was quite a coincidence that she'd happened to call at that very moment, for he'd been about to call *her*.

Oh yes?

Really.

Well?

Well, the fact was . . .

And once he got into his stride, the words just seemed to flow:

. . . The fact was he'd been evolving a plan of action guaranteed to be both life-changing and financially rewarding . . . The plan was already in its advanced stages of development . . . He'd been wanting to let her know but had been so *frantically* busy with—

Another philosophy paper?

'Let's be serious, DD . . .' He managed to make her derision sound like a joke in very poor taste, then went on to explain that his life to date had merely been a warm-up, as it were, for the course of action he was now committed to and would shortly be implementing.

Standing in the cold kitchen, in last night's oven-dried socks and underwear, he did his best to sound confident, decisive, and convincing. 'What I mean is, something quite new, something quite special.'

There was silence at the other end.

He continued, 'Yes, DD, you're right to be amazed.' He went quickly on, 'And to be really, really impressed. But it's under wraps, a secret for the moment.' He improvised quickly:

'Not a word more until everything's in place. I want to surprise you! Just give me another few days and . . .'

'Two days then. Call me.'

'Make it three . . .'

A pause. 'Okay. But not a day longer. Bye, Hume.'

'I'll be in touch as soon as—'

But she'd already hung up.

# 5

S T FRANCIS WAS woken by the sound of hailstones battering his window. Half-leaning on his elbow, he raised the
corner of the curtain a few inches – the sky was a solid mass
of grey cloud. The traffic on Bruntsfield Road had stalled to
a near-crawl in both directions. Morning rush-hour? Evening
rush-hour? His wristwatch lay on his desk, too far to reach.

He turned over. There was another, less exhausting way of
working out the time. He could try to get back to sleep – if he
succeeded, then it was probably still morning. If not, he'd get
up, put on the kettle and start preparing dinner.

Then all at once he jerked up, wide awake. Today was
Friday.

He grabbed his watch. Two o'clock. He was going to be
late.

A half-step forward . . . long pause/a half-step forward . . .
long paus/ a half-step forward . . . long pause – five dishevelled
chorus lines performed this slow-motion, scuffed-shoe shuffle
towards the metal counter. There was no music, no singing.
Not a theatre, more like a joyless church filled with joyless
communicants. St Francis and his fellow shufflers approached
the altar rail to receive their weekly sacrament, a reminder
that they were still part – the lowliest part, to be sure – of the
national congregation.

The officiating priests looked even wearier. Grim though it

was for the communicants, at least they were usually in and out the door within the hour, two hours max, but the staff of the employment exchange remained stuck in their dismal church all day, five days a week, forty-eight weeks of the year. Bad air, stained plastic seats, the counter slimy to the touch, the cracked lino sticky underfoot. The walls were institutional green and decorated with posters threatening prosecution for false claims.

A three-quarter-hour's shuffle later, St Francis reached the head of his queue and handed over his UB40.

Without looking up, the official riffled through the card drawer beside him and took out a file of papers held together by a rubber band. 'Take a seat and wait, you'll be called.'

Taking a seat and waiting to be called meant *problems*. Something was wrong with his claim? Routine harassment? Whatever, having shuffled his way through Limbo, he was now to take his seat in the anteroom of Purgatory. It could mean the first stage of permanent damnation, or it could mean nothing at all.

There were no free seats and so he joined his fellow sinners slouched along the back wall. The Government, at least, would be happy – everyone in this waiting room of the damned looked truly humiliated. No one smiled, no one talked. A couple of the lucky few on plastic chairs screwed to the floor were asleep.

'I've nowhere to live. Can't you give me something? HELP ME!'

The chorus lines perked up. It was show time! At the counter, one of the damned was about to go berserk. Usually these outbursts took place only in that inner circle of hell – the Supplementary Benefits Office. Here in the dole office it was an exceptional treat.

'You should apply to the Social Security Office. They will—'

'I've been there already, I'm telling you.' It seemed to be a woman. Straggly blonde hair, an old donkey jacket that she'd probably slept in. She banged her fist on the counter. No, it was a young girl. A teenager, more like.

'I'm sorry, but—'

'FUCK'S SAKE! Can't someone see me? Can't somebody help?' She gripped the edge of the counter.

There were a few encouraging shrugs and shakes of the head from the audience, some sympathetic *tut-tuts* and mutterings.

'For the last time, miss, you're in the wrong office. You need to go to the Department of Social Security. You'll find them in—'

'JESUS CHRIST! They're the ones who sent me HERE! I've nowhere to live. No address means no SS money. No SS money means no address. What the fuck am I supposed to—'

'I'm sorry, but—'

'You're not sorry. None of you is. I've nowhere to—'

'If you'll just take a seat—'

'A FUCKING SEAT! It's a bed I want. A room. Somewhere to live. FUCK THE LOT OF YOU!' She turned and stormed out.

Their misery having been briefly enlivened, the damned gazed at each other as if suddenly surprised to find they were not alone in hell. But then, show over, their eyes were once again lowered in reverence, in contemplation of the abyss gaping at their feet between the cigarette ends and green-yellow gobs of spit.

Then it was back to a half-step forward . . . long pause/a half-step forward . . . St Francis's slow wait at the back of the hall was resumed.

Yet, even here, time eventually passed. His name was called.

*When did you last apply for a job?*

*How many jobs have you applied for in the last week?*

*Did you bring copies of your applications?*

Routine harassment then.

He answered the questions and looked on while the clerk stamped each one of the day-spaces UNEMPLOYED with his little wooden block of John Bull print. A minute later St Francis was back out on the streets of Tollcross.

As he neared the Co-op, he caught sight of Hume up ahead. Then, miracle of miracles, he saw his cupboard-dwelling flatmate take money from his pocket and give it to a beggar.

Hume? Couldn't be. But it was.

And the beggar? The blonde girl.

⚜

With Prussian regularity, the philosopher Immanuel Kant used to take the same walk at exactly the same time each day and keep so precisely to the exact same route, that his fellow Königsbergians joked they could set their watches by his passing. The freedom from the distraction of petty choice and decision-making allowed the great man to concentrate all his energies on writing his masterpiece, *The Critique of Pure Reason.*

Inspired by this exemplary fixity of purpose and method, Hume had been determined to do likewise. Realising that DD was in earnest regarding her deadline, he knew he had to come up with something, and something pretty impressive. So he decided to follow in his master's footsteps, quite literally.

The instant he put down the phone after DD's call he

moved into action. Shower, dressed, tea, toast and out the door. All that day and the next and the next again he tramped the streets of central Edinburgh, the same streets in the same order – Lothian Road, Shandwick Place and the West End, George Street, Castle Street, Frederick Street, Queen Street, Hanover Street – before returning along Princes Street, back up to Tollcross and home. Wind and rain, sun and rain, rain and rain. For three whole mornings and three whole afternoons, he got soaked and wind-dried, sun-dried and soaked all over again as he followed the exact same route, calling in with Kantian regularity at the exact same job agencies. First thing each morning he purchased the *Scotsman* and at lunchtime the *Edinburgh Evening News*. He scanned the Situations Vacant, took notes, made phone calls. Busy, busy, busy.

One day. Two days. Three days. Grim, Grimmer, Grimmest. Tomorrow would be SUPER-GRIM.

His time was up, his period of grace at an end. DD hadn't phoned to ask and he hadn't phoned to tell. The result of all this concentrated effort and expense? One big fat fucking zero.

He stood in Woolworth's doorway on Lothian Road and cursed the philosopher of Königsberg. It was all over. He was beaten. Three days of solid walking and he wasn't one fucking step forward with any plan, special or otherwise. Immanuel Fucking Kant had a lot to answer for.

His pace faltered as he turned into Tollcross. He dragged his feet. Nearer home meant nearer failure. Life as he knew it – Social Security, the crammer and the cupboard, but minus DD probably – now stretched out far, far into the future. Next to the Co-op he noticed the beggar girl he'd talked with a few days earlier. He was in no mood for conversation today, unless maybe to pick up a few tips on begging. He was about to cross the road when he noticed a woman approach her. After a few words, the woman bent down to give her a cup of something hot and what was probably a roll or sandwich. A genuine philanthropist.

He hurried past. Quick march.

A *beggar*. When Mrs. Thatcher stopped his benefits, was that how he'd end up?

Did his presentation skills let him down? Or was it his wardrobe – the jersey and jeans combo, topped off by the ex-Army and Navy Stores greatcoat? Perhaps he should revamp his appearance, invest in something more calculated to reassure a prospective employer re his character and dependability, his standing in the community. It would be worth one last try.

Tollcross boasted a wide range of charity shops with all budgets catered for, even his: from the ones whose rancid stench of unwashed clothes and mice-droppings caught at the throat, to the more upmarket Sue Ryder where he'd bought the disposable clothes he and the Cat had occasionally ripped off each other. Luckily, there was still some change left over from his purge session in Sandy Bell's. He'd ignore Thoreau's crack about avoiding any job that required a new suit. This would be an investment in his future, with no expense spared. For once nothing less than a top-of-the-range boutique would do. He headed straight into Oxfam.

However, he couldn't stop himself from first having a quick scan through the secondhand books. Mostly paperback horror, thriller, romance. The usual. Nothing of interest, but even if there had been he'd have resisted. Today he was on a mission. No revamped wardrobe meant no job, no job meant no DD.

Okay, over to the men's clothing rail. He was no sooner rummaging through the suits and jackets on offer – something smart? something casual? chic and trendy? classic? – when the heart-warming scene he'd witnessed a moment ago out in the street came back to him full-force: *The look of gratitude on the beggar girl's face, as if she'd been served a ten-course banquet with all the trimmings.*

But wait.

Wait . . .

There was *something* . . . Not the kindness, not the compassion . . . Not the beggar herself even, nor the street . . . But *something* . . .

The woman bending down, the woman offering . . . ?

Wait . . .

Almost there . . .

The book he'd just seen on the 10p shelf, a most unusual title . . .

Not only that, but over in the bric-a-brac . . .

All at once Hume experienced a moment of *satori*, of pure illumination. An epiphany to rival Descartes in his Dutch oven and Archimedes in his bath. Even better, this glorious vision came with a built-in soundtrack of tills being rung, of cheques being cashed.

Ten minutes later he left the shop with a large plastic bag under his arm, and a plan. A plan, life-changing in its implications! Next stop, the Co-op. Quickest shop ever, and out.

As he passed the beggar, he dropped a ten-pence piece into her cup – he'd write it off as an offering to the Gods – and raced up the road to Barclay Towers.

❧

'What's your name?'

'Megan.' She gave the man a smile. Why not? It might help. Easy to see this one wouldn't punch and kick. Not women, anyway. Blue eyes, sort of a crying blue. The slightest scratch would bring out the tears he was probably always holding back. She could almost see them, like looking through rain.

'Have you nowhere to stay, Megan?'

'The pavement here, till I get moved on.'

Give him the right answers and he'd ask the right questions. Needed guided was all.

Down on his hunkers now in front of her, saying his name. Francis. That sad Rain-Eyes look. She could tell he wanted to touch her, on the arm maybe, or her hair like she was a child. Wanting to believe it was only about being kind. Wanting to believe he'd touch her just the same if she'd been a man. To make contact. To show that he cared.

'What about the hostels?' She could hear real caring in his voice.

'Full of crazies and drunks. Fine if you want to get your stuff stolen and your face punched.'

His hand was trembling. His need to touch her was getting stronger. Sex was always there. She could see it in their faces, feel it in their touch. Contempt too. The sex and the contempt, whichever won out meant she got some money. Or else a kicking. Or else nothing.

*Where are you from?*

*Have you been begging long?*

*Did you lose your job?*

*What about your family?*

The right answers brought Rain-Eyes to more of the right questions.

It was always quicker with women. The kindness. Sometimes kindness and contempt mixed up. Like that woman giving her tea and a ham roll a short while back. Saying that if she could she'd take her home, but all the time not really meaning it. Like she was afraid to. Afraid of the usual – dirt, fleas, her husband, her good furniture, afraid that her children might catch something, afraid that a beggar might mess up the place, that a beggar might steal. She didn't really blame the woman – so tea and a roll it was, and everyone was happy.

Rain-Eyes was following her question-and-answer trail nicely. She told him she was from out in the country near Eyemouth and she had not been begging for long. No job anymore because the boss – a real slimy bastard – had always been trying it on with her (she looked away from him while she told this bit, like she was ashamed). It was a café, she told Rain-Eyes, then forgot and said it was a bar, but he didn't seem to notice. So she stuck to the café story and that she'd had to run to get away. She told it like it really happened, how one time in the kitchen after everyone had gone, he'd grabbed her hair from the back and . . .

When she said about the boss grabbing hold of her hair, she knew it would work because Rain-Eyes said how terrible, how awful . . . and touched her hair without noticing he'd done it. He just did. Couldn't help himself.

Then, seeing what he'd done, he quickly jerked back his hand like he could pretend he'd never touched her at all.

'Is that how you got the—?'

And he pointed to his own right eye, meaning hers, of course, the bruise. Unsure about being so close to her again, about touching her again. But still wanting to, very much.

'That was after.'

'Oh. You mean it was someone else?'

She looked away, like it was shame. Like it made her feel so bad she couldn't say anything more.

She wiped her eyes like she'd been crying with the pain of what she was telling, and the pain of what she didn't tell.

For a few seconds neither of them spoke.

Just then it began to rain. St Francis stood up.

'Where will you go now, Megan?'

The right question at last. All nervous-looking and trusting, she gave him a shy smile.

※

Hume half-vaulted, half-flew up the Barclay Towers stairs. Dumped both plastic bags on the kitchen table to deal with later. Getting towards five already. No time, no time. He'd people to speak to, things to do. A handbook to consult, things to learn.

First – the phone call.

*Fine, Mrs. Chisholm, and you?*

Pleasantries out of the way, he gave the old lady a message to pass on to DD. Asked her to repeat it, to be sure.

'But, Hume, wouldn't you prefer to speak to your girlfriend in person? I know she's in. It's no problem to fetch her from—'

'Thank you, Mrs. Chisholm, but I'm in a real rush.'

'It's no problem, you know. A couple of minutes and—'

'DD's been waiting for me to call. Please give her my message *verbatim* – and say I'll expect her tonight at eight, dressed as I've suggested.'

'A special evening?'

'Very special, if all goes well. And not just this evening either. Goodbye, Mrs. Chisholm.'

'My goodness, Hume! Don't tell me you're going to ask her to—?'

Next, the Electric Boy.

Up the carpeted stairs to the attic flat. Rapid *knock-knock-knock*. A shout from inside telling him to come in.

No Mohicans or Heavy Metal Men in sight, thank Christ, and no Coconut. Just the Electric Boy sitting cross-legged on the floor of his kitchen-cum-recording studio, labelling spools of tape. Hume told him what he wanted. Yes, or no?

Instead, he was invited to sit down. A set of headphones was handed over. If he didn't mind – this re-take of 'Tartan Terror'? Listen out for when the maracas—?

No time for maracas.

Only take a moment.

The headphones clamped to his ears. Some buttons pressed, some switches thrown.

The maracas sounded great. Yes or no?

The Electric Boy took forever to explain that he hadn't re-let the Cat's room because it'd take too much time and trouble. People trooping up and down the stairs all day, in and out the flat all day. People looking at this, looking at that. People asking things. Having to interview them, having to explain. Arranging terms, drawing up agreements. Anyway, punk bands were paying an arm and a leg to record in anarchic-style studios like his kitchen, so he didn't need the money. Simpler just to leave things as they were.

*Yes . . . Yes . . .* Hume showed as much patience as he could manage. *Yes, of course . . . Yes, he understood. . . .* He pressed the Electric Boy and pressed him hard. *No need to interview him.*

'The maracas, only take a moment. Can you listen again?'
*No need to show him the room . . .*
The maracas?
*OK, the maracas.*
Headphones, buttons, switches.
*The maracas are fine. No need to do anything . . .*
'Do you really think they—?'
*Even better than the first time. Just say yes . . .*
Finally the Electric Boy gave in.

Rent agreed at his cupboard rate plus two pounds, and Hume was already heading out the door: 'Thanks.'

Back down to the flat. So much to do, so little time. Some light dusting and hoovering. He'd keep the furniture-moving to a minimum, not wanting to catch *St Francitis.*

The room smelt stale and airless. It felt chilled, damp, musty. He opened the window to let in a refreshing blast of cold October. Only a short blast because it had started raining again. Later he'd switch on the electric fire. Both bars. This evening there'd be no expense spared.

⁂

Four flights up they got to the top landing and stopped outside a door. The rain was beginning to batter the glass cupola above the stairwell – solid rain she was well out of. The man called Francis turned to her and put his finger to his lips:

'*Hush.* You must keep quiet until we get into my room, Megan. OK?'

She nodded. Depending on what he was after, of course.

Depending on what she could get away with. Maybe he really was just being kind? With his wavery Rain-Eyes he looked weak enough for that.

Leading her straight down a dark corridor and into a room. His. A room with walls, floor, ceiling, windows. The rain was kept outside and so was the wind. She'd not be going back downstairs. No way.

He started fussing about. Giving her a towel to dry her hair, her face. Pulling over a big old-fashioned chair for her to sit in.

Lighting the gas fire.

Turning it up.

Turning it down a bit.

Then up again.

Fussing about with books and papers. Dropping them anywhere.

Switching the desk-light on . . .

. . . and all the while never stopping his talk-talk-talk.

'Sorry about the mess.' Picking up another book and putting it down on a low table beside her, next to a mug of cold, slicked tea. 'Wasn't expecting a guest.'

A guest? Meaning her. So she nodded and gave him a smile. Same as the right answers, the nods and smiles could be good too and sometimes led to more good.

'Some tea? Something to eat?'

Another nod, another smile. The fire was roasting red, warm and purring.

'Back in a few minutes. Make yourself at home.'

Make herself at home? *Want me to trash the place to what I'm used to?* But she held her tongue. His kindness seemed real enough. The gas fire had been switched on to warm her up. Full on, just for her. She could feel the warm-warm-warm sink into her, and hear its comforting *hiss*. From another part of the flat came the sounds of clattering dishes, running water. Francis was getting food ready. Also, just for *her*.

Letting herself sink back into the cushions . . . and immediately was so tired her eyes closed like she was a little girl's doll whose lids fell tight shut whenever she was tilted backwards. Couldn't stop them from shutting. Not here. Listening to the rain that couldn't reach her now, listening to the wind punching and punching at the window to get in. Like she'd fallen asleep in the street and woken up in a lighthouse, high up and safe from the storm outside, the sounds of faraway traffic breaking in waves down below on the shore where she usually . . .

'Milk? Sugar?'

She must've fallen asleep. But here was a mug of tea on a tray with two slices of toast, yellow and runny with melted butter, and Francis saying, 'Just to keep you going till the main part. You're not vegetarian or anything, are you?'

He was joking, right?

'Anything's fine. This looks great, thanks.'

'Back in a few minutes.'

Every time he went out of the room and came in again he was very careful to close the door after him. To keep the heat in, but also because he probably didn't want other people to know she was here. Good, she could use that.

'Ready?'

She must've fallen asleep again.

A fry-up . . . a plate for him and a plate for her. Sausage, bacon, eggs, beans. Brown sauce. Lots more toast. Lots more everything. Biggest feast ever.

When she stopped for breath at last, Francis started asking and so she started telling – 'This guy says he'd give me a pound if I went into a close with him. You understand? Not all the way, not for a pound. But—'

He was staring at her. Really shocked. Good.

She went back to tearing into the food again, hungry now even though she wasn't hungry at first. Sometimes she was beyond hunger. Francis had asked about her bruised eye and cuts. So she was telling him something, anything. Telling him everything. She sat across from him, speaking low like what she was confessing was really bad.

'It was on Drummond Street, that derelict tenement along from Rutherford's bar, where dossers've kicked the door in, just past the Indian place. A real mess of bins and stuff in the passage, but easy money. Said I'd be able to treat myself to a curry afterwards, if I wanted.'

'Megan! But he didn't—?'

Making sure it took her a long time to answer. Playing it out slow, a word at a time: telling how bad she'd felt saying she'd do it, and how down-and-out she'd felt that so as to get herself something to eat she would . . .

Then telling how, once she'd got the guy started, he'd put his hands on her shoulders and was pushing her down onto her knees, saying: *Go on . . . into your mouth . . . two quid.*

Telling it so slow. Making Francis have to drag the words out of her. How the guy pressed her shoulders, kept her there saying over and over: *Go on . . . on yer knees.*

She was looking away again. Like she was ashamed. Whispering so Francis had to lean really close . . . and before he knew it, he'd reached forward to touch her on the shoulder, like to steady her.

'No, Megan, no. It wasn't your fault. None of it.'

'Told him to fuck off, I did.' She was sitting up straighter now, looking him full in the face. Looking him full in his rainy eyes. 'Told him to keep his money, keep everything, to fuck off and leave me alone.'

'Megan, what a terrible—'

Francis was resting his hand on her arm – meaning to show her that sharing her misery between the two of them would help make it bearable. And the shame, too, and the hurt she felt. Saying her name each time – but in his voice she heard it was really *his* misery, *his* shame. The weight of it, like she could almost *feel* it.

'That's when the guy hits me. Shoves me hard up against the close wall and starts in with his fist.'

'Megan . . .!'

'Then tried forcing me again, the fucker, me with my eye swelling up, or maybe that turned him on . . . I'm screaming at him to fuck off when a door slams upstairs. Guy stops hitting me, stands listening, trying to hear if anyone's coming down. That's my chance, I shove him away and run to the street door before he knows what's happening.'

She paused. 'Then here comes the funny bit – he can't chase after me because his zipper's got stuck and it's still hanging out! He's shouting and swearing and hopping up and down the close trying to fasten himself.' She mopped up the last of the egg yolk with the last piece of toast. 'Could've hung around for a good laugh, but I'm out in the street, and soon long gone.'

There was a knock at the door. Francis jumped to his feet, almost sending the small table flying.

'Yes?' Putting his head out into the corridor to see who was there. 'Yes?'

Moving house took Hume less than ten minutes. Books snatched off their wooden shelf; shirts, jeans and his jacket yanked off their nails. Clean underwear and laundry bagged. His entire worldly possessions were bundled across the corridor an armload at a time, to his new home. His new and wonderful home. After his windowless dinner-gonging Hell, this was going to be Paradise. Never mind the limitations of inductive reasoning, when the sun rose tomorrow morning – he'd actually see it!

Socks, underwear and jerseys were stowed out of sight in wooden drawers; his jacket, jeans and shirts were given their very own hanger each, in a full-sized, grown-up wardrobe. His books were stacked in a bookcase with more than one shelf. Real chest of drawers, real wardrobe, real bookcase, real window – and all in a room he could actually stand up in. This was real life.

Having seen the trail to furniture-madness blazed by St Francis, he opted to leave the movables exactly where they were. No time anyway. At some point he'd probably get rid of Nelson, retire him to greener pastures. In the meantime the wooden sheep was advised he was on seven days' probation, one hoof out of line and he'd find himself rattled downstairs to the nearest charity shop. Then Hume gave him a reassuring pat as if to say he'd only been kidding.

DD was scheduled to arrive in just over two hours. Switch into overdrive.

Thanks to a shiny veneer that gave its surface an expensive-looking sheen, the discreet single-drawer writing table needed only a quick spit and polish. It would be centre-stage,

of course. Which meant shifting Nelson nearer to the window
. . . Which meant moving the wardrobe over to. . .

Jesus Christ.

Time to consult the in-house expert.

Five minutes later, when the wardrobe was being eased a
few inches away from the wall to allow them a firmer grip, he
heard St Francis's astonished cry:

'My God, will you look at that!'

It was the wall he was pointing to. Hume straightened up,
stepped back and looked.

He could hardly believe his eyes.

FUCK!

Then he remembered. When the Cat had originally moved
in she'd decided to re-paint the walls a no-fuss magnolia and
opted for the simple elegance of white gloss for the woodwork.
Her intention had been to create a bright and airy atmosphere,
one that would hold the light and make the room seem more
spacious than it was. Also, she'd wished to suggest a sufficient
hint of the great outdoors to comfort Nelson. From the start,
the original and truly hideous green-leaf-on-brown-back-
ground pattern that was repeated round the entire room, had
proved particularly stubborn. She told him that initial trials
had indicated the need for several coats of industrial strength
magnolia, laid on thick. The Cat, of course, was a busy woman,
a mathematics student with problems to solve, essays to write,
tutorial papers to give, exams to study for. Once she'd come to
a final decision on the most effective locations for her various
pieces of furniture, no doubt after painstaking calculations,
she would have intended her decisions to be definitive, and
lasting. No further furniture-moving anticipated, ever.

Which explained everything.

For, having found the ideal position for the wardrobe, the bookcase and so forth, she must have then simply painted around them. Witness St Francis's cry of surprise.

To move the wardrobe would result in a wardrobe-shaped silhouette of repeated green-leaf-on-brown, set in a field of magnolia. A ghostly after-image, like a soul separated from its body. Further investigations disclosed a chest-of-drawers-shaped silhouette, a bookcase-shaped silhouette . . .

Gradually the full implications sank in. Two options:

To move all the furniture out into the hall and repaint the entire room

To leave each item of furniture exactly where it was

No contest.

A few minutes short of eight o'clock, Hume switched the extra bar of the electric fire back on. Its no-expense-spared welcoming glow would set the tone for the evening ahead. As well as being a part-celebration (her diploma) and a part-apology (for his lifestyle to date), the next couple of hours were intended as an experiment that might very well determine the course of his entire life to come. Whatever happened, he'd give it his best shot.

After a final readjustment of the anglepoise lamp so that its soft illumination diffused evenly up the wall to spill fanwise out across the ceiling, he lit the single white candle that was to be the modest centrepiece of the small dining table. He switched off the main light. The 100 watt interrogation glare was at once replaced by candlelit intimacy, letting the furniture and its gallery of latent ghost-images recede into a murky backdrop. Perfect, more or less.

The doorbell rang. Cue one last top-to-toe check in the dressing-table mirror.

Haircut (self-trimmed)

Shave

Wing collar and bow-tie

Starched white shirt

Striped waistcoat

Black swallowtail jacket

Pressed (i.e. ironed) black trousers, seamed with black piping

Mirror-polished black shoes

*Ecco Homo!* as Nietzsche might have said. Hume gave his reflection the thumbs up.

Out in the hall he allowed himself an executive-style shooting of the cuffs to confirm himself in his new role, then opened the door . . . and bowed.

'Good evening, madam. Your coat and umbrella, please.' Refusing to meet her eye and ignoring her look of total bewilderment, he stood to one side to let her enter. He took her wet coat and hung it on one of the hall pegs. Her brolly was left to drip out on the landing.

DD had carried out his instructions to the letter, surpassing them even. Strictly formal, an ivory-coloured dress with long white gloves, high heels, a touch of make-up, a hint of perfume and her best jewellery. She was starting down the hall towards the kitchen as usual, when he touched her on the arm, coughed discreetly and ushered her into his new room.

Thanks to his painstaking efforts, the place had ceased to be haunted by the Cat's presence. Above, suspended almost miraculously in mid-air, low-wattage illumination fell like grace upon the shined-up veneer of the perfectly laid table.

Indeed, so subtle was the lighting that the 'dining table' itself was hardly more than suggested. It was all but invisible – a lake of near-darkness on whose surface lay the reflections of a less-illusory world, like so many drifting islands of the blessed. Candlelight was pooled in the curved shallow of the dinner plate while, further off, its soft brilliance faded to shadow in the corners of the room. The polished cutlery, plate, folded napkin and condiments had been laid out with butler-like precision as detailed in his Oxfam copy of *Domestic Servants and Their Duties* (Published throughout the Empire). Expectations of the evening's elegance were hinted at in the nest of three glasses and in the glittering ensemble of nearly matching knife, fork and spoon.

DD had never been in this room before. She paused to gaze around, noting the formality of the candlelit dinner table, the extravagance of the electric fire's two bars. One place setting only. One chair.

'Your seat, madam.'

*What the fuck was going on?* Was Hume trying to be romantic? Was this a belated celebration of her Diploma *with distinction*? Was he hoping to act out some obscure sexual fantasy? Lady and manservant, perhaps?

She sat down, removed her long gloves.

'Some wine, madam?'

She gave a nod of assent. Her glass was filled.

With a Jeeves-like shimmer, he exited.

He had hardly gone out the door when he about-turned and re-entered to switch on a small radio.

'The evening concert, madam.'

He Jeevesed himself out again.

In the kitchen Hume removed the prepared hors d'oeuvres from the fridge – an oval dish containing two headless sardines invitingly ringed with a complement of sliced tomato and cucumber. He gave the edge of the plate a wipe-round with the dishcloth to remove any excess fish-oil. A rather cold starter for October, but soup would have been simply asking for trouble. The handbook had been surprisingly emphatic on this point, explaining that when the servant bent down to present the guest with their brimming plateful, not only was there the increased risk of spillage, but also the more serious danger of 'thumbing it'. For the inexperienced footman, 'thumbing it' had ended many a promising career. And so . . . a brace of drained and stationary sardines, with all the trimmings.

Bearing the platter before him on his upturned palm, his arm extended as per the illustration in the handbook, Hume returned to the dining room and stood next to DD's chair to take up his serving position. He bent forward, held out the dish with spoon and fork towards her. For a moment she was clearly puzzled, then she reached up and served herself.

'Hume, what on earth is going on? I'm very touched to be waited on like this, but what exactly are you . . . ?'

'All in good time, madam.' Then silence. Having withdrawn to dispose of the serving dish, he returned to butler-stance himself behind her chair and become the perfect servant – in attendance, but invisible. And silent.

First course finished, he removed her plate, exited and returned to lay a clean plate for the main course. Withdrew and returned to serve a heated-up individual steak pie. Withdrew. Returned with a serving dish of peas and potatoes. Withdrew.

Returned. He poured water. He poured wine. Resumed butler-stance.

DD dined to most of a Mozart symphony. Dessert was two clementines on a bed of seasonal monkey nuts. Dinner was rounded off with the cheese board – several previously unwrapped segments of processed cheese and some cream crackers.

'Would Madam prefer to take her coffee in the drawing room?' He nodded towards the armchair that loomed in the nearby shadows.

Coffee was served.

Hume threw himself on the bed. The evening had gone well, very well indeed.

'Now, DD, here's the plan . . .'

⁂

*A few drops of rain, but so, so light. Then a few more. The drops getting heavier and heavier. She'll soon be drenched through—*

Megan jerked awake. She'd been half-dozing in Francis's armchair, her feet up on the fender. Checking everything was still there - the ceiling, the walls, the floor, the curtained window, the door. Safe from the weather, from the police. Safe from the crazies.

That falling rain was *him*, Francis, staring down at her. That was what woke her - Rain-Eyes, getting himself into her dreams.

'What do you want?' She sat up, her hands clenched into fists, arms crossed over her chest. 'What are you standing there for?'

'Nothing.'

'You were doing something.'

'Yes. I helped Hume next door get his new room sorted. You were fast asleep when I came back so I've been sitting here doing my crossword.'

'I could have slept a week.'

'Now he's moved out the cupboard you can sleep there, if you want.'

'A cupboard?'

'A boxroom really. There's a bed, well, a mattress. Low ceiling. Snug. Hume's lived there for years. It's all yours, for tonight. Only, you have to keep very, very quiet.'

Putting his fingers to his lips, he led her out of his room and into the dark corridor. He pointed to a frosted-glass door – the bathroom. Then tiptoed into the room opposite, clicked on the light. The kitchen.

'Some water?'

She nodded.

He filled a glass, then they went back a couple of steps along the corridor. She could hear voices coming from the door on the right. Pointing, he held up two fingers like the peace sign. Meaning there were two people in the room.

Then into the cupboard-boxroom. Waiting till both of them were inside and the door pulled shut behind him, he clicked on the light.

No window, narrow, and the slanted ceiling so low at the far end that with your head on the pillow you could probably reach up and touch the ceiling. No room here for anyone but her, making it the best room in the world. An empty shelf and some nails sticking out of the wall. A metal door, it looked like, hung sideways along the back.

'What's that?'

*Shushing* her with his finger to his lips, he whispered: 'It's an echo chamber.'

'A what?'

'Just don't touch it.'

Why would she?

'And you have to be very quiet, Megan. Nobody must know you're here.'

She nodded.

Another whisper. 'You have a sleeping bag?'

'In my pocket, you think? Someone stole it.'

'Sorry I've no extra blankets, but you can have my coat and some other stuff. It'll soon warm up in here.'

She nodded again, what else could she do?

After he'd gone back to his room, she went and washed, standing at the basin. Washed as silently as she could. No clean clothes so she put her old t-shirt, jeans, socks and underwear back on. They felt greasy and street-hard. A few minutes later she was lying on the mattress under a couple of coats and with a rolled-up jersey for a pillow. Warming up nicely.

Was there anything else she needed?

'I'm fine, thanks, Francis.'

What he really wanted, of course, was to touch her. She knew he wanted to hold her . . . and to be held. Even when he'd clicked off the cupboard light he still stayed in the doorway, in the pitch dark. Wanting.

'Comfortable, are you, Megan?'

'Thank you, Francis,' she whispered back. 'Goodnight.'

'Sleep well. Goodnight.'

Still standing there. Rain-Eyes – who couldn't turn away. Till at last he did.

St Francis returned to his bedroom, closed the door behind him.

*Megan*. Was she his act of contrition? Not genuine kindness – whatever he might like to pretend – but a calculated offering to God, a gesture of atonement for his shameful treatment of the Cat? Nothing more than a shoddy attempt to barter with Him?

Or had he been hoping simply to get her into bed? Because being a down-and-out, she'd be grateful to him? Grateful enough to let him—?

Wanting to kiss her goodnight in the cupboard – was that so terrible, so very shameful?

Should he go back? Tell her it would be better if she came and slept in his room? And *he* slept in the cupboard? Yes, he could do that. It would be right, it would be—

Before he realised what he was doing, he'd thrown his crossword book across the room – knocking over his tea on the way.

He stared down at the smashed mug, the puddle spreading out on the parquet. Why the hell had he done that?

Why?

Who the hell cared *why*?

Who fucking cared? On his feet now. The small table. Booting it over – CRASH!

Next, the spider plant. A single swipe with the back of his hand, and its clay pot shattered against the fender. Earth everywhere.

Sweeping the line of books and ornaments off the mantelpiece. CRASH! SMASH!

Kicking the mess of broken pot and clods of dirt across the room.

Philosophy next. Two shelves of it, Ancient to Modern, arranged chronologically from left to right. First in, first out – Heraclitus and the pre-Socratics went cartwheeling across the room, Plato's *Dialogues* followed, then Aristotle, Boethius and Aquinas; Spinoza was drop-kicked into touch near the fireplace. A few thrillers went slamming into the opposite wall, along with the Russians, half of Proust and all of Camus; Coppleston's 11 volume history brought up the rear. He clattered his homemade bookshelves onto the floor, them and the bricks they rested on.

Smug-looking Descartes with his smug-sounding answers, was ripped from the wall, torn in half, then in half again. Torn and torn until he was confetti. Fucking Descartes, fucking—

'Rearranging things again? A bit drastic, no?' Hume was standing in the open doorway, naked except for a towel wrapped round his waist. 'I did knock.'

St Francis gazed at the planks of wood, the bricks and books scattered everywhere, the smashed plant pots, smashed ornaments. His room was a shambles.

'All done.'

'And you, Francis?'

'Fine, thanks.'

'Glad to hear it. Goodnight.'


How long had he been sitting here on the floor? Minutes? Hours?

Clear up the mess?

Or what?

He got to his feet and started on a desultory tidy up.

A book here, a fragment of plant pot there, smashed mug. Picking things up, putting them down. Mopping up the spilt tea, most of it anyway. Crunching earth underfoot as he crossed the floor meaning to prop a couple of planks up against the wall. Then didn't. He shrugged, stood and had another look round.

It would take hours.

He wiped the dirt from his hands onto an old t-shirt which he then tossed into the mess. Went for a pee. Picked his way back through the debris and climbed into bed. Off with the light.

⌘

The cupboard door was shut. Megan hardly remembered ever being so warm, so dry, so safe. His man-scent on the coats and jersey - his kindness, she'd call it. Snuggling herself down deeper into the warm, knowing she was alone. Knowing that no one and nothing could get to her. Even better with low ceiling and no windows. What was so wonderful to see outside?

Good darkness, not like in the street at night. Keep quiet here and she'd be safe. Here, she'd survive. This darkness was *hers*. It was deep inside her and inside nobody else. She was her own company, the best.

She had her own place inside her where the screams came from. And here, if the screams did come, there'd be nowhere for them to escape to. Here, they'd be trapped. Before they could start clawing to get out, she'd catch them and nail them to the wall. Leave them behind her when she left.

No sooner falling asleep than jerked awake again. The crazies. They'd followed her. She could hear them crashing, bashing, smashing everything. Wrecking everything. Louder and louder like they were near and coming nearer. Like they wanted to break down the door, wanted to trample . . .

Don't scream. Don't breathe, even.

# 6

LIKE ALL CREATIVE efforts, Hume's crafting of Executive Service's first promotion leaflet quickly turned into hard labour – hard labour complicated by the too-many marker pens, coloured pencils, crayons, biros and bottles of ink laid out on his desk. Too many options meant too many choices, meant too many chances for too many mistakes – he was glad he had plenty of Tipp-ex, lots and lots of it.

Elsewhere in the city, the weak October sun shone its morning rays equally across the working-class estates, the middle-class suburbs, the stonewalled wealth of the Grange, Merchiston and the New Town. With the passing hours, its cold brightness soaked into the grassy slopes of Princes Street Gardens, the Meadows, Arthur's Seat . . . Not that Hume noticed.

No mid-morning coffee for him, no lunchtime break. He never lifted his head from the desk, not once. Tongue out, eyes squinting with effort, he smeared, he smudged, misspelt and swore his way through the hours. Again and again he forgot to allow for a margin, or else left too much empty space. His lines would turn out too cramped or too free-range, the words marching to the right in bureaucratic rigidity only to come to a sudden halt, crammed together at the edge of the page. Individual letters swelled, lurched, squatted, and were all-too-frequently stricken with blots. Some sheets got crumpled, many got torn. By early afternoon the floor was littered with the casual tumbleweed of screwed-up rejects. He rang the changes on dozens, on scores of possible slogans and catchphrases; his variations of tone and nuance sought to address the whole world while, at the same time, they endeavoured to speak to every individual in person. Too subtle? Not subtle enough?

A butler FOR YOU!

YOU NEED a BUTLR

The bsst dinners are

The BEST dinners are srved by . . .

It was past two o'clock when he finally slumped forward onto the desk, laid his head on his arms and all but wept. He could serve, he could pour, he could butler-stance . . .

But *this* . . .

He was on the point of scrapping his entire promotion campaign when DD turned up. She was shocked—

'You're not writing another essay, are you?'

Miserably he held out his most recent botch-up:

EVERYONE NEEDS A BUTTER

Thanks to his increasingly frantic use of correction fluid, the sheet made a crackling sound as he handed it over. DD glanced at it, binned it.

She took off her coat. 'A cup of tea to start with, perhaps?'

⚘

Megan woke to find she'd crash-landed into someone else's life, and that someone else was now her. No crazies had come during the night. No icy wind, no rain, no police. She wasn't getting shouted at, pushed, shoved, punched, kicked, spat at.

For once she had the chance to piece together who she really was.

So make it into something good.

Appearing every morning out of a nowhere of dreams within dreams, that was her. Not out of yesterday, not out of the days and nights stretching back and back so far that she didn't know when or where, not out of the skip either or the garage with the busted window, or that doorway in the Cowgate where the crazies had come one night with their blunt knives threatening to set her free. Appearing out of nothing was what it felt like being her. Until now.

Treat Francis as he needed to be treated and she'd have a mattress to return to whenever she wanted. Her own mattress. Her own place. Her own life.

Megan stood in the doorway and stared. What the hell had been going on here? Not crazies coming for her last night, but Rain-Eyes himself by the look of it, smashing up his own place. Was he some kind of stay-at-home crazy?

Then he was saying sorry about the mess, and he hoped the noise hadn't disturbed her? Would she like some tea and toast for breakfast, or coffee? That big bookcase - he pointed to a heap of books and bricks and wooden planks - had fallen apart as he was trying to fix it.

And the smashed plant pots, the ornaments? The earth everywhere?

'Tea would be great, thanks,' she told him. 'I'd have slept through the end of the world. I've a lot of sleep to catch up on.'

He nodded. Nervous - a bird easily startled and ready to flit out of reach if she moved or spoke too sudden. But best of all was the pleasure she'd seen rush into his rain-eyes when she'd come into the room. Not from hoping he might get to fuck her, but just from seeing her.

She drank the tea and crunched the toast. 'Really kind that you let me stay. If you want, I can go back to where I was begging and get some money to pay you.'

'No, Megan. Definitely not.'

'For tonight, maybe?'

He wouldn't send her out to beg for him, not Rain-Eyes. Here was her chance to get herself cleaned and rested, get her clothes washed. Not much really, but it was everything. Treat him well, but not too well.

On his feet again. The startled bird moving to where he felt safer, to where his kindness wouldn't get upset.

'No, Megan. Not begging. It's not good . . .'

'Nor's starving.'

'. . . and what happened with that guy who punched you, it'll probably happen again. Next time even worse.'

She stared down at the floor like he'd just made her feel ashamed.

A few more words from him and a few more silences from her was all it'd take. She picked at a loose thread dangling from the arm of the chair.

He was embarrassed. But, yes, it was okay for her to stay tonight, if she wanted. Maybe not in the cupboard though. It was a bit too public. Someone might go in. She was to give him some of her clothes in the washing machine and, if his flatmate went out, she could risk a quick shower. He'd clear a space on the floor for her mattress.

She would be safe. Yes, with him.

After lunchtime soup and a cheese sandwich, she hung

her newly washed clothes off the mantelpiece and over the backs of chairs to dry, then curled up on her mattress in front of the gas fire. She looked up and gave him a smile, a real one. Came easy now she knew she had the whole day ahead and another whole night of not being on the street. Of not being moved on. She could sleep and sleep and sleep. It was a start.

꧁

When Hume returned from the kitchen with a mug of tea, he found DD seated at his desk with a stack of print sheets of As, Bs, Cs . . . and a notebook laid out in front of her. There was no sign of his previous efforts. Put out of their misery, presumably.

'I brought these stencils with me – more professional-looking, don't you think?'

He could only agree.

First impressions were everything, she explained. Presentation was all. Forget being modest, being taste-ful, being understated. Don't waffle, don't explain – TELL them. Blow your own trumpet, and blow it loud. And in the fewest words possible. Be eye-catching, be direct yet devious, engaging yet subtle. But not too subtle. Lowest instincts are the strongest instincts. Insecurity, envy and greed. Aim low, and aim hard. The sense of superiority had to be flattered, the worst kinds of snobbery appealed to. Don't think of them as people, they are *clients*. They are targets, and you only get one shot at them.

It took her less than an hour. Hume made them more tea so they could raise a fresh mug to her skill and invention.

They sipped and admired the neatly stencilled flyer advertising Executive Service.

**YOU ARE THE VERY BEST?**
**THEN SHOW IT!**
**Be the envy of your business colleagues,**
**your friends and neighbours with**
**YOUR VERY OWN BUTLER.**
**Dinner parties a speciality!**
**CALL EXECUTIVE SERVICE: 316-2011**

Next he rushed off to PrestoPrint in Tollcross. Two hundred and fifty copies Xeroxed off, he rushed back to Executive Service HQ.

DD was waiting for him, her coat already on.

'I'll take seventy for the Grange. You do Merchiston this evening – take you a couple of hours at most. Then back here to practise and practise and practise. Tomorrow morning you leaflet the New Town. Then practise, practise, practise.'

A kiss and she was gone.

Strengthened by a restorative Pot Noodle, Hume spent the first part of his Saturday evening racing up and down the better-looking streets of nearby Merchiston, as well as upper Bruntsfield and lower Morningside, pushing his flyers through the most affluent-looking letterboxes of the poshest-looking houses. Then it was back to Barclay Towers for more Pot Noodle and the rest of Saturday night devoted to mastering the skills of his new profession, as described in the *Domestic Servants* handbook. Making a start on them, at least. Like some kind of labyrinthine system of German metaphysics, there seemed to be a vast amount of inter-related minutiae to keep track of. Using the pick of his charity shop wardrobe and the best of the assorted cutlery and plates from the kitchen, he ventured into the intricacies of—

How to dress correctly.

How to stand correctly.

How to walk correctly.

How to open and close a door correctly.

How to enter and leave a downstairs room (without knocking).

How to enter and leave an upstairs room (discreet knock, then wait).

How to set a table for breakfast/lunch/dinner (including the order of precedence in the seating arrangements).

How to lay out cutlery (first course on the outside and work in, knife blades always facing inwards).

How to fold napkins (mitres, lilies etc.).

How to arrange a nest of glasses (which glasses were appropriate for which wines etc.).

How to serve at table (starting with the guest at the host's right, then the host himself, then clockwise round the table to end up at 'tail-end Charlie', the temperature and quantity of whose share depended upon the number and appetite of the guests served before him).

How to select wine for the table.

How to serve wine (deft twist of the wrist at the conclusion of pouring to avoid drips).

How to care for wine.

How to hold a tray (for drinks, for canapés and at dinner).

How to press or iron clothes for immediate wear or for travel (including which suits/jackets/trousers/shoes were appropriate for which times of day and on which particular occasions).

How to lay out clothes.

How to fold/brush/hang clothes.

How to pack clothes.

How to unpack clothes.

How to prepare for shooting parties (from tigers to grouse).

How to prepare for fishing parties (river/lake/freshwater/sea).

How to address members of the Royal Family and their retinue, peers of the realm, heads of state, a duke, a lord, an earl, a marquis, a life peer, an ambassador, a consul, an honorary consul (and their ladies), members of the law, members of the government (national and local), commissioned officers of the armed forces, foreign dignitaries, members of the clergy (higher and lower).

How to address other staff.

How to address tradesmen.

He practised opening his bedroom door to greet and announce: Ambassador Nelson, Lord and Lady Nelson, Sir Nelson. *Open the door . . . and bow/Open the door . . . and bow/Open the door . . . and bow.* He walked round and round the room with a tray of glasses which he kept level at all times. The tray was placed on the small writing table, then lifted/replaced/re-lifted till his arms ached. Empty glasses first, then full. He laid and relaid the table for breakfast, for lunch and for dinner. He mastered the art of folding napkins and, having turned out six perfect mitres in a row, moved onto lilies. He packed and unpacked Ambassador Nelson's suitcase a dozen times.

Hours and hours later, he was exhausted. Utterly.

It was only just after midnight, but St Francis felt ready for bed. Apart from lunch and dinner – sausage, eggs and fried bread with tea and a chocolate biscuit to follow – Megan had slept through the day on her mattress in front of the fire. He laid aside his crossword puzzle book, yawned . . .

Then, quietly, ever so quietly . . .

. . . bent down close to the sleeping girl, and reached across to switch off the fire. Her blonde hair spilled over the cushion that served for a pillow. He almost let his hand drop to stroke the stray strands as she slept, brushing them aside from her cheek. But resisted. He stared down at her, his hand only inches above. Not a beautiful girl, not like the Cat, say. Not particularly attractive even. But she was here, with him. She had no one, but she trusted him. Finally, he stood up, went through to the bathroom.

He was about to switch off the desk light and climb into bed when he caught sight of some Perfect Forms scattered on the floor. Not once all evening had he even thought to slide his cut-out furniture around his cut-out room. It hadn't even crossed his mind. After weeks of constant usage, night after night, the pieces of card looked grimy and stained, buckled at the edges from being forced together. The ground plan itself was dog-eared, the bay window area Sellotaped where it had been damaged during a particularly frustrating evening. Without thinking, he picked up the sorry-looking scraps and tore them to pieces.

Less than five minutes later he, too, was fast asleep.

Next morning the sole owner and director of Executive Service rose early. After a working breakfast when he served himself a pot of tea and ate from a rack of triangular toast, he set off to the city centre. Now for stage two of his ES's advertising campaign – the New Town. And as he walked from letterbox to letterbox up and down the secluded Sunday-morning crescents, in and out of the cobbled squares, Hume began to think.

Theory was one thing, practice another. The propositions detailed in the *Domestic Servants* handbook could, for his purposes, be viewed as *a priori* rather than *a posteriori* – necessary rather than contingent, based on pure reason and not on experience (certainly not his). Many philosophers had spent their lives trying to distinguish between ontological and empirical truth – had he, so early on in his new career, come to a similar crossroads? The fact was that never having been to an actual cocktail party in his life – let alone a formal dinner party, diplomatic reception, weekend houseparty or shooting party – he was handicapped big time. The convivial get-togethers around the scuffed kitchen table were his only experience of gracious living, i.e. no experience at all. Perhaps a certain redefinition of terms could resolve this difficulty? If he were to impress a prospective client sufficiently to secure a booking, then a certain *flexibility of information* would be required. And so, in addition to practising his doors and bows, his trays, his table service, his napkins and his clothes, he would need to streamline this information and come up with a possible cover story that would justify his claim to be a 'highly experienced butler'.

Also, fixing a price list for cocktail parties, dinner parties, weekend house parties etc. was tricky. Obviously he wanted to charge as much as the market could bear, i.e. as much as he could get away with, but at the same time he didn't want to price himself out of a potential engagement. Here the handbook was of no use whatsoever. In all its 235 pages there was not one single mention of *money*. He knew he must never underestimate the snob factor – too cheap, and he wouldn't be taken seriously. They'd assume he was merely an out-of-work waiter. His price had to indicate his value.

Having thought and letterboxed his way around the New Town, Hume returned home in time for a working lunch of Pot Noodle, tea and toast. Executive Service was now up and running – it was a going concern whose phone might ring at any moment.

The rest of Sunday was practice-practice-practice.

⚜

St Francis's Sunday was perfect, the best in his life. Megan woke around midday, they had a brunch fry-up, then went out for a Sunday stroll. Him and Megan together. It was sunny-ish, not cold. They wandered through the Meadows, down to the Grassmarket, up past the Castle, looked across the city from the Esplanade, then along the sunless canyon of the Cowgate and into the open spaces of Holyrood Park. Rather than climb Arthur's Seat they sat on top of Salisbury Crags, their legs dangling over the edge. A companionable silence as they looked out over the city to the sea beyond. Then he delighted her by producing a surprise sausage sandwich each – he'd made them when cooking brunch and had slipped them secretly into his coat pocket. He'd forgotten to

149

bring water, but she gave him a big smile and said they'd just drink more tea when they got home. That was the high point of his day – when she said *home*.

Back in Barclay Towers she once more lay down on her mattress and was asleep in minutes.

Monday morning. When Megan awoke from her marathon sleep-in, St Francis made a late breakfast and then showed her a list that included warmer clothes and a couple of fresh blankets for her mattress. If she was up to it, he said, they were going shopping later. It was a short list. His meagre savings were rapidly disappearing. He knew that if she stayed much longer, he'd need to ask Hume about getting some cash-in-hand work at the crammer.

They returned home mid-afternoon after a tour of the Toll-cross charity shops. Over a mug of tea he asked if she'd like to try on something – that blue dress, the blouse, jeans, winter coat, scarf? Then, having checked that the coast was clear, he showed her into the bathroom to change.

He'd not cleared up the mess in his room as, until now, the noise would have disturbed Megan's sleep. But he intended to spick-and-span the place properly and soon. For the moment, he pushed some of the books and planks to one side and gave the middle of the floor a quick rub with an old shirt. He had just finished when she came in wearing the dress. He pointed to the space he'd cleared, and grinned at her:

'A catwalk, Megan. And all yours!'

Then wished he'd not said anything. He could see it all in the look she gave him, the hesitation, the uncertainty – a catwalk in this demolition site? Was he some kind of pervert expecting her to walk up and down in front of him, swaying her hips as if she was a fashion model? He shouldn't have cleared anything, shouldn't have suggested anything. He shouldn't have—

A loud knock at his door.

'Francis! Francis!' More loud knocks.

He put his fingers to his lips and went out into the corridor. It was Hume and he was frantic.

※

ES's chief butler had been in the middle of serving a very late lunch to High Commissioner Nelson (a soup plate of tapwater with a dish of sliced bread to follow) when he heard the phone ring.

'Please excuse me, your Excellency.' Hume withdrew to the kitchen.

'Executive Service. Hume speaking.'

'Mr. Cunningham here.' The caller had the correct accent. 'We're having some people round for drinks. Never come across you chaps before. Your staff are fully experienced?'

The *flexibility of information*, honed to a few well-turned phrases, was ready for immediate delivery: 'Absolutely, sir. The core of Executive Service, several butlers and footmen, has recently returned from a year's secondment to the consular service in the Far East - kind of *shuttle-buttle* diplomacy you might call it!' Pause for a shared laugh, then a shift into business tone: 'Now, sir, how can we help you?'

'Small cocktail do, drinks for twenty or so chaps and their wives. Catering's already arranged, but my wife's just noticed your flyer and thinks your presence might give the evening that special lift. Some extra topspin, as it were.'

'Very well put, sir.' A butler-type clearing of the throat. 'And what date did you have in mind?'

'Tonight.'

'Tonight?' *Jesus Christ!* He rallied: 'Normally such bookings are made well in advance, however . . . Please excuse me a moment while I consult our schedule.'

Hume understood from his handbook that a cocktail party meant wandering around with a tray of drinks, then wandering around again afterwards, offering re-fills. A couple of hours at most. Trousering the cash at the end, then home. Money for jam.

He put down the receiver and noisily riffled some pages of the telephone directory into the mouthpiece. Another well-timed throat clearing before he continued, 'As I feared, sir, we do indeed have a largish reception tonight – embassy do, in fact – which will take most of our regular staff. However, as I wouldn't wish to disappoint a first-time client, your evening will receive my personal attention.'

'Actually, my wife appreciates that it's very last minute but thinks *two* members of your staff would be more appropriate. One to greet our guests, take their coats and so forth, while the other chap manages the drinks till everyone's arrived. Could you rustle up one more as well? By the way, my wife thinks a manservant adds more tone than a maid.'

'You'd like a butler *and* a footman?' *Jesus!*

'Perfect.'

Hume took down the details. 'We'll be there at 5:30. Goodbye, sir.' He hung up.

He was the butler, but . . . the footman?

Also, he'd forgotten to fix the fee. Shit.

Mrs. Chisholm's spacious lounge could have contained the whole of Barclay Towers with a good few acres left over.

'Keep still, Francis.' The collar stud that had bitten him in the neck adjusted, St Francis felt like a work-in-progress, only part-assembled.

To help meet the emergency, Mrs. Chisholm had offered to lend selected items of her late husband's evening clothes. The new footman was grateful but felt very awkward in the dead man's wings and tails. At least they fitted him, almost.

'You'll look great.' DD was down on her knees working her way round the bottom of the new footman's trouser legs, turning them up inside and securing them in place with black duct tape.

Less successful was the line of safety-pins up the back of his waistcoat to take in a good three inches of slack. So long as he remembered not to remove his jacket, remembered not to bend suddenly in *any* direction, indeed not to make any sudden movements at all, the risk would be minimal. It was only for a couple of hours. Everything would hold together. Probably. With a bit of luck.

The starched shirt felt like a piece of reinforced cornflake packet, the wing-collar and bow tie were strangling him, the striped waistcoat strained against its line of safety pins.

DD got to her feet. 'Right, Francis. A final twirl.'

Round he went with a most satisfying flair-and-flourish of the jacket and tails. Brother Michael would have overheated himself in his dark little confession box!

'You'll do.' She sounded genuinely impressed.

'You look splendid,' added Mrs. Chisholm.

As he turned, he caught sight of himself in the large mirror above the fireplace. Was that really *him*, that elegant young man dressed like Fred Astaire about to step out on the dance floor of a whole new life? He gave his reflection a nod of encouragement – and the safety-pinned, duct-taped footman nodded back.

Hume hurried him to the door: 'Five pounds plus tips, remember, and as many canapés as you can grab. And Champagne, buckets of the stuff.'

'But what do I *do*?'

'Like I said on the way over, you just stand around with a tray. Could do it in your sleep.'

They began to hurry along the street.

'But the door-and-coats, you said—'

'Tell you on the bus. Look, we've got to move. You'll be back before you know it. Your girlfriend can wait.'

'How do you know there's a girl in my—?'

'We'll get a bus at the corner. Come on. Most important thing is – a good footman is silent unless spoken to. He's supposed to be invisible.'

'Invisible? Dressed like this?'

꒳

Having taken their seats on the 41 as casually as anyone could when togged up in full evening dress, Hume wished he'd brought a newspaper to hide behind. School kids, being unable to keep their observations to themselves, were the worst. But this was no time to be squeamish – he had a crash-course to give on the duties of a footman:

'You'll start by doing the door-and-coats.'

'Which is?'

'Easy. Open the door – *Good evening, sir/Good evening, madam.* Take their coat, their fur wrap or whatever. Then point them towards the drawing room.'

'And what do I do with the coat?'

'Christ, Francis, you hang it up.'

'Where?'

'They'll have hooks, or something. It's the New Town. A whole cloakroom, most likely. Plenty of pegs. We'll see when we get there.'

The traffic was slow, they were going to arrive late.

They got off amid the rush-hour bustle of Queensferry Road, then crossed to enter the New Town proper. Less than a minute later, they were hurrying through the elegance of Georgian crescents and squares, partly-cobbled streets and mortice-locked private gardens. As they turned into Moray Place, the first-time butler and footman could almost *feel* a glare of Georgian disapproval coming from the floor-to-ceiling windows and mausoleum-heavy stonework.

The door was answered by a brisk five-foot nothing of wispy silver hair and jewellery, Mrs. Cunningham in person. She greeted them and uttered two statements, the first worthy of Heraclitus, the second of Cleopatra:

Statement 1: 'There is no time anymore, one of you must remain and the other must wait.'

Statement 2: 'The Champagne is in the downstairs bath.'

With a rattle of precious stones, she hurried off.

A score and more bottles of Champagne lay in a large Victorian bath, partially submerged like so many dark green islands adrift on a sea of broken ice, a shifting archipelago of wealth. Hume had never before been this close to a bottle of Champagne, let alone held one, let alone had a sip from one. The parties he gate-crashed usually started after the pubs had closed and were fuelled by cider, cans of McEwan's, chemical reds and acid whites out of paper cups. On the TV news he'd seen Champagne bottles being smashed over the keels of ships, and magnums being mock-ejaculated by racing drivers – unfortunately, however, he'd never witnessed a bottle actually being opened properly, and the handbook had failed to devote even a single line to the subject. He lifted one out. Surprisingly heavy. Slippy with moisture and trailing droplets of water. There was wire, gold foil, and no instructions.

'Probably just Cava.' A badly stuffed sack of evening clothes with a bow-tie choker round its neck to keep it from bursting open stood in the doorway. 'Anyway, I do the drinks.'

Another butler? A real one? A good twenty years older than himself, at least. Though aware that the sack had waddled across to him and was reaching for the bottle, Hume continued to study the label: 'And you are?'

The waddler came to a stop, dropped its arm and slumped.

'Greaves. Billy Greaves. My wife does for the Cunninghams and, when they have drinks, I get asked to help.' He sniffed. 'You'll be the special butler they've brought in?'

'Yes. From Executive Service. I'm Hume, the head of Executive Service.' His glance turned to the older man: 'Right then, Billy. . .' he handed over the bottle, 'you can open this one and the rest in batches of three, ready to be brought through as required.' Having paused long enough to watch Billy unwind the wire, unpeel the foil and start easing up the cork, he moved towards the door. 'I'll check on the guest situation and be back shortly.'

No more worries about opening the Champagne then.

A few minutes later, he took up position just inside the reception room with a tray of glasses that were full almost to the brim. Had Billy poured them like that just to be awkward? As he'd struggled to lift the tray without spilling, Hume had been aware of a rather nasty glint in the older man's eye.

The room was filling up and the guests gathering in small clusters of civilized restraint. They sipped, they smiled, greeting, air-kissing and murmuring to each other. Now and again someone laughed. Was this how wealth enjoyed itself? Nobody swilling down the free booze as fast as they could in case it suddenly ran out, or snaffling up the canapés before there were none left? Nobody cruising the room to check for available women?

The doorbell rang every few moments and he could hear St Francis reciting his welcome speech like a recorded message on legs: *Good evening, sir. Good evening, madam./ Your coat, sir? Your coat, madam?* Guests kept coming through the door in a steady stream. He had three glasses left on his tray, then one, then none. Time to head back to the bathroom for another load.

'Could I have some more Champagne, please?' A nearby roll of chins that seemed to ripple all the way down to the floor was extending an empty glass.

'Certainly, sir.' He offered his tray. 'If you give me a moment, I'll be right back with a full—'

'Same glass is fine, thank you. Just a top-up, and for some of the others too.' The man gave him a friendly smile, and clearly believed he was being helpful.

Which meant he'd have to bring back a full bottle. Fine, but he knew he couldn't manage a bottle *and* a fresh trayload of Billy's brimming glasses, certainly not at the same time. Certainly not pouring it as well. He'd need to make two trips. Meanwhile, new guests would be streaming in through the door, all of them expecting to be served their Champagne.

Back in the bathroom, the dozen glasses waiting for him this time were all so overfilled he could see a Champagne meniscus trembling at nearly every brim. He'd be slopping it everywhere.

Fucking Billy.

Hume picked up one of the worst offenders and poured a quarter of it into an empty glass. Then turned to the sack of malevolence:

'Re-pour the rest of them likewise, *Billy*, I'll be back shortly.'

He grabbed an opened bottle and returned to the room to top up Multi-Chin and his friends. A job well done. He glanced towards the door. The hostess had just finished greeting a fresh intake who, without a glass in their hand, now stood around, idle and aimless. Back to HQ.

This time the trayload awaiting him in the bathroom was a gathering of the worst examples of an 'Edinburgh cup' – each glass was now considerably less than half-full. Without saying a word Hume emptied the remains of the Champagne in his bottle into some of the glasses and then looked his persecutor straight in the eye:

'Let me tell you something, *Billy*. People who can't fill Champagne glasses properly . . .' he paused for effect. From down the corridor came the sound of the doorbell announcing yet another batch of thirsty guests. '. . . will never get to drink from them. They are life's losers, *Billy*. Stick to uncorking from now on. Seems you can manage that.' A good exit line.

Half an hour later, each with a bottle cradled in his right-hand palm and with index finger crooked stylishly in the base dimple for better balance as per the handbook's illustration, he and St Francis circulated the crowded room topping up freely. A nod, a murmured 'Thank you', and the flow of Champagne was turned on, then off, with a drip-free twist of the wrist. No one so much as looked at them, it was the bottle they addressed. Hume and St Francis had achieved complete invisibility.

'Wearing green shoes, can you imagine! . . . The country's more than ready . . . Thank you . . . The miners asked for it, and they got it! . . . Oil, I tell you, look at Norway . . . Just a spot, please . . . Money should earn its keep, put it where it'll sweat . . . Green shoes and a red bag, for God's sake! . . . Railways, telephone, electricity, gas – once Mrs. T gets into her stride they'll be for the taking . . .'

By now, the room was warm-going-on-tropical. A trickle of sweat ran down Hume's back. His bottle emptied, he returned to the bathroom for another. The disgruntled bottle opener rose from the closed toilet lid on which he had been sitting and pointed wearily to the marble-topped washstand:

'Another live one.'

'Thank you, Billy.'

'Managing all right are you, Mr. Hume? I can pour, mind, if things get hectic.'

'Open two more. My colleague Francis will be through shortly.'

He left.

Before going back into the party, Hume paused in the doorway to take a good look round the generously proportioned reception room. A glass chandelier hung from the ceiling like a waterfall cascade arrested in midair, individually lit paintings – not a print or poster in sight – were displayed on the walls. Wealth was at home here. And doubtless, too, was power. The mock-baronial fireplace could have contained his former cupboard twice over, and the mirror set above made the room seem twice as large. Traced on its surface was a soundless choreography of wealth and power played out amid antique furniture, floor-length curtains, thick-pile carpet, art and servants. In the room itself, all of life's doubts, uncertainties and ambiguities had been resolved into the correct tone of voice, accent, dress, gesture and attitude. And money. Into the right conversation, jewellery, perfume. And money. Laughter. And money. Kant's *Critiques* and Hegel's dialectic had not been invited. Time to let the dead bury the dead – here indeed was *The Appearance of Reality and the Reality of Appearance*, here was philosophy in action.

As the party reached its peak, he and St Francis wandered through the babbling hubbub like a pair of invisible deafmutes. Champagne, olives, mini-pastries, prawns, micro-strips of smoked salmon and roast beef – the two of them were in a boiler room, stoking forty furnaces at once.

The guests' eyes shone wetly; their mouths were fleshy and slack and their hands agitated, no doubt eager to grab whatever might be coming their way – more canapés, more drink, more stocks and shares. Was life really so very straightforward? What you don't take, you don't get – was that all there was to it?

To make the future his, would he, too, merely have to reach out and take it? His grasp would make it happen, and make it *right*. Easy as that? In one of his greatest dialogues, Plato had emphatically maintained that might *did* not, and *could* not, imply right. Indeed, he argued most convincingly that—

Plato? Also not on any guest list for late-twentieth-century Britain. It was time for the future, his own future, to begin.

Hume strode across to the nearest clump of businessmen, four suits tailored to accommodate the entrepreneurial energies he could see seething within.

'Gentlemen, more Champagne?'

❧

Having safety-pinned and duct-taped Footman Francis together and waved the two party-going penguins goodbye and good luck, DD had been invited to stay and share an early supper with Dora. Afterwards the two of them played through some duets. The supper was delicious, the piano perfectly in tune and the sitting room soporifically warm. Several Mozart waltzes and part of Schubert's F *Minor Fantasy* later, she had to leave the land of central-heating cosiness.

'Night, night! And thanks again for supper, Dora, and the music!'

A lot colder outside. Weighed down with an armload of penguin day-clothes, she hurried down the path then raced across the lawn to the summerhouse.

Such had been the communal panic to deal with Hume's footman emergency that she'd forgotten to light the wood-burner. The place was chilly going on very chilly. At least the fire was already laid and would need only a quick match.

She dumped the clothes on the chair, pulled on a jersey and crouched down in front of the open grate. She struck a match.

It didn't light. A trail of red smeared across the scratchboard. Fucking damp. Same with the second one.

The third match flared and the firelighter caught, then the dry twigs began crackling. Thank Christ.

She had to get both the summerhouse and herself heated up before Hume returned, prepare a warm room and an even warmer welcome – anything less than 65 degrees Fahrenheit was sure to promote a host of residual cupboard-man/philosophy-fuckwit traits. Having at last prised him out from under the stairs and got him pointed in the right direction, she intended to keep him on course. It was for his own good.

Flames blazing up at last, she slammed the fire door shut. On with her fingerless mittens. The opening bars of the *Revolutionary étude*? Her hands thundering up and down the keyboard, she battered out Chopin's noisiest effort at full volume. Romantics made for good kindling.

Several études later she was warming up nicely. Some hardcore Baroque to confirm the temperature rise? Bach's *Chromatic Fantasy*? Not the exact notes so much as the general drift – improvised, of course. Or else one of Beethoven's real thumpers? She started banging out what she could remember of the *Appassionata's* opening chords . . .

❧

The party was at last showing signs of winding down. Guests had begun leaving. St Francis was back at the door-and-coats, this time operating in reverse. Hume was discreetly collecting empty glasses. He was making one last circuit of the room with a newly-opened bottle when Multi-Chin beckoned him over.

'Do you have a card?'

'I'm afraid . . .' began the proprietor of Executive Service, 'We've been out of the country for the last year and haven't—'

'What's your name?'

'Executive Service. If you'd care to—'

'*Your* name.'

'Oh. Hume.'

'Right, Mr. Hume. I'm Melville. I don't do cards myself, but you write down your phone number and I'll be in touch. Might be able to put some business your way.'

Success. Then two other guests approached him offering cards.

Success. Success. Success.

Back in the kitchen he found Billy in the act of downing a glass on the sly and putting himself aside a snatched handful of prawns and bite-size quiches. In WealthLand, it seemed that losers got the leavings and had no one to blame but themselves.

The Bottle Opener met his gaze steadily over the heaped plate.

Finally Hume spoke. 'Thanks for keeping the Champagne on tap, Billy.'

No reply.

'The evening wear, is it yours?'

'What do you care?'

'The jacket, bow tie and all – are they your own?'

'And if they were?'

'Right. We have some other evenings to cater for in the coming weeks. Jot down your telephone number, Billy, we might give you a call.'

'Sure, Mr. Hume, of course. Be delighted. Get to serve next time, will I?'

'We'll see, Billy, who knows?'

Not the usual hauling himself and his permanent exhaustion up the four flights of ever-steeper stairs for St Francis, not tonight. Fiver in his pocket, Champagne bottle in one hand, bag of rescued canapés in the other, he hurtled himself upwards at maximum velocity – the stairwell twisting him round like he'd been fired out the muzzle of a gun pointed directly up at the top floor and aimed straight for Megan's waiting arms.

He closed his bedroom door soundlessly behind him. And stood, amazed. The mess had been tidied up. The books, planks and bricks were now stacked neatly against a wall; the ornaments that had survived were set out on the mantelpiece; his papers had been piled on the desk and the floor swept. The gas fire was on. She had turned his demolition site into a genuine *living* room. It felt welcoming. Without stopping to put down the Champagne and bag of canapés, he tiptoed across to where Megan was stretched out on his bed, fast asleep. Not only that, but she was wearing the blue dress he'd bought her.

Megan must have done it for him, for them both. Why disturb such a perfect scene? For a few moments why not let himself pretend that this was his everyday life: his day's work done, he'd come home in triumph to his woman, bearing gifts?

Dare he lean over and wake her with a kiss? Would she

open her eyes and be pleased to see him? Raise up her arms to give him a welcoming hug? Or else, tell him to fuck off?

Her blonde hair straggled loosely across her face, half-covering the bruise around her eye, and he had to resist an urge to reach down and smooth it aside. Her left hand was under her cheek, her right resting across her stomach, the red scratches still visible on her pale skin.

Best plan of all, perhaps: simply pour the Champagne and wake her, saying *Cheers!* as he handed her the glass?

She'd not seen him yet in his bow tie and tails and was bound to be really impressed. She'd be delighted.

*Sorry about taking your bed*, she says as she begins to sit up. *Do you want me to move . . . ? Or would you like to join me?* She eases over a little, inviting him to lie down beside her. *I feel so very tired.* Her warm, welcoming smile. *It's so good that you want to take care of me.* She's tilting her face upwards to be kissed . . .

A sudden gust of wind rattled the bay window, and rain like a fistful of nails clattered against the glass. Megan stirred in her sleep.

Poor girl. Still exhausted and completely worn out. Here she could let go of her tiredness, and sleep for as long as she needed.

She was safe here with him. Wasn't she?

His gaze moved over her bare arms, her hands, the rise and fall of her breasts, her slightly parted lips, her eyelids, the fading bruise . . . Her dress had rucked up slightly along her thighs.

He could feel himself getting hard.

⁂

Having let himself into the garden, Butler Hume navigated a passage through the darkness, across the lawn, through the archway and then safely past the koi pond. Finally he entered the summerhouse, bearing Champagne and generous canapés.

'Greetings, Love of my Life! Glasses! A dish!'

The smoked salmon and prawns were soon laid out on a dinner plate, the thin strips of roast beef and tiny pastries arranged on a couple of saucers. Having opened the front of the woodburning stove, they picnicked by firelight. He poured the Champagne. His first cocktail party had been a triumph, he told her, and already there was the promise of more business to come. Still wearing his full evening dress, Hume was on a high.

With DD playing maid, however, the Director of Executive Service was soon down to nothing but his bow tie and happily eating out of her hand, quite literally.

Afterwards, he was invited to share his future business plans. In particular, what opening might there be in his new company for a completely naked maid-cum-concert-pianist? The comely applicant lay on her back saying she was willing to be interviewed whenever the director felt inclined.

As he proceeded on a close assessment of the young hopeful's experience and special talents for the post, Hume all at once realized that his life had indeed truly changed. Less than a week ago DD had told him that he needed to grow up. And here he was. In a few days he'd not only created an occupation for himself, but started up a totally new business from scratch. Executive Service's first-ever booking had gone without a hitch and proved a significant earner. Potential clients were already clamouring. He employed staff. Come to think of it, he was actually a boss. A CEO, no less!

The applicant certainly seemed to be doing her very best

to secure her position in the new enterprise. And rightly so. After tonight's success, they might soon be making the world their oyster. Their oysters and Champagne.

༈

'Wondering what you'd get away with, eh, Francis?' Megan had opened her eyes and was staring up at him.

'I'm just back.'

'Been standing there long?'

'Came in a moment ago and I've brought us—'

'Getting turned on, were you?' Megan made no move to straighten her dress. She lay quite still.

He said nothing. Nervously shuffling from foot to foot, him and his dripping bottle of recorked Champagne, his bag of greasy leftovers.

'Saw me lying here on your bed . . . and thought, why not? A grope while the going's good?'

'No.'

'Don't fancy me?'

Trying not to stare at her exposed thighs, he gave the bag he was carrying a little shake. 'I brought us something . . . from the party . . . for us to share. Something nice.'

Megan glared: 'Think I'm street-trash? Frightened if you touch me you might catch something?'

'No, of course not.'

'Go ahead if you want. I don't mind. A quick feel, just this once. Like it was rent. Fair dues really, seeing as how I've been lying here on your bed, wearing out the sheets.'

'I was just hoping we would share . . .'

'Help yourself, go on.' Megan lay down again flat on her

back and pulled the hem of her dress a few inches higher up. 'Special Offer, for one night only.'

Forcing himself to turn away, he put the Champagne and bag of canapés on the small table, then went through to the kitchen for a couple of glasses and a plate – and also give his erection the chance to ease off. When he returned, she'd swung her legs round so she was sitting upright on the bed.

'I'm sorry, Francis. Shouldn't have said all that.' She moved a little to make some room. 'Sit next to me?'

His hand shook slightly as he poured out the Champagne and gave her a glass.

'Cheers.'

He offered her a piece of smoked salmon on toast.

'Is that how you'd serve it to a lady? Maybe I should ring for you next time.' She took a sip. 'Let's try again: Ring-ring, ring-ring.'

St Francis picked up the plate and held it out to her.

'Very good, Francis.' Her put-on posh accent. 'Thank you, my man.' She leant back to let the pink slice slide into her mouth, and grinned.

He could feel himself beginning to relax. He took another sip, silently toasting this moment of real happiness. His new job. The fiver. The Champagne. Smoked salmon. His woman?

She held out her glass for a refill. 'So, how did the first-time footling go?'

He told her about doing the door-and-coats and the drinks trays, and by the time the canapés were finished, they were down to a last glass each.

St Francis wondered if he should now get up from the bed

and go across to sit on the armchair. But he felt good where he was. He felt at ease. He felt happy.

Leaning forward to replace his glass, he was about to stand up when he was aware of Megan's hand on his arm.

'Francis? Don't go and leave me.'

'I was just . . .'

But she'd placed her finger on his lips to silence him. 'Stay for a few minutes. Just the two of us sitting here together. You don't have to say anything . . . or touch me, or any stuff like that.'

She was leaning against him now, her face pressing on his chest. It seemed quite natural to put his arm around her. A comforting gesture, nothing more. For nearly a full minute they sat in silence while from far in the distance came the purr of the gas fire and muffled traffic noise from the street below.

Her words were indistinct at first.

'Sorry, Megan, I didn't quite catch . . .'

She looked up, her face almost touching his. Was she inviting him to kiss her? She didn't flinch as his fingertips traced the bruise.

Did it still hurt? He was about to ask her when she whispered: 'Do I seem real to you?'

Not the words he had expected.

'I don't understand . . . Of course you're real, Megan . . . Of course you are . . .' Speaking slowly so as not to break the spell of being so close to her, of holding her.

She slid herself round in his arms and kissed him on the cheek.

'When we're alone, Francis, caring for no one and no one caring for us, nothing is real.' She was looking straight into his eyes: 'I know all about that – and so do you, don't you?

Without other people, we're not really here, we're not really anywhere. I need you. You need me.' She kissed him lightly on the lips.

Suddenly he was very aware of his room – the books, desk, wardrobe, the ornaments, papers. It was like taking a farewell glance around familiar surroundings, as if he knew that his world was about to change, and would never be the same again.

'Close your eyes, Francis . . . Let's make each other real.'

PART THREE

T HE COMFORTING WREATHS of Lebanese black were sucked in deep and held-held-held until the Cat had felt them uncoil inside her, spreading their soothing ease, relaxing the last of that block of solid misery, and dissolving it. A couple more hits and the previous night's misery would have become so much expelled air drifting away to nowhere on a midsummer's afternoon. Good dope can be kind and merciful.

The handclapping, the whistling, the 'Big Spender' chorus, the adolescent girl whose teasing play at the very edge of the roof would surely end in—

But then, for one brief instant, she'd glimpsed her twin-sister Kirsty in the stance and gestures of carefree young Josie—

Dizzily getting to her feet, dizzily slow-motioning herself across the flat stretch of roof, the Cat had started to go towards—

When her left foot snagged on a trailing cable —

Yanking her off-balance, stumbling her towards the open trapdoor—

Twenty years later, the Cat could sometimes still feel the wrenching ache in her arms, the sudden agony as, about to swallow-dive clean through the open trapdoor, she'd managed to grab hold of the metal frame. Managed to hold on for dear life, dangling in midair. Would her childhood and adulthood have passed before her eyes? The choices she'd taken/not taken?

Instead, someone had screamed, slamming her into action.

The decision must have been building up inside her for months because, next thing, her hand grabbing the top of the ladder, she'd felt for one of the lower rungs with her foot. Other hand, other foot. Then she'd quickly scrambled herself down into the attic, out into the corridor, through the Electric Boy's studio and down the carpeted stairs.

Her own room. Quick glance round – her unmade bed with its sun-yellow duvet half-thrown aside, the pile of maths books on the small table, her lilac silk scarf trailing out of an open drawer, the small tree of jewellery and a clutch of photographs on the dressing-table, her shoulder bag on its hook behind the door, the staggered line of her shoes laid out along the wall – sensible to the left, high heelers to the right. Each of her things as she'd touched them last, the unfinished gestures of an unfinished life . . .

One-eyed Nelson had looked at her in surprise: Back so soon?

No time to talk, no time to think even. Just grab . . . grab . . . grab . . . Her thesis in its boxfile. Washbag. Make-up. Favourite cotton jacket, necklace, skirt, jeans stuffed into her rucksack. T-shirts, handful of socks, tights, underwear and *Mathematics: A Historical Perspective* crammed into her shoulder bag. Money, passport, purse, handbag. Farewell pat for Nelson. Her hand resting for a moment on the top of his woolly head . . .

Then straight out the front door and clattering down the stairs. The main street. Tollcross. Next bus into town.

Back in those pre-digital times it had been so much easier to disappear. Which she did. With bullet-point efficiency:

- A letter to the university notifying them of her immediate change of circumstances, giving her mother's house as her new address
- Graduating a few weeks later, with her anticipated First, *in absentia*

- London (a dishevelled squat/crash pad in Acton), working for cash-in-hand at a pub on the High Street while applying to various universities in the UK and abroad as a PhD student/undergraduate tutor
- Accepted by Melbourne
- To Melbourne she'd gone

In 80s Britain it had seemed to take all of everyone's time and energy to keep the days and weeks from falling apart. Jobs, relationships, families – nothing seemed to last. Thatcher had held the country together by going to war with Argentina. The Falklands – where were they? And who cared? A last triumphant wave of the Empire flag. Then war at home – defeat the miners, smash the unions. The future? Forget it. No time for the future. Now was what mattered – and the whole country clung on, one day at a time.

In the upside-down Land of Oz, however, she had found solid ground. Never mind the funnel-web spiders, poisonous snakes and the rest of it, in that laid-back, sun-and-surf: Melbourne people seemed to take each day as it came, and take it for granted. There, the future was something to be relied on. Something to be looked forward to, even. No worries.

- Doctoral thesis accepted four years later
- Lectureship in Pure Mathematics
- Marriage
- No children
- Divorce
- Having to fly hurriedly back to North Berwick to care for her dying mother . . .

## SUNDAY 3rd JULY 2005

The Cat planned to spend the week before she was due to fly back to the Land of Oz travelling around the country, saying her last goodbye to Scotland. She intended never to return. First, though, there was the whole weekend in her now more-or-less empty childhood home to get through.

The place cleared of furniture, she felt like a ghost haunting the deserted house – tip-toeing far too quietly, she wandered in and out of the stripped rooms, up and down the echoing staircase. As the weekend progressed her unsettledness grew. Come Sunday evening, the pizza and red wine on the bare kitchen floor that was meant to be a fun picnic turned out to be cheerless and solitary-feeling.

Later, as she got ready for bed, she found herself standing in front of the bathroom mirror about to lean forward and breathe on the glass . . . Was she hoping to glimpse the future awaiting her back in Melbourne? But she wasn't a little girl playing at the afterlife anymore; she was a grown-up professor of Pure Mathematics. Childish nonsense, she snapped at herself. Time for bed.

Afterwards, she lay on the mattress in the curtainless bedroom as cold moonlight soaked into the floorboards. An owl hooted nearby. Someone's dog barked. She was so, so tired. The months spent caring for her mother, the heart-breaking final days, the funeral, the lawyer, the estate agent, the furniture, the house. There'd been no rest, no respite. When her head touched the pillow she expected to fall asleep instantly . . .

And perhaps indeed she did.

But then again . . .

She fell asleep eventually – but not before walking for hours through the hollow-sounding, comfortless rooms bearing six-year-old Kirsty in her arms, searching for a place to lay her down.

The first Monday in July promised to be a lovely summer's day for her final farewell to Edinburgh.

Taking the side exit from Waverley Station onto Market Street, she headed straight up the stone steps set in the narrow eighteenth-century close behind the old *Scotsman* building. Eight foot wide, if that, with a medieval-style gutter running down the middle and high soot-blackened walls on either side – up and up she went, like walking up the inside of a chimney. Then she stepped into the warm splash of colour and brightness of the Cockburn Street sunshine. Time to catch her breath. Then onto the Royal Mile. The tartan, the tourists, the bustle. It had been twenty years, but now she was here, it felt like she'd fled only yesterday from Barclay Towers.

For the next hour she strolled through the Southside, ticking off her old student haunts – from the historic grandeur of the Old Quad to the Brutalism-with-bells-on of redesigned George Square, vandalism that said it with breeze-blocks. A quick glance into some of the pubs she used to drink in – Sandy Bell's and Greyfriar's Bobby seemed much the same, others had been turned into designer wine bars no self-re-specting student of her day would have been seen dead in. For old times' sake she started through the Meadows in the afternoon sun, intending to cut across the open grass, past the cricket pavilion, over the road, the pitch-and-putt course and up towards Bruntsfield, and check out her old flat.

On Middle Meadow Walk she stopped for a good look round. People, people, people – sunbathing, playing foot-ball, having picnics, cycling, dog-walking, eating ice-cream. Shouts came from the tennis courts and playpark over towards Newington. Several kites were dipping and swooping above a clear stretch of grass. There was a busker who must have pushed his weathered piano all the way from God knows where, to give the Meadows ragtime. Even this far from the city centre, Edinburgh was a picture-postcard of a Scottish capital – Arthur's Seat to the left, the park on all sides, and the avenue of Japanese cherry trees leading through its shaded coolness to Marchmont. Maybe here was where she should call a halt to her nostalgic stroll? After all, she could almost see Barclay Towers in the distance and the tenement itself looked much the same as ever. She raised her hand in a half-embarrassed farewell, then turned to set off towards Tollcross when—

What was *this*?

She went over to the low wall topped with iron railings. Peering through a gap in the blue fence-boards, she stared up at the palace-sized Victorian stone building with its grandeur of towers and balconies now a derelict near-ruin of smashed windows, boarded-up doorways and graffiti. The place was a demolition site, a demolition that seemed to have been aban-doned halfway through. There were heaps of rubble and timber everywhere, sand, broken brickwork; rusting machinery, torn plastic sheeting and tangles of electric wire littered the long grass. Large sections of the roof were missing, exposing a smashed ribcage of uncovered rafters where the slates had been stripped away. Pigeons flew in and out, or fluttered down to perch on solitary chimneystacks and shit-stained windowsills. A large sign announced:

**'Luxury Apartments Development on the site of the former Edinburgh Royal Infirmary. Three, two and one-bedroom flats. Completion date – late 2007.'**

Edinburgh had once been a world centre for medicine with a history and tradition that went back centuries. The closure of hospitals had begun before she left, the site of each closure commemorated by a plaque. At this rate, there'd soon be a lot more plaques than hospitals. Was this modern Britain? Wars abroad and luxury apartments at home?

Enough. She was ready to head back to Waverley. The train to North Berwick, pick up her overnight stuff for a few days' bus and B&B around the Borders, then the rest of Scotland, saying her last goodbye. Walking faster than before, she continued towards Tollcross and then made her way down Lothian Road. What a transformation! – on the wasteland that had once been the old Caledonian railway yard stood the Sheraton Hotel looking like a no-frills ducal palace flanked by lesser stone-and-glass palaces set back from the road and sharing their very own mini-piazza in front. Not only that, but—

*Helicopters.* She realized that for the last few minutes or so she'd been dimly aware of hearing distant helicopter sounds, and now they were getting louder and louder. And the emergency sirens she'd heard but not really noticed properly were blaring almost continuously.

She turned sharp right into Princes Street. And came to an abrupt stop. Where was the traffic? A Monday afternoon in the city centre – and no traffic? Pedestrians wandered up and down the empty road, strolled across the central aisle. Bus stops were deserted. Traffic lights continued through a meaningless sequence of red, red-and-amber, green . . . What was going on?

No buses. But even at an easy-paced amble she'd make Waverley in twenty minutes and be in good time for the next train back to North Berwick. It was then she noticed that many of the shop windows were boarded up and had large block lettering scrawled on the wooden shutters: BUSINESS AS USUAL/WATERSTONE/ HM/ BOOTS . . . Roads were blocked off, diversion signs and barricades were everywhere. She glanced over the black railings and down into Princes Street Gardens – the usual picnickers on the grass slopes, ice-cream sellers, tourists – and Edinburgh Castle pasted high on its rock like an illustration from the country's biscuit-tin history. Further along the street she could see the Scott Monument looking like a rocket rusting on its launching pad. All very normal. Except for the police cars and the helicopters. Every twenty yards or so, she passed another van-load of police. Some kind of massive demo? A riot? A bomb scare?

The nearer she got to the foot of the Mound, the more the helicopters sounded like they were tearing the very sky to shreds as they circled above. And the noise! Shrilling whistles, police loudhailers, emergency sirens, bagpipes. Bagpipes? She went up the front steps of the Royal Scottish Academy to get a better view.

The entire scene looked staged, a film set. Immediately in front of her were the main players – a handful of clowns and fairies dancing a ragged Strip the Willow, a dozen at most. They were surrounded by an army of police. Several armies, it seemed like. A demo, obviously. Nothing to do with her. Meanwhile, at the foot of Hanover Street, hundreds of extras, ordinary men and women, had been penned behind a massive steel barricade as if waiting for their cue to come on.

So many people crowded together, watching. Too many. She'd have to push her way through. Her next train was in less than quarter of an—

'Get over there with the clowns, madam.' Black-tinted visor. Faceless. Militia-style black uniform. Riot stick. Shield. Boots.

'What—? I'm not part of this. I'm going to Waverley to get my—'

'Over there, I said.' Shoving her with his heavy-duty shield, shoving hard. Forcing her back . . . and back . . . and back: 'With . . . the . . . clowns.'

## 2

MONDAY 4th JULY

THE WHUP-WHUP OF another low-flying security helicopter shook the reception room from cornice to skirting and made the windows rattle in their frames. Since Saturday's Make Poverty History demo, helicopters had been ploughing the Edinburgh sky back and forth, day and night near enough, and their most southerly end-of-the-furrow turn seemed to be directly above Executive Service's headquarters. To Hume it sounded like they'd been circling overhead all weekend. Suited him. Every time he thought about Melville and his threats he felt he wouldn't mind settling for a whole squadron of helicopters circling round and round permanently. Holding back the birthday celebrations. Holding back the rest of his day, the rest of his life.

Part of him felt like it, anyway.

The butlers, footmen and maids, mobiles at the ready, were getting restive. The moment had peaked. Once again, he straightened up from trying to blow out his birthday candles, and this time his what-else-can-I-do shake of the head raised a laugh at least. A nervous laugh, awkward. It was an awkward situation. He was waiting. They were waiting.

The helicopter screamed into its turn.

And where the hell was DD? Her long-ago flair for organisation and good time-keeping was ancient history and then some. These days she was always late – and often when she did finally show up, she wasn't really there. Be down for five to eleven, she'd been told. And she'd promised. Today of all days, his loving wife should be at his side. The oak-heavy, galleon-sized dining table had managed to sail across from the far wall and moor itself in the middle of the room. The massive bass drum of a birthday cake had managed to get itself baked, triple-layered no less. Almost his entire staff, including even Billy Greaves, the Champagne-popping star of Executive Service's first-ever cocktail party, had managed to arrive on time. But DD . . . ? The Champagne was getting warm. There was a general shuffling of feet, the occasional cough, snatches of conversation . . .

Had an invisible servant of his very own been following behind him, snuffing out the moments of his life as soon as he'd lived them? And now, was this all that remained – fifty red candles planted in their wintry icing and rapidly burning down, their flames hot against his face?

Where the fuck *was* she? Orbiting Planet Prozac? In the summerhouse perhaps, sitting at her piano and picking out single-note tunes with one finger? Or had she already crash-landed back on earth and was lying stretched-out on the bed or the floor somewhere? Seneca had said that love was friendship gone mad. Well, the man had got it spot on re the *madness* factor.

So here he was, marooned. Waiting, as usual. Alone, as usual. Except, of course, for the dozen or so staff that had assembled, including the latest in the seemingly endless line of delectable Polish girls taken on to train as maids. The most recent – Marta, or was she called Violetta? – was blonde and curly-haired, delicate features, cleavage, black skirt. Hardly twenty, if that. Her eyes had caught his a moment ago. Innocence? Invitation?

The *whup-whup* faded as the helicopter headed back to the city centre, the room fell silent. Blow out the candles? Part of him wanted to lift the cream-clotted, chocolate-gorged confection high above his head, blazing candles and all, then hurl it and all the years it represented far away into a never-never future that could carry on without him. For a half-beat he imagined himself stepping out of the moment and into another life altogether. Walking out the door, simple as that. Take the money and run, and he knew where the money was.

Once again he leant forward, once again he took a deep, deep breath . . .

⚜

DD stood in front of her bedroom mirror surrounded by the birthday-wife outfits Tanja had laid out for her, some on their hangers, some spread across the bed, on the nearby armchair – her embroidered white blouse and dark blue skirt/several tops and black jeans, blue jeans, white jeans/her red dress, her green dress, her black dress. She seemed to have been here for hours, for days, weeks, months. Forever, near enough. Trying them on, holding them against herself, and putting them down again. Slipping in and out of dresses, skirts, pulling jeans on and off. Everything was crumpled now.

She should have been downstairs ten minutes ago, and here she was – still in her underwear. Everyone would be gathered in the hall. They'd be waiting. Hume would be waiting.

*Wear anything. What the fuck does it matter? Anything.*

Her hands balled into fists, white-knuckled to punch her way to a decision. *Fuck's sake. Pick something! Anything. DECIDE!*

She grabbed the nearest top and held it up. Ivory silk. Insipid. She wasn't anyone's fucking auntie. She wanted to chuck it back on the bed, which would mean deciding she definitely *didn't* want it. Maybe that was the best way forward? Toss aside anything she was certain she absolutely and definitely did *not* want, then pick something at random from whatever was left? Simple really.

The silk's liquid smoothness seemed glued to her hand.

When she'd worn that top at the Provost's Christmas Party, she'd felt her jet-black hair take on an extra sheen from its ivory glow. She'd felt good and looked good. And had known it. She'd done the supporting wife-biz over the wine and olives in the City Council's main chamber, cleared of its usual chairs and desks to form a most imposing and elegant reception room with its chandeliers, wood panelling and floor-length curtains. Chatting to Cllr. This and Cllr. That, to Lord and Lady Whoever and the rest of the city's Great and Good, she'd noticed being noticed. Once they'd returned home, Hume had kissed her and told her how proud he'd been of her.

Yes, that had been a really good day. A two-tablet day. She'd been sure to keep to two for the occasion, knowing she could count on a few glasses of Champagne to give her that little extra lift. Perfectly relaxed and in control, she'd drifted at her ease from group to group, carried by the natural social flow. Floating, not drowning. Getting introduced to Provost Hinds. A really good evening once she'd sorted out that it was actually the *woman* who was the provost. Obvious really, the one with the gold chain round her neck. Still, she'd covered her mistake well, and no one seemed to notice. Instead, the Provost's husband had kindly asked how she was doing and said it must be a great life being looked after by a houseful of butlers, maids and the rest of it. A bit like being Mr. and Mrs. Provost, she'd joked back. No need to lift a finger unless she—

*Christ, it was almost quarter past!*

What the fuck was one of her favourite silk tops doing lying on the floor, like so much trash? Fucking Tanja. She picked it up, smoothed it out on the bed. Beautiful material, beautiful workmanship. Ivory was fine – for evenings.

To celebrate, she'd allow herself tab number three. Sensible really. She wanted to feel relaxed, in control, and with no risk of slip-ups. There'd be the toast to his birthday, that was all, and she didn't need to drink down every last drop. Just a sip, for politeness. For Hume.

Tab number three sorted out, her day was about to fall into place.

The red top. The black jeans. Obvious really.

Give herself a few seconds in front of the antique cheval glass for a final checkover. The jet-black darkness of her hair, the smoothness of her not-a-wrinkle-in-sight complexion, hardly even a hint of Botox. She looked good for forty-three? Hell, she looked good for thirty-three, thirty even. She smiled at herself in the mirror, and caught her eye. And held it. She didn't look away. Embarrassed almost, to be standing like that in an empty room, she gave herself a wink and a thumbs up. It was a good feeling – *like she was no longer alone.* Because she wasn't, was she? She had *herself.*

Perfume! Fuck. The nearest. A few quick squirts. Back of the ears, throat, wrists. Perfect.

She'd only be a few minutes late, if that.

His welcome speech over, Hume felt the pressure of someone's hand on his arm - trembling, uncertain. A familiar scent. DD at long last. Thank fuck. For how long now had their togetherness been reduced to a series of hesitant gestures like this?

He blew out the candles and everybody clapped. Executive Service was back in business. But for a split-second after the candles had been extinguished, he'd been aware of the briefest silence, a silence he had felt *inside* him - as if someone had touched that echo chamber all those years ago back in his old cupboard-room . . . and the very last reverberations were only now reaching him.

He straightened up, and DD kissed him. To his left, he saw St Francis nod to the latest Polish recruit and Marta/Violetta stepped forward to cut the first slice of the chocolate-and-cream gâteau. No wonder the girl looked so nervous - only a few days into her new job and here she was centre-stage, everybody staring at her. He could see the knife shaking in her hand.

'Have good birthday,' she murmured, and her eyes met his. Such beautiful eyes.

Too late he realised the slice of cake was sliding off the plate . . .

Fuck. DD would be furious.

The white linen tablecloth. She'd probably shout at the girl, humiliate her in front of the entire staff.

'I sorry, sorry, sorry!' The girl was nearly in tears.

He turned to DD, 'That was *my* fault. I was too excited! My birthday cake! My Big F, eh!'

He smiled, kissed her on the cheek before she could reply

and whispered that he loved her. Which he did, really. Quickly he picked up his glass and said aloud, 'Thank you, DD! Thank you, everyone! And I'd like to take this opportunity to say that Executive Service is poised to go from strength to strength. Starting with the high-profile Billionaires' Banquet on Thursday, we will go forward together. All I'll say at this point is that I'm looking at London. Watch this space! I am proud of Executive Service and proud of everyone here. Thank you. And thank you all for coming today. I really appreciate it.'

Finally he raised his glass: 'Cheers!'

After the applause people relaxed and began chatting. Fifty years down, his next fifty had begun. A crisp and spotless linen napkin had been placed over the smear of chocolate-and-cream, and Marta/Violetta was now offering him another slice.

&

Too shocked to move away when she was told, the Cat had been shoved again. Harder.

Knocked off-balance, forced back another step until she was jammed right up against one of the stone pillars at the front of the gallery, unable to move.

'You'll be safer over there with the clowns.' Another visored face. A woman's voice this time, but no mistaking the tone of command. 'We'll be clearing the area. You'd better move . . .' Another firm push in the chest, the woman's shield. '. . . Madam.'

Hard see-through plastic. POLICE written across the front of it, forcing her to stagger round the side of the pillar. To step down onto the street.

From nearby came a harsh *rumble-grumble, rumble-grumble* like the clattering of small stones – a pair of clown-faced drummers. The air was filled with the shrilling of whistles, wailing sirens, bagpipes. A helicopter wheeled round to continue circling less than a hundred metres above, its engine a relentless *whup-whup* roar.

'But I'm not part of this. I'm trying to get to—'

'The clowns. Over there.'

Directly in front of her now were the clowns and fairies, most of them with painted faces, and all of them dancing. In the centre, a piper (well over six-foot, red-and-green-striped cheeks, blue hair, black t-shirt, tartan kilt, bare legs and trainers) stood with legs apart, blasting Strathspeys and reels the length of Princes Street. Two drummers battered out *rumble-grumble, rumble-grumble*. Some of the fairies had plastic wings.

To her left and right, riot police had been drawn up in two lines to face each other, fifty metres apart. Between them, and completely trapped there, were the dancers, the musicians and now *her*.

The police lines had started marching towards each other. Fifty metres, forty, thirty . . . abruptly speeding up, double-step. Behind them were police on horseback, the horses wearing blinkers and protective armour.

She'd have to dash right across the street, straight in front of the advancing police. Only a few seconds left. All she could see were barricades, boarded-up shopfronts, faceless visors, shields, batons, boots. Yellow police vans were parked two rows deep, blocking all exits.

The drummers were *pound-pound-pounding* so loudly she could feel it in her bones.

'This way!' A fairy with star-sprayed cheeks and a rainbow of spiked hair had yanked her arm. 'NOW!'

'But the police are—'

'NOW! Before they batter the shit out us.' The girl screamed at her. Grabbed her. 'NOW!'

Following the fairy into the open street. The riot police less than twenty metres away.

Starting to run. Halfway there . . . stumbling.

Stopped. Standing in the middle of the street. Waiting. Waiting for – what?

Megaphones, the *tramp-tramp-tramp* of heavy boots, *thwack-thwack-thwack* of batons striking against shields . . .

'Don't turn into a FUCKING RABBIT!!'

The police less than ten metres away. Raising their batons.

Her arm grabbed again. 'FOR FUCK'S SAKE, COME ON!'

Next moment, they squeezed round the side of the metal barricade . . . and into the safety of Hanover Street.

A chance to catch their breath. 'Thought you'd frozen back there.'

The Cat started shaking. 'Thanks. Don't know what happened to me. If you'd not grabbed—'

Abruptly they were on the move again, swept along by the crowd retreating up towards George Street.

'Come on! Run!'

The two lines of police they'd just escaped from were now charging up Hanover Street, right behind them. Their shields held up, their batons raised . . .

'RUN! RUN!

The Cat ran.

When, on 7th July 1776, James Boswell had interviewed David Hume on his deathbed, he'd found the Scottish philosopher as firm as ever in his conviction re the non-existence of God. Right up to the very end, in fact, the philosopher remained true to his beliefs and passed away peacefully. As an apprentice philosopher living on tea and Pot Noodle all those years ago, Hume had read his namesake's inspiring *Treatise of Human Nature* from cover to cover a half-dozen times and more. He'd worshipped him and revered such total integrity, such uncompromising, unwavering commitment to the search for truth.

Earlier in the year and with the approach of his fiftieth birthday, Hume had found himself taking stock. By any measure, he was a success – from understairs cupboard to a four-storey townhouse in the Grange, from out-of-work philosopher to successful entrepreneur running his own company.

And yet . . . ?

Money and a townhouse – that was *it*? Over the years things had changed, *he* had changed.

After much thought, he'd come up with the idea for the Billionaires' Banquet and, as a covenant between him and his re-awakened conscience – a very private covenant, as it were, between himself and David Hume – he'd scheduled the event for that historic date: 7th July. That it would be less than a week after the Make Poverty History demonstrations taking place world-wide, was an added bonus. The world and Edinburgh would be focused. A good omen for a fresh start – and he needed all the good omens he could get.

Businesswise he'd been very lucky. Executive Service had appeared on the scene at exactly the right time. If the Eighties had been awash with cash, the Nineties were one flood after the next. Boom-bust/boom-bust – the drumbeat of good times. PR had become an end in itself and received budgets to die for. What better way to give a veneer of respectability to the latest dotcom speculation, takeover-cum-asset strip rip-off, merger or stock flotation, than put on a high-profile PR event complete with real-life butlers, attendant footmen and serving maids to add the perfect *tone*? Executive Service suggested wealth and confidence, and class.

DD had kept in touch with Mrs. Chisholm and when the old lady moved into a nursing home, Executive Service acquired her house as its headquarters. The creative accountancy involved in the purchase had also helped turn some of his ever-accumulating liquidity arising from off-the-books, cash-only, dealings – which he'd stash under the Barclay Towers floorboards, calling it 'insulation' – into en-suite bedrooms, a conservatory and a modest swimming pool. He and DD occupied the upper floors, waited on hand and foot by a full complement of liveried staff who did everything from running their morning bath to turning down their bed last thing at night. Servants served them breakfast, lunch and dinner, servants laid out their clothes and cleared up after them. Servants did the cleaning and laundry, answered the door and dealt with tradesmen, all in the name of *staff training*. They were chauffeured wherever they needed to go. Few millionaires lived as well as Mr. and Mrs. Hume.

More and more, however, he'd come to feel something was wrong. Bertrand Russell's definition of work as being either moving things over the face of the earth or telling someone else to move them was all very well, but was this really *it*? Epictetus the Stoic had started off as a slave and ended up a philosopher. Was *he* going backwards? From philosopher to lackey for life – in his case, super-lackey?

It would be very easy to blame Melville – the Big Bad Gangster Man and his Big Bad parties with enough food to feed a continent; enough booze to flood an ocean; enough drugs to remix time and space; enough boys and girls of every sex. OK, so he'd blamed him and then done his best to sever all ties with the psycho. Not so easy, and Melville hadn't taken it kindly. Psychos never do.

But he also blamed himself for having gone along with the easy money. And for what? To live in a grand house and be waited on hand and foot? The thrills had gone, and so had his life.

Bearing in mind Seneca's dictum on corruption, he knew that he could not blame Melville. He had corrupted himself. End of story.

His fiftieth birthday reception a few hours ago had been intended to mark the official cut-off point, the opportunity to announce the end of the old and the start of the new. Executive Service would be re-branded and become a name to be proud of. No more Melville, no more letting ES be used as a front while he pretended ignorance of what was really going on. No more self-deceit. His off-the-cuff hint of a possible expansion to London had been a surprise, even to him – but why not?

Then, of course, there was DD. The drink, the pills. Rehab/relapse . . . rehab/relapse . . . What was all that about? For more years than he could remember he'd tried to be understanding, tried to help. And failed. Or, let's say, had not yet succeeded. The Billionaires' Banquet was taking place on Thursday evening; come Friday morning she would be his number one priority. He'd get her the very best that money—

What the hell was this? Glancing over at the muted TV he saw men and women being chased along . . . Princes Street, was it? No traffic, and police vans everywhere? A ten-foot high barricade at the bottom of Hanover Street? Police in riot gear, clowns with painted-on smiles and plastic-winged fairies?

Close-up – a clown with blue hair and a green-and-red-striped face was walking up and down the line of police and seemed to be serenading them with bagpipes. A girl clown was blowing them kisses.

Hundreds of police. Thousands of them, it looked like. State power versus the clowns?

He cut the *mute* button.

Yells, screams, shouts, chants, emergency sirens.

The helicopter noise was pure *Apocalypse Now*, but this wasn't Vietnam in the Sixties. It was central Edinburgh, July 2005. Live coverage from only a mile or so down the road.

The reporter's voice continued very calm and unhurried. So many arrests, so many injured. Heightened police presence, foreign anarchist groups, containment, kettling, anticipated trouble.

Fucking anarchists and their demo. Self-defeating rabble by definition, as any real philosopher could have told them. He pressed the *mute* button again, leaving the riot to play itself out in silence. Back to the Billionaires' Banquet.

꧁

Shortly after Hume's company had purchased Barclay Towers from the Electric Boy, St Francis and Megan were relocated upstairs into what had previously been the recording studio.

The old downstairs flat was completely gutted. Walls were knocked down, doorways sealed and new doorways opened. Central heating installed. The entire place had been rewired, re-plumbed, repainted and refurnished.

When the neighbouring flat was acquired a few years later, the knock-through created an extensive apartment occupying the entire top floor of the tenement. Melville supervised the work, free of Council involvement. This streamlined approach helped avoid unnecessary paperwork, cumbersome planning regulations and a whole catalogue of Health and Safety issues re fire doors, hard-wired fire alarm systems, window-to-floor ratios, wheelchair access etc. etc. The result was a labyrinth of rooms that afforded his clients their complete privacy at all times. Within a society increasingly dependent on debit cards, credit cards, electronic bank transfers and the like, Barclay Towers remained a cash-only haven.

Megan came down from their apartment every morning to oversee the daily cleaning, provisioning and so forth of the establishment. It was a thriving concern. Some of the younger Executive Service employees moonlighted there. When called upon to provide staff, Hume insisted their involvement be restricted to drinks parties and private dinners. He wanted to hear no details of what went on and rarely put in an appearance himself. At night, St Francis and Megan closed the door of their attic flat. And locked it. Triple-lock.

Having dragged himself every last step of the hundred miles and more back from the Co-op, St Francis let himself in through the street door. Ahead of him soared the usual four pitiless flights rising higher and higher ever upwards to the very roof of the world. His supermarket bags were stuffed to near-bursting and arm-wrenchingly heavy . . . and, praise the Lord, one of the plastic handles had stretched. It would very likely snap at any moment. Perfect timing. Couldn't be better, in fact.

And so, four flights of stairs . . . but not today.

What a shame!

Melville had installed the Barclay Towers lift in the stairwell ten years previously to save his clients risking a heart attack or stroke before their evening had even got started, and to ensure the safety of their late-night descent when their post-partying minds were often very, very elsewhere.

The door slid open. He stepped inside. Pressed for the top floor and relaxed, his conscience clear. In one minute max, he'd be climbing the carpeted stair to their flat, then laying down the bags for Megan to unpack. Off with the shoes, wash the hands and on with the kettle for tea and a slice – no, *two* slices – of the Jamaica Ginger cake poking so invitingly out the plastic bag. After Hume's birthday reception, followed by some Billionaires' Banquet preparation rounded off with a trip to the supermarket, he was ready for some quality decompress watching his new tape of *The Simp*—

'Don't turn round!' A man's voice. Commanding. Threatening. The lift door hadn't closed like it should. Without thinking, St Francis began to turn—

The blow sent him into the wall in front of him, almost cracking his teeth.

'I'll not tell you again!'

The bags slipped from his hands. His shopping tumbled to the floor.

'Your man, Hume, he's owing 150k. Tell him.'

'What? Who does he owe—?'

'Knows fine. 150k.'

Behind him, the lift door jerked fully open once more before beginning to close again. St Francis was about to pick up the bread, the bottle of cooking oil—

The man had stepped back into the lift. St Francis could feel his too-closeness when—

A brick-thick brown brogue stamped down onto the cardboard carton and ground it into the carpet as if stubbing out a cigarette. 'Pity about the eggs.'

Next moment, the door slid closed again and St Francis was alone. The lift started its glide up to the top floor.

❧

No longer a crowd of men and women running to escape the swinging batons and trampling boots of a police charge, but a river, a flash-flood surging up Hanover Street, the force of it carrying forward everything in its path. The current was so strong it swept straight past Rose Street. Some overspill trickled down the basement steps of Milne's Bar, but the main flow continued to cascade miraculously uphill. When it reached George Street it would surely burst its banks.

But it didn't. It couldn't.

The top of Hanover Street had been dammed, blocked solid by a six-foot high barrier of black uniforms, visors, riot shields, batons. The barrier held firm. Contained between four-storey buildings on either side and the threat of riot sticks straight ahead, the first men and women to reach the barrier were forced to turn round, colliding with those immediately behind – but still more and more continued to press upwards.

People stumbled, lost their balance, sometimes slipped. Small whirlpools formed here and there, cross-currents streaked the surface searching for other channels, other possible run-offs. People scrambled onto higher ground as best they could or rushed into shop doorways. Only to find the doors always closed, locked.

From the top of a short flight of steps, the Cat gazed down at this river roiling below her in full spate. She could easily pick out the clowns and fairies borne along by the current, some carried this way, some that. The barrier at the top had begun advancing downhill, while a second barrier was now march-march-marching up from Princes Street to meet it. Cut off top and bottom, the river spread in any direction where it met no resistance, mostly into east and west Rose Street. Split in two, it began losing power as it ebbed away. The shouting and yelling became fainter. The two approaching ranks of police met in the middle. The street was cleared, law and order were back in charge.

Slowly the Cat descended the steps. No flooding river now, only small puddles of twos and threes that were quickly draining away.

'Hi there!' It was the spiky-haired fairy. 'We meet again!'

'So we do! Thank you for—'

'We'd better move. The Orcs are taking over,' said the fairy. 'My getaway pumpkin's already on its way. Fancy coming along?'

'Can't, I'm afraid. But thanks again for everything. Really. Goodbye.' The Cat smiled, turning away to walk in the direction of Waverley Station.

Instead, she walked straight into two riot police.

'You're booked, dear. So's Tinkerbell here.'

'But, Officer, I'm not part of—'

'Name?'

The fairy stepped in front of her. 'I'm Mickey Mouse, she's Minnie.'

'Had a sex-change, did you?'

'No, officer, we're the first gay-mice couple.'

'You what?'

Next moment they were sprinting up the centre of Hanover Street and across George Street, the policemen pounding after. They ran downhill towards Queen Street.

Just then a minibus screeched to a halt beside them. The door slid open.

'Get in!'

The fairy dived headfirst through the opening.

One foot on the running board, a clown was leaning out extending his hand. 'In! In! Jump!'

Behind her, the Cat felt someone grabbing for her shoulder. She jumped.

⚜

The all-too-familiar chilled glaze had spread over every surface, a lacework of ice-hard crystal lay across the steel chairs, shrouded the paperless desk, the computer screen, the printer, the telephone. How long before Hume's entire office was a complete glacier? When she walked across the floor, how soon before it creaked like the surface of a frozen lake? Even now DD expected to see her breath turn to mist. She coughed to get his attention.

Hume looked up. 'Yes?'

'I said: I wondered if you fancied having a private

birthday tea-party – just you and me, the two of us together?'

The briefest flicker of irritation. But then he was smiling at her. The laughter-wrinkles around his eyes like fine cracks.

'Tea? I'd really love to, but . . .' He gestured to the on-screen spread sheet, and explained that he was working on the final details of the Billionaires' Banquet. He'd been at it for hours. She wouldn't believe how many small—

'I assumed Melville would be taking care of—'

'Not anymore. From now on Executive Service will be doing without him.'

'He won't like that.'

'Maybe not. But he's been told. I was firm. There'll be no more Melville. No more of his parties.'

'Nor his money? Paid for this house.'

'We'll manage.'

'He won't like it.'

'Tough. Like I've been saying for the past few months, things are going to change. Somewhere back along the road we've taken a wrong turning and . . .'

DD stopped listening. A wind had sprung up, blowing his words all over the room. So many ice particles. Outside, she could see the city swept by the same chill wind. How soon before an ice age descended, bringing traffic to a standstill, freezing pedestrians into position where they stood, pinning the helicopters to the sky . . ?

It was getting to be an effort to breathe in, and then out. The cold air was painful, scouring her throat and lungs. Behind her Hume's voice continued to drone on like a held note . . .

In . . . and then out. In . . . and then out. Like she was

forcing her heart to start beating again. Then her tears began.

His breath, its chillness freezing her tears. Arresting them in their fall.

She started sobbing, couldn't seem to stop herself. 'The summerhouse . . .'

'In the garden, DD?' His arms were around her now, his voice warm.

'Yes.' She swallowed, got control. 'Repainted it . . . if we repainted it . . . repainted it . . . and . . .'

'Have you been taking your meds?'

'Of course.'

'*All* your meds?'

'I think so. I try to keep . . . I really, really try, but sometimes I just . . .'

'Let's go over to the couch, DD. I'll ring for them to bring us something. There's birthday cake left, I think.'

She allowed herself to be led across the room, helped to sit down. Hume was so kind, so considerate and caring, that he must still love her, he *must* do. If he'd wanted, he could have abandoned her at any of the private clinics where she—

He was speaking on the phone . . .

He was answering a knock at the door . . .

Placing a tray on the glass table in front of them. Pot of tea, milk in the jug, sugar bowl, cups, saucers, side plates, small forks. Some slices of birthday cake.

The two of them were eating, drinking, and chatting once again. Quite as normal. Tea and a slice of cake - how easy it was to be normal.

'Yellow,' she heard herself say. 'The summerhouse is yellow and has to stay yellow. A really happy colour . . . like sunflowers, like . . .' She was smiling now. Wasn't she? She was sure she was smiling. It *felt* like she was smiling.

Lying out at full-stretch on the couch now. A cushion under her head. Feeling so relaxed, so at peace. Across the room she watched Hume silhouetted in the glow of his computer screen, tap-tap-tapping away at the keys. A busy man. She loved him. Body, mind and soul, head and heart, happiness and sadness – everything. All she was – was her love for him. With nothing left over.

More than anything at that moment she wanted to tell him how much she loved him. She wanted to tell him *now*, to call out the words across the room . . . or, even better, go over to him and put her arms around him, whisper them into his ear.

For the time being though, the effort to get up from the couch and make her way across to the other side of the room was beyond her. She'd tell him later. Yes, that was a promise. And she'd tell him how happy she was. How wonderfully happy.

※

'Floor it, Simon!' called the clown as he snatched the Cat from the arms of the law.

The minibus shot forward. Its sudden acceleration sent her colliding into him.

'Hold on, madam!'

To what? There was no seating, no hand straps. The floor was covered with mattresses and the mattresses covered with clowns and fairies.

'Say goodbye to the nice policemen, boys and girls,' Driver

Simon called back to the rest of the minibus, his dreadlocks shaking as he powered everyone over the cobbles.

Hands were waved and kisses blown through the window, the spiky-haired fairy gave them the finger.

The minibus ran the Queen Street lights, bounced *clatter-thump, bumpity-bump* downhill towards Stockbridge. Parked police vans lined the pavements.

'Nice of them to clear the streets for us!' shouted Simon, gunning them through another set of lights.

At the bottom of Howe Street they swung left through Royal Circus, catching the lights at amber to go hurtling over the Water of Leith.

The Cat finally managed to disentangle herself from the clown. Matted blue hair, red-and-green-striped cheeks, painted-on smile, kilt. She recognized the piper.

'I'm sorry for—'

'My pleasure. You can grab hold of me any time!'

'I'm Lucy.' The fairy with the spiky-rainbow hair was holding out a bunch of bananas. 'Fancy one? Plenty of potassium – helps to lower stress levels after a hot pursuit. Bank robbers swear by them.'

The Cat was still shaking, but she gave a smile. 'Thank you. I'm Cat.'

'So you two don't really know each other then?' The piper looked closely at her: 'And where have you suddenly appeared from, *Cat*?'

'Edinburgh.'

'We're all coming from Edinburgh, *Cat* – where d'you live?'

'Melbourne.'

'Right.' His smile didn't ease. 'Committed, eh! I'm impressed. At Genoa, were you? Seattle?'

'I *live* in Melbourne. I'm here visiting.'

Now that it was clear there would be no pursuit, the minibus slowed down to a more normal speed. The driver called back, 'He's just anxious you're not filth.'

'Simon's right.' Lucy nodded at her. 'Mr. Anarchism here, aka Danny, doesn't believe in anything, or in anyone.'

'I believe in my pipes.'

Cat unpeeled her banana and took a bite. She'd finish it, get her breath back, then when they reached Queensferry Road she'd ask to be dropped at the nearest bus stop.

One of the fairies had just clicked off her mobile.

'Seems there's ten thousand of them guarding the fuckers. And get this - Bush has even brought his private army!'

'That's illegal!' a clown called out. 'It's violating British sovereignty to have a foreign—'

Danny punched the air. 'Bring it on!'

This was surely her cue to say, *Maybe you can let me off here, please?*

⚶

'Smashed our eggs? They'll be smashing our heads next time,' was Megan's greeting. 'The sooner we're out of here . . .'

*Shells and yolks crushed underfoot—*

'. . . need to grab what we can, Francis. Get the hell away as fast as . . .'

*His face being slammed into the wall—*

Kneeling down in front of him now. Her hands holding his, her eyes pleading: '. . . not exactly sure where . . . the cash Hume's got stashed here . . . get us far, far away . . . a new start . . .'

*Was she meaning they steal Hume's—?*

'. . . and under the floorboards. We'll need our passports and bank cards. The other stuff doesn't matter . . .'

*Abandon their home? Leave everything and—?*

'. . . taxi to Waverley, out to the airport and . . .'

St Francis laid his hands on her shoulders. At least he was no longer trembling. He pulled her towards him and explained the situation. 'It will be okay. Hume knows there's a few things still to sort with Melville, like who actually owns the flat downstairs. But this must be some kind of a mix-up. I'll tell him. We'll be fine. No need to—'

'Even you can't believe that.'

He said nothing.

'Melville's like the crazies when I was on the street. The total head-bangers. It wasn't money they were hassling for, not really - I never had any - they hassled *because* they were crazies. Money was just their excuse.'

St Francis gave her a quick hug then stood up. 'I'll phone Hume.'

'Fuck's sake, Francis. Melville's another crazy. The hassling's just getting started.'

⚜

Still in the minibus, the Cat was crossing the Forth Road Bridge on her way to take part in the protest against the evils of capitalism.

A cause close to her heart?

A sense of new-found agit-prop camaraderie with Lucy and the others?

She fancied one of the clowns?

Wanted to dress up as a fairy?

No, none of these. So why *hadn't* she asked to be dropped off as she'd planned, on Queensferry Road or anywhere out towards Barnton where a city bus could've taken her back into town? Why hadn't she made the slightest effort to say her goodbyes and leave them to carry on and save the world, but without her?

She'd only half-listened as the others continued to discuss clown-and-fairy tactics for the approaching demo. With the police likely to be herding them here, there and everywhere, the consensus was that they'd be lucky to get anywhere near the G8 at all. Widening the field of discussion, Danny dismissed London's bid to host the Olympic Games as 'the usual bread and circuses.' Others chipped in about *Britain becoming a police state . . . more CCTV here than anywhere . . . multinationals pulling everyone's strings . . . the melting ice-caps . . . more slavery in the world now than ever . . .* So much conviction, so much feeling – but what, really, did it all mean to her?

Very little.

So why, she wondered, was she still in the minibus? She stared out the window down at the Firth of Forth. Its grey-green waters were scored white by small yachts tacking to and fro as their slack sails felt for and clung to the least wind. A warship was moored across the water at Rosyth docks. Out toward the open sea, beyond the intricacy of red girders whose perfectly tied knots had held the Forth Rail Bridge together for over a century, a tanker was approaching the oil terminal standing stilt-legged in the middle of the estuary. The minibus wheels went *slap . . . slap . . . slap* over each succeeding length of prefabricated strip of road. *Slap . . slap . . . slap . . .*

Her plan – saying a last farewell to Edinburgh and Scotland

before flying back to Melbourne and getting on with the rest of her life – had come to an abrupt halt halfway across Princes Street. If spike-haired Lucy hadn't grabbed her and pulled her to safety, would she really have remained there? Between two lines of riot police bearing down on her, their batons raised?

Because the fact was . . .

. . . she had *not* been the least afraid. She realised this only now. Contrary to appearances, she had *not* panicked. Had *not* frozen. In fact, having run halfway across the street, she now remembered coming to a stop *quite deliberately*. Then, and in her own good time, she'd turned to face the approaching riot police. As she'd stood there, the city centre seemed to fall silent around her – no shouts and yells anymore, no pipes, whistles and loudhailers, no *whup-whup-whup* from the helicopter circling overhead, no *stamp-stamp-stamp* of approaching steel-capped boots. Anticipating the blow from the first baton, had she been seeking to become a martyr to the cause of anti-capitalism? No, for there was neither righteousness nor self-righteousness here, no strength of conviction, no grace of sacrifice. Instead, there'd been an *acceptance*, it had felt like – an acceptance so total that she'd been quite unable to move. As if a spell had been cast on her.

Yes, that was it – a spell. And so, so familiar. It was only as they'd stopped-and-started their way through the bottle-necked Stockbridge traffic that she realised what that sense of familiarity recalled to her. It had been the very same as when she used to let herself get picked up at parties all those years ago. No wonder she never saw any of the men again, nor had ever wanted to. They'd meant nothing to her. It had been the spell alone that mattered.

And the instant the spell was broken, she would gather up her clothes and leave. How well she remembered it now – that rush to get away. Back home, she would feel herself *reclaimed*. Often, instead of falling asleep, she would then sit up in bed and work with refreshed clarity on a maths problem – as if the intimacy of sex had been mere foreplay to better mathematics. No wonder her marriage hadn't worked out. But some things just didn't bear thinking about – how much easier to run off with the clowns and fairies, and go and save the world! It would be her farewell tour of Scotland, though not quite as she'd planned. At any rate, she'd avoid more nights in her emptied-out shell of a childhood home. It was win-win.

Meanwhile the minibus had *slap . . . slap . . . slapped* itself across to North Queensferry. They were flagged down at a police checkpoint shortly after crossing the Forth Road Bridge and told to turn back for their own security. The driver had to show his licence, everyone had to give their name and address and wait while it was checked against an unspecified national database. Half an hour further on they were stopped again, same routine. This time an army sergeant told them a bomb had been found on a minibus similar to theirs – and they all had to get out. The mattresses were dragged out, too. A Golden Retriever, aka Leila, clambered inside and sniffed every corner, then every mattress, and then each one of them in turn. Finding nothing, Leila eyed them with disappointment. Again they were told to swing round and return to Edinburgh. For their comfort and security.

Three road blocks later, a signpost said *Auchterarder*. 'This is as close as we'll get,' called out Simon.

It was nearly eight when they pulled off the road and into a field already packed with caravans, camper vans, cars and tents. Camp fires were burning. The Cat climbed out, stiff and with a headache from the relentless throb of the engine.

As she stood stretching herself, Danny came up to her. His red-and-green face only inches from hers, his paint-crusted stubble, dirt-crusted blue hair. Touching her lightly on the arm and leaning so close she could feel the brush of his lips: 'I'm watching you, Mrs. Plod.'

'In your dreams.'

# 3

## Thursday 7th July

FOR YEARS NOW they had been warm, dry, and safe in their house at the very top of the stairs, their house in the sky. In winter, Megan would lie awake listening to the wind tear across the roof immediately above their slant-ceilinged attic bedroom, she'd hear it tug at the slates, the chimney-stacks, satellite dishes, hear it whip-lash the TV cables. Rain would hammer down for hour after hour. On hot summer nights, the skylight needed to be jammed half-open to let the room breathe, to let them breathe. Winter storms, summer heat – Megan had lived them every night, held onto them every night.

To fall asleep was to trust. Which she didn't. Lying awake, letting go their bedside table, their wardrobe, their shelves of clothes under the eaves . . . Lying awake in the darkness, listening to the *tick* . . . *tick* . . . *tick* of the alarm clock. The next *tick* . . . and the next . . . and the next . . . until . . .

*Tick* . . . *tick* . . . *tick* . . . Waking up, but keeping her eyes tight closed. Picturing everything around her, each piece of furniture in its proper place – her home as it should be, her world as it should be. Then her relief as she opened her eyes and saw it all again. Her home, her world. Waiting for her. Welcoming her.

Like it had done for year after year.

But not anymore.

For that was the very last night and this was the very last morning. *Melville*. His threats had already demolished their home, turned it into an overnight skip, turned their twenty years in Barclay Towers into a single night's doss. It was time to get out, time to move on. They had to.

Francis was still asleep. Good. He was clever. Too clever. He trusted. Which was the same as asking for it. She never asked for it.

The first time Melville had appeared in the downstairs flat, she'd seen him at once for what he was. Not that she'd ever met him before, didn't need to. His name didn't matter. Take away the suit, the haircut and shoes, Melville was—

'Good morning, Megan. Need to get up soon. Big day today, remember.'

'So, we are getting out of here?'

'No, I'm meaning the Billionaires' Banquet.'

She said nothing. Better to save her breath and let him tell her how this and how that, and how wonderful . . . how they were doing something worthwhile . . . She stopped listening. If the two of them were to get through this, it was going to be up to her.

They got up. Showered and dressed. Breakfast.

'Have a good day.' She kissed him goodbye at the top of the stairs. Mr. Off-to-Work one moment, Rain-Eyes the next. Suddenly not so sure about leaving her alone? Not really believing his Billionaires' Banquet-saving-the-world spiel? Seemed he did and he didn't – that's what came from thinking too much, from trusting too much.

'Everything'll be fine,' she told him. Because—

Because, with him out of the way, it would be. She'd make sure of it. She'd got a hammer and a chisel and the whole day ahead to make it fine.

The screen showed a London double-decker with its entire roof ripped off as if some deranged giant had taken his tin opener to it, then gone on the rampage, smashing up the nearby buildings, scattering rubble and debris everywhere. Police and emergency vehicles were parked at crazy angles wherever they'd slowed to a stop on the road or half-up on the pavement. Ambulance men carrying stretchers zigzagged their way around cordons of yellow tape, stepped over firehoses and electric cables. The injured lay on the ground waiting to be attended to, survivors wandered around in shock, dazed. There was a close-up of a teenage boy sitting on the pavement, weeping.

When he turned up the sound, Hume could hear the panic in people's voices, the fear and anger, the bewilderment. And the sirens, and the loudhailers.

Jesus Christ. What the hell had happened? If that was London, then forget ES setting up shop down there anytime soon.

Through the open window came the pulsing *throb-throb* of yet another helicopter. Police, Army, Special Forces, MI5, MI6, CIA, SAS – who knew anymore? The whole fucking alphabet could be up there keeping the skies safe for democracy.

Ten minutes later, he muted the TV. There'd be no can-celling tonight's Billionaires' Banquet due to any 'high alert status', or out of respect. To be on the safe side he'd get some heavies for the door. More for show than anything else. No

Melville-type psychos. That was all behind him now. He wanted muscle that was squeaky-clean legit and came with a security firm's logo. Short of a suicide bomber walking into the building and blowing the place to Kingdom Come, tonight's event was definitely going ahead. Need to give it some spin, of course – 'ordinary men and woman determined to carry on as usual, refusing to give way to terrorism'. Spirit of the Blitz sort of stuff. The War Against Terror gag had worked for Bush, and it would work for him.

After years of profiting from the unhealthy appetites of the city's high earners who attended Melville's parties, it would mark a fresh start. It felt good – cleansing, almost – to be raising money for a worthwhile cause, even if the subscribers would likely consider it small change and probably write it off against tax. Whatever, it'd be a treat to watch most of them living off rice and water for a couple of hours. When it came to helping the world's poor, the half-million he'd be raising, less a few thousand for expenses, was a drop in the ocean, but at least it was *something*. More was probably spent every ten minutes bombing and slaughtering in Iraq, Afghanistan or wherever. Make Poverty History? Dream on. There was already enough food to go round – starvation/poverty was a political issue and always had been. If the whole world turned vegan tomorrow, the same people would likely be starved of grain.

With one eye on the TV screen, he googled 'Edinburgh security firms' and ordered up a dozen rentacops.

※

The sound of doors opening and closing all over the house, footsteps padding up and down the stairs, someone vacuuming, a telephone ringing. Another morning already. Tuesday? Wednesday? Thursday? DD turned over to see the bedside clock. Nearly 10:00. She had to get up or Hume would start worrying. God, how that man worried. If it wasn't for him and his non-stop worrying, she'd manage to get through her days a lot easier.

First things first. Best way to start was by getting a fix on her location. Gone were the days when she'd wake far out at sea, the water sometimes so electric blue she'd feel its high-voltage charge surging through her, lifting her onto crest after dizzying crest, and with no shore in sight. Or worse, she'd find herself already sliding deeper . . . and deeper . . . and deeper . . . to where the ocean's darkness and its full weight – every single drop of black water and fleck of spume towering and thrashing above – pressed down on her. Other times, other mornings – not a breath of wind, not a surface ripple. On good days it was calm. Soothing, consoling. Dry land, almost.

Forget Hume. She could depend on her little pink tablets. When she was out at sea they were her compass and her sails, they controlled the weather, set the tides. They positioned the moon and stars and helped her plot her course. Also, thanks to them, her journey's end was always well within reach. If need be.

10:30. Would she make it a good day, or a very good day?

She didn't have bad days anymore, those terrible days when her whole body was so fizzed up with adrenaline she couldn't keep still. Hardly able to breathe or to speak, or find her way among the rush and clatter of chairs, tables, doors, corridors, stairs, people. Her poor mind threatening to slip under at any moment, and take her with it. Mercifully, all that was history.

In the bathroom mirror her reflection smiled at her, gave

her a wink of encouragement. Her hand trembled as she opened the medicine cabinet and lifted the blister strip of tablets from off the glass shelf. Her very own Advent calendar, she called it, her chemical countdown to a good day or a very good day. Her day, her choice. She popped a couple of the little pink beauties out of their plastic bubbles and laid them on the rim of the washbasin. So little, so pink, so round – the shape and colour of the future. For prophecy read pharmaceuticals – the correct dosage, and navigating the day really was that simple.

One tab might still have her strung out, edgy, unsettled; her mind like an agitated bird peck-peck-pecking at nothing, and flitting here and there in alarm every few seconds.

Two tabs steadied her. Two tabs soothed, but didn't dull. Her mind calm once more, her body at ease, she'd feel confident enough to go about her familiar daily tasks – running the house and, more importantly, helping Hume to run the business. Two tabs and everything would be sure to function at maximum efficiency, herself included. Teaching little angels the piano was long behind her, she now had an office of her own with her name plate on the door – DIANE HUME, Human Resources. Her laptop with its heart-lifting screensaver – a field of yellow sunflowers. The colour of happiness. Hers.

Three tabs could mean an even better day, too good a day, perhaps. An occasional indulgence, but only if she deserved it.

Four meant a too-kindly, too-easy-drift of a day.

Five tabs meant an ever-slowing-to-complete-shutdown day.

Six tabs meant no day at all.

She ran the tap and filled the glass. One tab. Swallow.

Second tab.

Swallow.

She pressed the plastic bubble and popped tab number three. So little, so pink, so round, and lying almost weightless on the palm of her hand, weightless as the day ahead was about to become.

Fuck it, why worry? Let the morning blur a little at the edges and go soft-focus, leaving her free to glide effortlessly from one anxiety-free moment to the next, and to the next after that . . .

Allow herself the third? Tempting. So, so tempting. A day of well-earned ease to wind down after the strain of the recent birthday celebrations and all that noise and disturbance in the city centre. It had been a good day. The whole staff. The birthday cake. Her and Hume's impromptu private tea party together. So intimate, so loving, that shared togetherness . . . A busy, busy time. No wonder it was taking her a day or two to recover. Which made today – Wednesday?

Or was it Thursday?

Two tabs would be enough. She'd be strong. She'd impress.

But maybe just an extra half tab for luck, a bit of fine-tuning. She snapped it in half along the handy indentation, and swallowed.

To be on the safe side she slipped the other half tab and a couple more for emergencies into the breast pocket of her blouse. Not that she'd be rushing to take them, of course. Indeed, her resistance, her not-taking them, would show how strong and well she really was. But it would be a comfort to know they were within reach, if needed. Yes, as they say at the airport – *for her comfort and security.*

Yesterday had been a two-tab day, hadn't it? She deserved a treat.

11:30 already. Time to get into gear. She picked up the cordless from the bedside table, pressed *internal*.

'Hi there, Michael. You can tell Marta she can do the bedroom now. I'll have breakfast downstairs, thank you.'

Hume next.

His line was busy. Surprise, surprise. She left a message telling him she'd shortly be in the morning room, if he fancied dropping by.

It was when she was taking her first few steps down the staircase that the tabs really started to kick in. She paused to savour the moment. Her left hand gripping the polished wooden banister, her feet on the carpeted stair, she felt wave upon wave of that delicious calm wash over her. No longer a staircase, but an easy step-down waterfall of unhurried mini-cataracts, a slow-motion cascade that carried her along with it. Sunlight on her face, its warmth soaking into her bare arms . . .

If she let go of the banister, she would surely float away on the current! Had she really taken only two tabs? Yes, this was going to be a good day. A very good day.

Only two tabs and she was so very relaxed, so very, very relaxed, yet fully alert at the same time. She must be getting better! She had her feet firmly on the ground for step after step. A tab and a half in reserve, for *herself*. But it would be her choice, she knew exactly what she was doing. She was in control, in *total* control. She—

'Mrs. Hume? You all right?'

It was the new maid coming upstairs.

'Fine, thank you, Marta. Never better. A lovely summer's day today.'

*A two-tab day.*

The girl's upturned face was actually brimming with sunlight, her clear eyes shining, her smooth skin and cheekbones glowing. Yes, that was the word – they *glowed*. Another couple of weeks and she'd be ready to hire out for the events at Barclay Towers. Whatever Hume thought he had sorted out with Melville, the parties would continue and the girl would earn herself some good money. She was pretty enough for that. The girls from Eastern Europe were born for Executive Service. They worked hard, were polite and eager to learn, and they were grateful. Those who weren't, she fired.

Marta had taken her arm. 'We go down, yes?'

The individual stairs were cascading a little too fast, making the girl stumble, which then made *her* stumble. What an awkward, clumsy girl. But she herself at least did her best to stay on course. One of them had to. The varnished oak banister swept alongside her in a downward run-off of reflected light. She held onto it more tightly, determined to keep them both on an even keel all the way down, down, down to the main hall.

Above the roaring onrush, DD could hear the girl calling out the steps in Polish . . . each meaningless word taking her that little further into the day.

And into the morning room.

In front of her – a cup of tea, a rack of toast, butter, milk, marmalade. The tea had been recently poured, its light brown surface was still swirling. Had *she* done that? Had she poured and stirred? She was quite alone.

Wasn't she?

A glance round to check.

Yes, of course she was. She knew she was alone.

She felt in the pocket of her blouse. One and a half tablets all present and correct. She could relax. After her hectic descent – white-water rafting almost, thanks to Marta's clumsiness – she'd reached this tranquil pool, this most welcome *quietude*. From its accumulated stillness, from the pleasing arrangement of perfectly laid out breakfast things on the coffee table, from the motionless furniture attractively positioned around the room and the dependable stability of the framed paintings on the walls – from each of these in turn, she could draw a deep and solid confirmation of her own recovered calmness. Her surface *and* inner calmness. No threatening weather and no uncertainties, for here was the security of a familiar room, a shut door, and double-glazing that gave onto the same reassuring stretch of lawn day after day.

She sipped her tea, selected a piece of toast and buttered it. Now that she had completely recovered her sense of ease and repose, she'd sit back and let the morning take over. The thick-cut bread crunched deliciously in her mouth, the sharp-but-sweet coolness of the orange marmalade and the melting butter mediating between the toasted crispness outside and the soft fluffy whiteness within. Tea and toast. How enjoyable were the simple things in life. Her tea was not quite as hot as it could be – a tad too much milk, perhaps? She laughed to herself, a shake of her head. No one's perfect. Easily fixed – a top up straight from the pot. English Breakfast tea at just the right strength and temperature, what could be better?

In fact, she would be content to spend the rest of her day sitting here, savouring this perfect moment – sipping and crunching, and feeling good. A modest enough wish. Wanting nothing more than what we already have – is that not true happiness? She must tell Hume. He used to worry about such things: human happiness, appearance and reality, the existence of God, and all the rest of it. But really, life was very simple – it was people who were complicated. Not her, though, not any more. Another slice of toast, thickly buttered. Maybe she should take it to him, to show him? An audio-visual aid to prove just how perfect, how truly perfect, life could be? She laughed again. Truth be told, she'd rather eat the toast herself! It was *hers*, after all! Like the whole new day ahead, and all the days still to come! Every single last one of them! Astonishing thing was – it had always been like this, only she'd never realised it before. Not properly. Quite amazing really, that for her entire life to date she hadn't realized how—

A siren screamed the length of the street outside.

The police, most likely, keeping them secure. But the Make Poverty History demo and then the rioting anarchists, that was all done and dusted – no? The circus had left town, hadn't it?

She was about to pour a second cup when the door opened. It was Hume.

How was she? Had she slept well? Did she need anything?

Best to keep things upbeat. Light and conversational.

'Some tea?'

Banality was all it took. Without waiting for his reply, she poured out a fresh cup.

'There's some toast, if you fancy a slice. It's really good.'

'I'm fine, thanks. Just popped in to see if you were—'

'Perfect day, by the look of it. The acceptable face of global warming! How's things shaping up for the Billionaires' Banquet?' Which proved she knew what was going on – proved it to him, and to herself. Two tabs, and she was good. Two tabs, and she was completely on top of *everything*.

Hume sat down. 'There's been a really serious bombing in London, with dozens dead and hundreds injured. Up here the cops are everywhere, and on full alert. The city centre's all barricades and traffic diversions, which'll mean things running a bit late and some security problems for us. That aside, everything's on track. STV plan to mention the Billionaires' Banquet in the 'and finally . . .' slot at the end of their news, which is great coverage. You'll be able to watch some of the opening live on cable this evening, around seven.'

*This* evening? The Billionaires' Banquet was tonight?

'Watch it? I'll be there.'

'DD, we've been through this a dozen times. It's best if you stay here, my love. Nice and easy with your feet up and—'

'I can help you, can't I?'

'That would be great, but . . . Look, DD, everything's taken care of. There's no need for you to—'

'Maybe some background music while the people are coming in, help settle them, and then while they're dining? I could play some "relaxing classics", sort of – not Bach or anything like that, but easy listening.' Yes, she'd be at his side adding that little extra to the event, giving it a soundtrack that would hardly be noticed and yet help hold everything together. Yes, it was going to be a really great day! 'Or else Themes from the Shows, that kind of thing. Easy enough to hire a baby grand for the evening. Set just the right tone.' Yes! Yes! Yes! It'd be great! It'd mean looking out scores, of course, and she'd need to practise and . . .

'I'm sorry, DD, but—'

'Come on, Hume. No problem to arrange. I'll see to everything. A quick call to hire a—'

'A real shame. If only you'd mentioned it earlier . . .'

'Never too late. I'll sort out everything. Be no problem . . .' The calm surface of things was becoming agitated. 'Hume, please, I want to be there by your side. To take part. To be of some use. Please . . .'

'But you are, DD. You are.' His reassuring smile looked stuck-on. Another siren went screaming past the house. 'You hear *that*? I want you to be safe and keep safe.'

'Bet you didn't even think of having music. You never do.'

He said nothing. Which said it all.

'You don't want me there, Hume. Do you?'

'Of course I do.' He reached forward, moving into sincere mode. 'Anyway, it really is too late to start making new arrangements. I'm very sorry, but . . .'

She tuned him out. Let him talk. Talk-talk-talk. Once he was gone, she'd take that extra half tab. Why the fuck not? She'd tried her best, hadn't she? She'd been having a good day till he turned up and spoilt it. Come to that, why not take the other tab as well? Then stretch full out on the couch and let the rest of the morning lap gently against its sides like she was on a small boat floating somewhere out in the middle of a peaceful lake, a really vast, vast lake with no land in sight. Close her eyes, and let the gentle rocking of the boat carry her from nowhere to nowhere . . .

She would be all by herself, but not alone. Not any more. *Herself*, remember, she still had herself. Like a secret friend. Invisible, imaginary – but quite real. Which was what counted. For fuck's sake, *she* was real, wasn't she? She managed to get through the days and nights, didn't she? Every single day, every single fucking night. Face the facts – she trusted *herself* a lot more than she trusted anybody else. *Herself* – the only person in the whole universe who was totally on her side and had her interests at heart, *her* interests only, completely, totally and un-reservedly. Even God, so she'd heard, struggled to be that loyal.

Hume was still talking, still blundering through his repertoire of explanations and excuses. The way his mouth kept opening and closing, he could be a fish swimming round and round, his eyes searching out hers just like the koi she used to feed, gazing up at her from their pond. Needing to be fed was all. With Hume it was his needing to be sure she wouldn't bother him.

Which she wouldn't. She wouldn't bother anyone, and no one would bother her. Fair was fair. Three tabs, four tabs, five, who was counting?

She held up her hand for silence:

'Fine, Hume. No problem. Run along now. Bye. Hope everything goes well.'

The instant she heard the door close, she reached into her blouse pocket.

❧

The Cat stared out the minibus window. If she'd stuck to her original plan and changed her flight ticket instead of doing a farewell tour, she might at this very minute be sitting out in her Moonee Ponds garden, enjoying the last of the evening warmth before going to bed. Gleneagles had been a complete waste. Total fiasco. A demo all right – of police power, of state power. Bush really had brought his own private army with him. The clowns and fairies never got anywhere near the G8. Instead they were chased up and down country roads and lanes where the only traffic was security services, or else were herded in and out of fields where TV gave them world-wide coverage – see the protestors trampling down crops, see them blowing their whistles and behaving like a bunch of clown-and-fairy losers!

They were approaching the Forth Road Bridge when several phones seemed to ring at once. By the time they'd begun speeding up along the dual carriageway towards the city, everyone agreed that this bombing sounded big and would change everything. It was the UK's 9/11. While the clowns and fairies talked and talked about Britain getting payback for Iraq, about Blair and Bush being war criminals who promoted the weapons industry, the Cat could think only of getting the hell out the country and as far, far away as possible. She still had one last night in North Berwick to get through. Then it was off to the airport and—

The minibus swerved suddenly, throwing her forward. She grabbed onto the nearest clown to steady herself.

'Sorry, folks. Everyone all right?' Simon called back. 'We'll have to stop. Feels like a puncture.'

On its three good tyres and one that was definitely flat, the minibus limped slowly to the side of the road.

'Everybody out!'

※

'Yes, the whole crew'll need to be there for two o'clock, Francis. See you.' Hume put down the phone. Good. Everything was ready.

But DD? Was she lying happily stoned somewhere, orbiting Planet Prozac again? Might be for the best. For the time being anyway.

Come tomorrow, with the Billionaires' Banquet behind him, apart from the post-event admin, he'd be able to give her his full attention. Doctors, specialists, therapists, counsellors, analysts, detox clinic, detox holiday, no expense spared. Some of his undeclared cash could be put to good use. To healing. A genuine updating of Nietzsche's transvaluation of all values. It would be a rebirth for them both – post-Prozac for her, post-Melville for him.

She'd actually wanted to come along and take part, her and her piano? Her and her Catherine-wheel eyes? Not after last time. No way.

He tried her mobile.

Switched off.

Which most likely meant she really was crashed out somewhere. Fingers crossed. Best to track her down though, and make one hundred per cent sure she'd be staying put. He'd 'mak siccar', as someone had once said. Robert the Bruce?

The Venetian blinds in her office had been pulled half-shut against the sun. Plenty of paperwork spread everywhere. An opened bottle of water stood next to her computer on her desk. He clicked the mouse and her screensaver of yellow sunflowers was replaced by a page of Google search results. Piano Hire Edinburgh. By the looks of it, she'd not got as far as clicking any of them. Good. He logged off, put the computer in hibernate.

The morning room where she usually had breakfast?

He was going downstairs when he met Marta/Violetta coming up. Her cleavage rising a step at a time to meet him.

'Good morning, Mr. Hume.'

He nodded, said hello and tried not to stare.

Five minutes later he crossed the lawn to the summerhouse. Shading his eyes, he rapped on the glass and peered inside: 'DD? You there, DD?'

No reply . . . not that he really expected any. Just as well he'd thought to have the lock removed several years ago. He turned the handle and pushed open the door. 'DD?'

⁂

While Danny and Simon set about dealing with the blowout, the others sat in the sun. There was music from a penny whistle and guitar. Everybody agreed that an hour's downtime on the grass verge of the dual carriageway beat their wasted days in Gleneagles.

But not the Cat. An hour's halt was an hour too long. By now only a made-up mantra was getting her through: *Waverley-North Berwick-Airport-Amsterdam-Dubai-Singapore-Melbourne-Waverley-North Berwick . . .*

Lucy had been speaking on her phone. 'Seems all is not lost, *compadres*. One door closes and so on. There's a party tonight. A big-big-big one. All the fattest cats gathering to get fatter at a mega-do they're calling a Billionaires' Banquet. Not the politicos this time, but the ones that pull their strings. We've all been invited, but our invites must have got lost in the post. Who fancies it?'

Turned out everybody did.

But not the Cat. . . . *Waverley-North Berwick-Airport-Amsterdam-Dubai—* . . . She'd had it with saving the world, with the class struggle, anti-capitalism, anti-globalisation or whatever. *Singapore-Melbourne-Waverley-North Berwick-Airport . . .* She'd had it with her childhood home. She'd pick up her stuff, drop the keys into the lawyer's then stay in a hotel tonight. Problem solved. *Waverley-North Berwick-Airport-Amster—*

'Everybody back on the bus!'

DD opened her eyes. Hume was staring down at her, talking talking talking. Hume and his words words words. The usual. Concern/reassurance/anger/resignation – take your pick.

The summerhouse slipped in and out of focus as too many colours leaked into each other, framing his head and shoulders with a hazy backdrop – the curved sweep of the raised piano lid, the off-white of the painted wall behind him, the half-closed yellow shutters, the blue of the summer sky outside. Only his face remained untouched, its smoothness cracking around the mouth and eyes as if his expression had been hammered into place.

DD reached up, letting her fingertips stray across his cheek until they brushed against his lips. Then she pressed gently. Maybe his words would run onto her fingers and stick to them like so much honey she could lick off later, as and when the mood took her. Or else if they came alive, they'd be tiny word-ants, sentence-marching themselves in straight lines down onto her palm. Then she could close her fist around them. Feel them scurry blindly in panic, squeeze them tight, shake them out like so much harmless dust.

So many words, so many grains of sand.

Hume was another person, another country, another planet almost, and always a lifetime away.

Better to simply tune him out?

Yes. Always, always yes.

# PART 4

# I

BEFORE HUME HAD moved into his Barclay Towers cupboard all those years ago, he'd lived in a basement-burrow just off Morrison Street – and how the area had changed! No more soot-blackened tenements or the butcher's shop where animal carcasses swung on their metal hooks getting bumped into when he queued for offcuts from the bacon slicer; or the baker's where he'd get a fresh-made Scotch pie from the back door at 4 in the morning. The licensed grocer's and the chip shop had gone and so had that windowless pub, the gloriously named Barley-Bree. No Co-operative Dairy, no blinkered horses clip-clopping the cobbles as they pulled the milk carts out through the massive black-iron gates to begin their deliveries, breath steaming in the early morning cold.

Had a sorcerer from the *Arabian Nights* or a witch out of an old Scottish folk tale turned all the noise, clutter and bustle of Seventies' street life into this steel-and-glass severity of twenty-first-century business grandeur? With one wave of a corporate wand, the shops and flats had been turned into ice-palaces of dark-tinted or mirrored glass, each set well apart from the others. Offices, and more offices. Banks, insurance companies, pension firms – who else could afford sorcerers these days? A little further along the street, an arched bridge spun from the most delicate steel thread hung weightlessly in space, joining one airy glass palace to its neighbour across the way.

At the very same moment as the whine of an emergency siren came from the Lothian Road end of the street, the predictable helicopter roared into view, its wheels almost touching the roof of the ice-palace opposite. The emergency siren's two-note snarl was so persistent and the helicopter's *whup-whup* so steady and unchanging as it hovered above, that time seemed to have stopped. Like a piece of old-fashioned celluloid film that had got jammed in the projector, the present moment threatened to curl in the heat, to blister and melt to nothing.

Then abruptly, the film jerked forward – the police siren faded trailing off towards Princes Street and the helicopter lifted itself higher into the air. Next moment was indeed straight out of a silent film as more than a dozen butlers and footmen emerged from the back of a medium-sized furniture van, each in his Executive Service livery of bow tie, waistcoat and tails, and each carrying a large cardboard box. A retro, camped-up version of the Keystone cops?

A hundred-foot sheet of water had stiffened into clearest ice, a motionless glacier with not one single handhold on its sheer face except for an occasional outcrop of ornamental red sandstone – the headquarters of an insurance company. Through the glass could be seen a very wide staircase whose generous sweep tapered as it rose to a mezzanine floor some twenty or so steps above, like a new-style drawbridge. All that was missing was the moat and portcullis.

Hume felt a thrill of genuine pride as he led his staff into the hi-tech castle of wealth that he had secured as the ideal setting for the Billionaires' Banquet.

Ascending the staircase to the spacious mezzanine where the event would be held, he saw the early afternoon sunlight pour though the glass frontage and onto the heads and shoulders of his butlers, footmen, maids and himself, its touch falling as a blessing almost.

❧

The minibus pulled into St Andrews Square. Police were everywhere walking in pairs, standing in groups, sitting in parked vans. Radios crackled, phones clicked on and off. But nothing was actually happening, not this time. No riot, no demo.

'All these cops, the London bombings have got them on edge. Thanks to Mr. Sincerity Blair, we're at war and probably always will be, from now on.' Danny slammed the door shut. 'Only it's not just Iraq anymore, is it? The front line runs right through the street where we live.'

A helicopter's drone became louder as it banked into a turn before starting on another sweep across the city centre. The air was so clear that the Cat could imagine the Fife hills were within walking distance. She heard one of the clowns, a self-satisfied slab of Scottish grimness, mutter to himself: 'Aye, right enough. London today . . . Edinburgh will be next. You can bet on it.'

She was less than five minutes from Waverley, thank goodness.

The clowns and fairies were discussing how best to disrupt the Billionaires' Banquet that evening. It was some kind of charity do, a conscience-saving event, according to the Scottish Slab, and strictly for the wealthy. 'Mind you,' he added, 'the whole country's a billionaires' banquet.'

The Cat interrupted to say her goodbyes and give a big thank-you all round for so hospitably having her along and

233

making her feel so welcome. A few quick hugs and wishing everyone well. Then she was off, her riot-free, demo-free life beckoning. *Waverley-North Berwick-Airport—*

She'd only gone a couple of steps when she heard:

'Hume will have plenty of heavies tonight, extra muscle.'

*Hume?* A couple more steps.

*Hume?* She paused. It couldn't be?

Could it?

⚜

By 4:30 everything was ready. In Kitchen Centre, set up in one of the conference rooms off the main hall, St Francis ticked off his checklist—

White plastic bowls for 500 (25 packs of 20, plus one pack extra) stacked next to the back wall.

Plastic forks for 500 (2 cardboard boxes, plus 50 forks extra).

250 litres of still water, in their plastic wrapping.

2 cases, Château Margaux '85.

50 cases, Bollinger Champagne unpacked and stacked in the several fridges specially installed for the day.

1 case each, white and rosé, Entre Deux Mers and a superb Chilean (in fridge).

Case of mixed soft drinks.

Butter, cheese, grapes, milk (in fridge).

6 hot plates in position on trestle tables, wired up and good to go.

Pre-cooked, four-course dinner for ten, confirmed to arrive at 6:15pm, requiring only to be heated up

Time to return home, shower, get into the wings and tails. Back here for 5:30.

Airy and elegant, the mezzanine was the size of several tennis courts – the perfect setting for the event. Hume had chosen well. The translucent glass ceiling allowed natural sunlight to filter down as though from the open sky directly above, screened by a thin haze of summer cloud. This 'outdoors' theme was reinforced by the trimmed bushes and potted palms scattered here and there, each in its own patch of decorative gravel, like so many miniature oases to refresh the desert expanse of sand-yellow tiles. The inner walls of this sun-drenched landscape were transparent, and through them St Francis could see men and women seated in their open-plan, floor upon floor of toiling office-workers stacked one on top of the other, and reaching all the way up to the man-made sky.

Near Kitchen Centre a small herd of tea trolleys was gathered in readiness around a grove of palm fronds. A metre-high stage-in-the-round had been set up in the middle of the hall. Centre-stage, the dining table looked superb with its creaseless, immaculate white linen cloth. Each place-setting comprised forks, knives and spoons laid in perfect array, all solid silver, a side plate, nest of three glasses and folded napkin. The centerpiece would be an ice-sculpted billionaire's yacht sailing on a base of frozen waves and flying a tricolor flag decorated with the currency signs for the dollar, the pound and the euro. Scheduled for last-minute delivery, it was created to melt only during the dessert, a symbol of acquired wealth being as one with the natural world. On the tiled desert below, techies were setting up the audio and visual equipment needed for such a large hall. Feedback whine and sudden static crackled from loudspeakers as a voice called out, '1 . . . 2 . . . 3 . . . Testing! Testing! 1 . . . 2 . . . 3 . . . Testing

Testing!' A television crew was getting itself installed – one man carrying a camera, another with rolls of black cable slung over his shoulders like he was a mountaineer; a woman was ticking off items on a list pinned to a clipboard, while at the same time speaking into a lapel microphone. A sound boom on a long pole was being erected to hang over the diners; cables had been taped to the floor and a microphone set up at the front of the stage. Freestanding in the middle of the hall were two large plasma screens, and a couple of men on a ladder were adjusting the angle of the nearest; a third screen had been fixed against the far wall.

Having positioned their music stands to one side of the stage, a woman and two men were unpacking their instruments while a cellist, already seated, bowed a few chords to check the acoustics.

'No crappy *muzak* for this do. That's the Edinburgh String Quartet – touch of real class.' Hume had come up to him and was holding out a bottle of Champagne: 'Take this for you and Megan to share afterwards. It's going to be a great night, but a hard one. See you in an hour.' Then he rushed off to speak to a techie.

As he turned to leave, St Francis nearly went smack into a solid wall of dark blue uniforms and tattoos. A dozen of them, all wide and heavy-looking. The Security Hume had ordered.

Clutching his bottle of Champagne like when he'd returned from his first ever footman gig all those years ago, St Francis let himself in from the street. He also had good news to tell Megan, to set her mind at rest. Hume had explained to him about the £150,000 and Melville, told him that everything was sorted out. Hume had assured him that Melville wasn't involved in the Billionaires' Banquet nor would be working with them again, ever.

Key in the Barclay Towers door, and up the stairs. Hume had reminded him the downstairs flat was owned by Executive Service in name only and would now be sold lock-stock-and-barrel to Melville for the nominal sum of one pound. Problem solved. Apart from using the same entrance, he and Megan need have no further dealings with what went on there. More good news.

Maybe when he returned after the Billionaires' Banquet, it'd be like that very first evening all over again, when he'd come home to find Megan sleeping on his bed? Let's make each other real, she'd said – well, tonight they could reaffirm their vows.

He opened the door and stepped inside. 'Hi, it's me!'

No reply.

Okay, he'd surprise her.

⚙

Spike-haired Lucy was standing a little apart from the others while re-tying her Doc Martens, one foot on the low wall that ran round St Andrew Square Gardens. The Cat went back up to her:

'I just heard Danny mention someone called Hume?'

'Yeah, he's the guy putting on the Billionaires' Banquet.'

'He's a billionaire?'

'No, just organising it. With him, though, charity will begin at home and stay there. Hume's half-businessman/half-crook like the rest of the crème de la crème. A real Edinburgh Del Boy.'

237

'How old is he?'

'Bit older than you. Late forties. Fifty maybe. Bright guy, by the sound of it. They say he's got a PhD in philosophy. Set up his own catering company years ago. Caters for anything, so I've heard. And I mean *anything*. Tonight's a real obscenity. Fat cats feeding their faces to save the world's poor? Give me a break!'

Philosophy? Hume? The same. Had to be.

'When's your demo?'

St Francis entered the living room, and came to an abrupt stop. Horrified.

'Megan?'

When they'd moved into the old recording studio they'd stripped the place, papered and painted the walls, laid fitted carpets throughout, even in the awkward tower-shaped recess in the kitchen where the Electric Boy had stacked his banks of recording equipment. They had done all the work themselves, putting their heart and soul into every square metre of their new home.

And now?

The carpet had been ripped up and dragged to one side, and the floorboards beneath attacked with an axe, it looked like – gaping holes everywhere and lengths of splintered wood sticking out like hacked limbs. The furniture had been shoved to one end of the room to stand derelict – the huddle of displaced chairs, the coffee table and lamp stand staring out at the devastation. The wallpaper hung in tatters exposing gouged-out plasterboard and smashed lathes.

'We can leave now.' Megan had come through from the bedroom, a canvas holdall in each hand.

'What? *You* did this? What the hell's been—?'

'Seventy thousand in each, give or take.' She raised one of the holdhalls. 'Hume's black money, as much as I could find anyway. DD once joked our flat was probably worth more than their house in the Grange, an exaggeration, but good enough. Enough here for us to go and stay gone.'

'But Megan—'

'Our passports as well, and bankbooks, credit cards, laptops and overnight stuff. We stay here any longer and Melville and his heavies will be—'

'Hume's spoken with him. Everything's sorted.'

'And you believe him?'

'Hume? Course I do.'

'I don't care about him. I mean Melville. He's a crazy, and crazies never let go.'

'Melville's a businessman. If there's no profit to be—'

'God, you might be clever, Francis, but you're really stupid sometimes. Book-stupid. Hume's finished. Hospital, if he's lucky. No need for us to join him.' She kissed him. 'Come on.'

'We can't just walk out and—'

The phone rang.

'Excuse me.' St Francis stepped over a gap in the floor-boards and reached to pick up when—

'Leave it.'

'It'll be Hume about tonight's—'

'I said, leave it!' Next moment, Megan had dropped her bags and clamped her hand down on the receiver: 'LEAVE IT!'

It rang and rang. Then stopped.

'Hume would try your mobile first. That's Melville checking to see if anyone's here or not. The moment you answer they'll be round.'

'I'll try 1471.'

'Jesus Christ, Francis! WE NEED TO GO!'

She started towards the door. 'You want your head smashed in? Mine? I'll book us into a hotel for the night. Call me. See you soon. I hope.'

'Megan, you can't just—'

But she'd gone. The phone started to ring again.

Half a dozen rings later, it stopped.

And now? Stay and get changed into his wings and tails? Follow her?

The phone rang again.

⚬⚬⚬

How many pills have you taken? HOW MANY/HOW MANY?/HOW MANY?

DD could still feel the words resonating inside her, coursing through her body like so many micro-blood clots ricocheting up and down her veins.

Finally, though, she absorbed them. Absorbed the lot – the pills, Hume's words, his kindness, his irritation, his concern. A delicious soothing followed. Question was – had she absorbed Hume too? He was nowhere to be seen. Judging by the angle of sunlight between the half-opened shutters it must be hours later. Five, six o'clock, easy.

No pills left in her blouse pocket? Fuck. Her emergency stash over in the sugar jar? There should be a blister strip bulging with the little pink lovelies.

Her fingers fumbled around in the jar like in a bran tub – the Lucky Dip for the Advent strip. And, yes, there it was. Hallelujah!

Pulling it out. Licking the sugar off her fingers. A sweet apéritif.

Two rows of punched and sagging plastic – two rows of skin blisters already popped. Fuck it. Except . . . in one of them, thank goodness, there was still a half tab hiding under the torn lid. A pink one. Forty mgs. Which meant 20. Better than nothing.

Her mouth was so dry she needed two swallows of voddie to get it down. Soon it'd begin its good work. Like an up-draught, the vodka would lift her. As well it should. Why spend what was left of the day slothing it on the couch when there was work to be done? Hume would surely need her help.

Another swallow to set her on her way, get her firing on all cylinders.

A shower. Fix her clothes. Fix her face. When she was ready – call CityCabs.

If she felt herself drifting off-course, a sip of voddie would keep her on track. But only a sip. She smiled to herself, she knew what she could do and what she couldn't. She was in total control.

## 2

HAVING TOLD LUCY she'd catch them all later, the Cat went straight round to M&S. After her three days on the road wearing and sleeping in the same sweatshirt and jeans, she needed new clothes. Afterwards she treated herself to a good long session in the Balmoral Hotel's spa centre.

She arrived late at the demo, and the event had started. The full circus ring of clowns and fairies plus at least fifty other protestors were gathered on the pavement outside. They'd been locked out. Not that they seemed to care – after the frustrations of their G8 demo up at Gleneagles, Danny was blowing himself to vein-bursting blood-red and beyond, his pipes going full-blast; Simon and the Scottish Slab were giving their side drums a workout the skins would be lucky to survive; Lucy and two other fairies charged up and down the length of pavement in front of the entrance, leaping in the air, high-kicking, twirling and prancing a free-form bal-let-cum-ceildh – *The Rite of Spring* meets the Gay Gordons – while the rest of the crowd gave out the highland *och-ayes!*, whooping and hand-clapping in time. The glass doors were closed, guarded by a security man standing eyes-front and unamused.

Lucy pulled out of the dance and strode up to the main door. Hands on her hips, she half-chanted, half-shouted at the top of her voice: 'CORPORATE BASTARDS! SNOUTS IN

THE TROUGH! CORPORATE BASTARDS! SNOUTS IN THE TROUGH!'

A backing chorus of 'CORPORATE BASTARDS!' was quickly taken up.

Instantly, the guard stepped forward and shoved her away.

She yelled into his face: 'Get your hands off me, you FASCIST BASTARD!' Then nodded in the direction of the CCTV camera set above the entrance. 'Smile, Big Brother is watching you.'

The guard stepped back immediately. 'Riff-raff, the lot of you! Vermin. Away and have a bath somewhere. Go and drown yourselves!'

Danny gave a loud fart on his pipes, stopped playing and swung them rifle-style over his shoulder. He addressed the circus, 'Oooh, listen to Rentaplod. He's a Scary Man!' Then he led them in a new chant: 'SCARY MAN! SCARY MAN!'

Clutching his hands in schoolboy-nervousness, he shuffled forward, right up to the headmaster-guard. A high-pitched schoolboy voice: 'Mr. Scary Man, Mr. Scary Man, I'm sooo frightened.' Stopped only inches from him: 'Look!' Abruptly the clown's hair stood up on end in rigid blue tufts. The chorus laughed and applauded.

Lucy yelled: 'Back to your sty, RENTAPIG!'

Which he did, closing the ice-palace door behind him. Danny went up and banged his fist on the plate glass. The rentacop stood arms folded and stared out at him with a half-smile on his face. Danny banged his fist again.

'Locked. It'll be reinforced like the rest of this fucking Fort Knox – built to keep out the financially undesirable.'

Lucy: 'So that's that?'

Danny: 'We could crash the minibus through it – all in a good cause.'

Simon was quick: 'No you don't. Me and Sally are living in it.'

'Fair enough.'

Simon: 'But won't there be some kind of back entrance, some kind of . . ?'

The Cat stopped listening. One way or another the circus was going to force its way into the event. Was she really that desperate to catch sight of Hume?

Surely time for a discreet exit.

She was edging away when a taxi pulled up and a woman got out. Botox, business suit and heels, she pushed through the circus ring without a word, went straight up to the entrance and rapped her knuckles on the glass door. The guard shook his head and kept shaking it, mouthing a big NO-NO-NO and gesturing her to go away. The woman wasn't giving up, though. Started rapping louder, more insistently.

Finally the door was opened the merest crack.

'Sorry, madam, everyone invited has arrived. The event has already started.' He flourished a clipboard. 'Here's the list . . .'

'The organizer, Mr. Hume, is my *husband*. I don't need to be on any list.'

Lucy said in her ear: 'That's must be DD aka the Drug Doll. Hume's wife. Been in and out of rehab for years – no wonder, being married to him. She helps run Executive Service, smearing caviar over all kinds of dodgy stuff.'

The woman was smashed out of her head. DD . . . ? DD . . . ? Wasn't that the name of the girl who'd turned up and dragged Hume off to the disco that night? And he'd gone and married her! Jesus Christ.

'My apologies, madam.' The door was opened wider.

Once inside, DD carried on up the staircase and across the crowded hall, nodding here and there to familiar-looking blurs of the great and good, to footmen and maids. Toilets located, she headed in for a reality check. Quick touch of lipstick, quick comb through the hair – and she'd be ready to rock'n'roll!

❧

The instant Hume's wife had stepped through the entrance, Danny slipped in behind her and shoved the guard aside. The circus of clowns and fairies came in surging straight after, sweeping the Cat along with them.

'Easy as that, eh, Cat! Told you we'd be invited!'

The drummers stood to one side and started their *rumble-grumble, rumble-grumble* while the others ran up the staircase. . . only to find a six-man security barricade waiting for them at the top. Shoulder-to-shoulder, barring their way.

'. . . SHOW WE ARE NOT AFRAID, THAT WE WILL NEVER GIVE IN TO TERRORISM . . .' boomed out from a very large screen some ten feet to Cat's left. She could see the hall was crowded. A large cocktail party, it looked like, with hundreds of men and women, standing, drink in hand, while waiters and maids rushed about offering refills. A pretty well-heeled crowd, too, judging by their clothes. The guests were listening to someone giving a speech. The camera now showed a dining table, in front of which stood a man in evening dress, at the microphone. There was a butler in attendance behind each empty chair. The camera zoomed in on the speaker.

'TODAY'S BARBARIC ATROCITY IN LONDON WAS . . .'

'That's Hume,' said Lucy. 'Listen to him, Cat. London's getting bombed – but who cares? Business as usual . . .'

She could see him quite clearly now, filling the screen. Evening dress, bow tie, touch of grey. *Hume?* Older, of course. Could it really be him? Sleek and successful-looking. *Hume!* Jesus Christ!

'. . . RAISE HALF A MILLION POUNDS IN ONE NIGHT, ALL THANKS TO YOU GOOD . . .'

*Rumble-grumble, rumble-grumble, Rumble-grumble, rumble-grumble . . .*

'. . . THE FINANCIAL CRÈME DE LA CRÈME, AS EDINBURGH'S VERY OWN JEAN BRODIE MIGHT HAVE . . .'

*Rumble-grumble, rumble-grumble, rumble-grumble . . .*

The security line was being pressed, but it pressed back and had started advancing, forcing the protestors to retreat a few steps down the staircase.

*Rumble-grumble, rumble-grumble, rumble-grumble . . .*

'. . . THE LUCKY WINNERS, TEN MEN AND WOMEN OUT OF FIVE HUNDRED, WILL DINE LIKE BILLIONAIRES. . .'

*Rumble-grumble, rumble-grumble, rumble-grumble . . .*

'. . . STARVATION. SO MUCH SUFFERING WHILE WE WHO ARE . . .'

Lucy was yelling: 'Think your money'll save you? When the plane crashes you think Business Class stays up in the air? Assholes! FUCKING ASSHOLES!'

*Rumble-grumble, rumble-grumble, rumble-grumble . . .*

Behind them, a vigorous chant had begun in time to the drumming:

*Rumble-grumble, rumble-grumble* – 'PUSH!'

*Rumble-grumble, rumble-grumble* – 'PUSH!'

At every cry of 'PUSH!' she and Lucy found themselves being shoved up onto a higher step.

'We're winning, Cat!'

'. . . AND CAN BE DONE. LET US MAKE POVERTY HISTORY!'

The hall broke out in loud applause.

*Rumble-grumble, rumble-grumble* – 'PUSH!'

*Rumble-grumble, rumble-grumble* – 'PUSH!'

Forced to retreat several steps, the guards had now formed a twelve-man wall that completely blocked the narrow entrance, stopping any advance into the hall. They stood firm. The front line of multi-coloured clowns and fairies faced the line of black-uniformed security, with only a metre between them. Total stalemate.

꧁

Having fixed her face and hair so she'd look her very best for the gala evening ahead, DD was putting away her lipstick when she caught sight of something quite unexpected. Something quite wonderful, in fact.

Peeking out almost shyly from one of the side pockets in her handbag was—

An Advent strip!

She almost jumped in the air for joy. Of course! It was her mobile stash for trips away from home – and three of the advent blisters were still unpopped. Three whole 40mg tabs!

Her lucky day, right enough!

Just to celebrate, she popped tab number one. Which left two of the pink little beauties snug and inviting in their plastic bubbles, a reward for later on. A reward for good behaviour, for conduct above and beyond the call of duty, wifely or otherwise. Even one tab was quite enough to be going on with, of course. She'd be sensible; tonight of all nights she needed to keep her wits about her.

Which she was doing . . . and how!

Back in the hall, she was in time to catch the end of Hume's speech of welcome. Behind him, the table, the butlers and footmen. No piano in sight, of course. But there had to be something she could do, something that would help him and show how much she—

Of course! Only a few feet along from her, in the wings as it were, stood St Francis, preening himself, getting ready to walk onstage as the official quaich-bearer. Straightening his lapels, his waistcoat and tails. Smoothing down his jacket, centering his clip-on bow tie, giving himself a last-minute spit-and-polish . . .

. . . and yes! Yes! YES! On the trestle table next to him stood the silver quaich itself. So silver-smithed and glittering, so curly scrolled and elegant, so brim-brim-brimming with five hundred pink slips, one for each of the five hundred guests now giving Hume their full attention. The Quaich, standing there and waiting . . . waiting for her.

Her lucky, lucky day!

With a sudden swoop and snatch, she grabbed the bowl.

Couldn't have been easier; perfect timing! Then quick-stepping it through the crowd while Hume's microphone voice boomed in the background. No slowing down till she reached the foot of the stage.

At the bottom of the short flight of steps she paused long enough to calm herself, preparing to switch into *public* mode. So far, so good.

Now for her big entrance. Seemed a few of the lottery slips had fallen out on the way. But not many, a handful at most. No one would notice. The random element was surely only to be expected in a lottery. Random, in fact, was what it was all about.

She took a deep breath. In a moment all eyes would be on her. Placing her foot on the first step, and with a well-judged sense of ceremony, she began to make her way up on to the stage. Slowly-slowly, arms outstretched in front of her, she bore the silver bowl with a dignity that would be seen as true stateliness. She reached the top. Stood still. Another pause, for dramatic effect.

Making sure to give the attendant butlers and footmen stationed behind the empty chairs a wide enough berth so there'd be no danger of colliding with any of them, she proceeded at a measured pace, all pomp and circumstance. She glanced down every few steps, extra-careful not to miss her footing. It would be a disaster were she to go tumbling over the edge, the lottery slips sent fluttering like a host of butterflies onto the crowd below. But she wouldn't. No chance.

It seemed a long, long way to the front of the stage where Hume stood waiting for her at the microphone.

Cautiously, cautiously. Taking her time. Every breath controlled, every movement precise. Every step deliberated. Poise. Balance. Careful, careful. Five hundred people who'd each paid £1,000 were watching her. The world's TV cameras were zooming in on her. She focused . . . she ignored everything else and everyone. All that mattered was what she was carrying and to whom she was bringing it. The silver quaich, and Hume. She was doing this for *him*. It was an offering – really it was *herself* she was carrying to him. Showing she could help, showing he could trust her to play her part.

She was almost there. Only a few steps more. Her hands trembling ever so slightly, she held the quaich out to him. It was filled with half a million pounds' worth of lottery slips, but it was far more precious than that. It was a silver pitcher brimming with her love.

⁂

Standing at the top of the stairs, the Cat was able to see the screen again. And there, walking unsteadily towards Hume and holding a silver dish shaped like a punch bowl, was his wife DD. She stumbled across the stage, scattering clouds of paper slips as she went.

'Looks bombed out her skull!' She shouted into Lucy's ear.

'Right enough. And holding the hopes of the world in her hands – pretty much sums up late-stage capitalism, eh?'

She'd only seen DD that once and for a couple of hours at most, sitting at the Barclay Towers kitchen table. A long time ago – a dim memory of straight black hair and Hume trailing off after her, his tongue hanging out. She'd seemed a nothing-special sort of girl. But this was the same person twenty years on, drugged to the eyeballs and getting blown from side to side across the stage by a wind that only she could feel. Poor woman. The Cat almost felt sorry for—

'What d'you fancy – clown or fairy?' Lucy was holding out some small tubes of facepaint.

'Clown, I think.' She reached for a tube of red.

'No, I'll do it. Easier that way – you can give me a re-spray at the same time. Clown for you and fairy for me. Touch up the stars on my cheeks with some silver and blue, then dab a yellow sun on my forehead. Got to look our best for the *Ten o'Clock News!*'

⚜

DD's hands were trembling so much as she offered Hume the quaich that she nearly dropped it.

The look of fury on his face. The utter rage.

Her hands wouldn't stop shaking, and more of the slips went spilling onto the floor.

Without missing a beat, Hume gathered up the nearest and returned them to the bowl. Her love was once more intact.

Leaning close to her, he hissed in her ear:

'Don't fucking move! Don't breathe even!'

What could she say? Nothing. Nothing, and everything.

'I wanted to—' she began. But that look on his face . . . She stood rigid-still and clutched the quaich in her hands as tightly as she could. In the whole wide world, what else had she to hold on to?

His showman's smile firmly back in place, Hume had already turned to face the audience and the cameras.

'Now for the big moment, ladies and gentlemen. Who will sit at the billionaires' table and who will starve?' He drew out the first slip:

'Cameron McClay of McClay, Donaldson and McClay – one of our most respected law firms. Congratulations, sir!'

There was a burst of applause. Out the corner of her eye DD saw a tall, fair-haired man make his way out of the crowd, up the stairs and onto the stage, grinning. He was shown to his seat by his own personal butler, and a fresh glass of Champagne was poured for him. Meanwhile, another name had been drawn, then another and another. Not once did Hume even glance at her.

*Rumble-grumble, rumble-grumble, rumble-grumble . . .*

But she couldn't look over to see what was happening. She daren't. She had to concentrate, concentrate her whole mind and body. She had to make sure she kept the quaich steady so that Hume could call out name after name, draw out ticket after ticket. She would hold it out for him for as long as he wanted, until the bowl was empty even. She would show him her love would never run out. . .

*Rumble-grumble, rumble-grumble, rumble-grumble . . .*

That anarchist rabble she'd seen outside – they must have got in somehow. Concentrate, concentrate. Clenching her fists and pressing her fingernails into her palms to keep herself safe.

But the quaich . . . ? The silver quaich of lottery slips that she'd been holding securely in her hands . . . where was it?

The final winner's slip had been drawn – a forty-year-old business suit with a public-school complexion clasped both hands above his head, boxing-champion-style, and strode onstage. Much less applause than for the first few winners – the remaining 490 subscribers now knew for certain they were each a thousand down and condemned to represent the world's poor living off rice and water for the rest of the evening. Some of them were already drifting towards the exit.

But St Francis hardly noticed. Not even when DD dropped the quaich. All he could think of was:

*Megan – the gutted flat*
*Megan and the money she'd taken*

*Phone her – he had to phone her*
*Megan – the gutted flat*

'A nice touch,' remarked the final winner, indicating the envelope that he'd found at his place setting. It contained a cheque for £1,000, signed and dated with the space for the payee's name left blank. There was an accompanying note:

### CONGRATULATIONS!

Your status as one of this evening's ten billionaires
demands that your subscription be returned to
you. Please write your own name as Payee
—and be sure to take your cheque with you when you leave!
However, should you wish to reconfirm your initial
donation, please tear it up. Thank you again for helping to
make BILLIONAIRES' BANQUET such a success.
*Bon Appétit!*

DD watched Hume lead the butlers offstage, taking the quaich with him. Without a word or even a glance in her direction, he'd simply walked off. Behind her, she could hear the diners chatting among themselves as they sipped their Champagne.

Had Hume meant her to follow him?

With a wave and a 'Bon *appétit*, ladies and gentlemen!' she wandered past the dining table, a cloud of pink slips swirling up around her feet. They were so much waste paper now. The ballot had been chosen. Billionaires' Banquet was going to be a great success. That was all that really mattered.

Once Hume had a chance to calm down, he'd see that she'd only been trying to help. Trying to do her best. Each time he'd reached his hand into the bowl it had felt like he was reaching into her, into her very heart, to sound the depths of her love. Until, that is, the quaich had somehow slipped from her hands . . . But he would understand. He would forgive her. Forgiveness – *that* was surely what love was all about. *No point in crying over a spilt half-million*, he'd probably joke. To which she'd answer, *So long as we have each other. Which we do. We're very lucky people.*

Yes, today was her lucky, lucky day.

As it turned out, going down the short flight of steps couldn't have been easier. What a relief! One moment she was on-stage, and the next she was half-gliding, half-strolling across the sunflower-yellow tiled floor of the hall. It was all so effortless. She was doing fine despite the loudspeakers blaring out on all sides, despite the trolleys of rice and water that kept getting in her way, and the endless people who kept bumping into her. Yes, she was doing fine. Never felt better.

A two-tab day, a perfect day.

'Are you all right, Mrs. Hume?' one of the maids asked before drifting off into the crowd, pushing her trolleyload of rice and water.

*Never felt better,* DD had meant to say to her. She was sure she'd heard herself saying it. Quite, quite sure.

'Never felt better!' she called after the girl.


Walking into Kitchen Centre was like walking into hell itself. Around St Francis, steam swirled in clouds, a line of gas burners flared, rice pots bubbled. Chefs, butlers, footmen, maids – everyone was shouting at the top of their voice. 'Bloody protestors, police'll sort them out. No half-measures after London . . .' Everyone getting into everyone else's way.

'My daughter's somewhere down there, the phone networks have all crashed so I can't reach her . . . and instead I'm pouring out fucking Champagne . . . The Clown Army? What the fuck's that all about?'

Silver serving dishes were laid out on a trestle table in the centre and a chef was working his way along them, filling them from a trolley pushed by one of the footmen.

'Getting paid, at least. Unless anyone fancies giving theirs to charity? Fucking right!'

A tureen of rice, a stack of plastic bowls, forks, bottles of water and paper cups on each, the maids' trolleys were being loaded up and wheeled back out into the hall.

From the centre of hell, St Francis heard himself issue instructions and give advice, but at the same time he was being jerked in an accelerated zig-zag from scene to scene of vivid flashbacks and flash-forwards: the gutted flat, Megan waiting in a hotel room somewhere, the bags of banknotes, Megan holding down the phone . . . When he tried to fix events in their proper order, to make sense of them and see where they might lead, they at once speeded up again zig-zagging back and forwards, taking him everywhere and nowhere—

*His face getting slammed into the lift wall . . .*

*The money . . .*

*Phone Megan . . .*

*Their gutted flat . . .*

'We're all ready, Francis.'

Stepping out into the hall, he could see that some of the maids, wearing their sponsored costumes logoed HSBC, ROYAL BANK OF SCOTLAND, CLYDESDALE BANK and the like, had already begun distributing rice-and-water portions, as calculated by Oxfam to be in accordance with accepted minimum starvation levels. Joining in the spirit of things, some of the poor forked up their rice as if their very lives depended on it. He gave the musicians a nod, their cue to begin.

The opening bars were struck up – an arrangement of 'Food, Glorious Food' from *Oliver!* – and he led the procession of butlers and footmen, each bearing a covered serving dish, round to the short flight of steps. There was a burst of spontaneous applause. A cameraman took up position near him, filming their progress.

The procession made its way around the table. The dishes were laid before the guests and the silver covers removed to reveal the first course: one dressed lobster in its shell per person, with trimmings. While the cameras zoomed in to catch the delight on the diners' faces, the Champagne glasses were refilled. A toast was drunk to the crowd gathered below, the poor who were paying for it all.

*Rumble-grumble . . . Rumble-grumble . . . Rumble-grumble . . .* The two drummers – the Scottish Slab and Simon with a painted-on skull-grin – faced the line of security men while Lucy and two other fairies strolled up and down in front of the guards, smiling at them and winking as they sway-hipped past, blowing them kisses.

Drumming more and more softly, Scottish Slab and Skull-Grin then stepped back.

*Rumble-grumble, rumble-grumble, rumble-grumble, rumble-grumble . . .*

Danny took their place. The fairies withdrew.

Without a word, he clicked his heels together, then walked the length of the security cordon as if they were soldiers on parade.

*Rumble-grumble, rumble-grumble, rumble-grumble, rumble-grumble . . .*

Midway along the line, he halted in front of a guard who was slightly overweight. Then yelled sergeant-major-style right into his face:

'Private Pig, your nose is too long!' He tweaked it.

'YOU SCUM!' The guard yelled and took a half-step forward. 'YOU FUCKING SCUM!!'

With the guard's screamed-out words filling the crowded hall, a silence fell. Everyone looked over towards the entrance. Champagne in hand, the diners paused. Waited.

Waited . . .

But then nothing more seemed to happen. No more yelling, no more drumming or chanting. No more raised voices even. Had the protestors been overcome, had they been arrested and taken away?

Only when it seemed certain there would be no further disturbance did the crowd and the diners regain their confidence. 'Tea for Two' was picked up from the top by the string quartet, conversations were resumed, Champagne glasses emptied and refilled. Red and white was offered, and poured. Everyone relaxed.

'Scum is right,' remarked Cameron McClay, nodding in the direction of the protestors. 'Anarchists, terrorists, socialists – same breed, same garbage. Same scum.'

Now that the first course had been served, it was agreed that their privileged seats at the feasting table came with a heavy responsibility. Their duty was clear – to take their courage and their lobsters into both hands. They had to grit their teeth, tighten their jaws and eat as if they meant it, every mouthful a stand against the threat of barbarism!

The string quartet glided into a stately minuet.

'Save something for me, Cameron,' one of the starving multitude called up a few minutes later, his hands extended palm-upwards in mock-supplication. His neatly-tailored suit added poignancy to the appeal.

Some of the nearby poor laughed and joined in: 'Me, too! Me, too!'

'Listen to them! Enough to put a man off his lobster!' remarked a diner breaking off a piece of breadstick and tossing it down. 'Have some Foreign Aid, my friend. *Bon appétit!*'

The neatly tailored suit made a grab for it, but missed. Another of the poor retrieved it and pretended to gnaw on this scrap from the rich man's table, then threw it back . . .

'Debt repayment!'

. . . hitting one of the women diners. 'What the—? Where did this come from?' Without pausing in her conversation, she tossed it over her shoulder, down to the floor of the hall.

Seconds later, the same breadstick came flying back up again.

'Debt repayment, with interest!' This time it was accompanied by a sprayed spoonful of rice pellets flicked up catapult-style.

Rich and poor shared a good laugh.

Within a few minutes, World Bank loans, international development and foreign aid packages were good-naturedly flying back and forth. The increase in frequency and amount soon meant increased levels of debt and interest repayment, and ensured a vigorous exchange of breadsticks, water and rice between rich and poor. Trade was flourishing.

The rentacop who'd had his nose tweaked, was grabbed by his colleagues on either side. The twelve-man security line closed ranks and linked arms to form a solid barrier.

Sergeant-major Danny addressed the overweight guard directly: 'Before I became a member of the Clown Army, I was training to be a doctor, and in my medical opinion a belt as tight as yours . . .' he tugged at the guard's buckle, '. . . can damage the internal organs.'

'You clown-faced scum! I'll—'

'And so, in the interest of promoting good health . . .' Danny reached forward.

Next moment, the guard was standing in his shirt-tails and underwear, trousers around his ankles.

'FUCKING SCUM! FUCKING . . . FUCKING . . . FUCKING . . .'

Danny moved on to the next guard.

The instant the security line broke, the fairies and clowns swept past them into the hall.

To allow the butlers and footmen safe passage to begin clearing the plates at the end of the first course, a brief truce in hostilities between rich and poor was agreed on. Unfortunately, the far end of the table mustn't have heard the full terms of the ceasefire for, within seconds, one of the diners got to his feet and mimed pulling out a pretend pin with his teeth. He hurled his empty lobster-shell grenade into the crowd below:

'Howzat for *clawing* back our investments!'

A couple of his neighbours raised their glasses in salute. Then threw their own grenades. The grenades were lobbed back almost immediately, the bombardment intensified by a sudden upsurge in rice and water.

After suffering a direct hit, one of the diners began to shower the nearest poor with his *Entre Deux Mers.*

In reply, an empty rice bowl landed on the table knocking over a recently poured glass of Margaux '85.

*Rumble-grumble, rumble-grumble . . .*

'My dress!' Drenched red, a lady diner jumped to her feet: 'What the hell's the matter with you down there? Ruined. My dress is RUINED!' She snatched a carafe of water out of the hands of a footman who'd been about to refill her glass, went to the edge of the stage and emptied it out over the nearby poor.

*Rumble-grumble, rumble-grumble,* RUMBLE-GRUMBLE . . .

Rice bowls were soon coming thick and fast. And fistfuls of rice.

More carafes of water, more Margaux. Some of the crowd started pushing back to get out of range, while others pushed forward to get in on the action.

RUMBLE-GRUMBLE, RUMBLE-GRUMBLE . . .

The police had arrived. TV cameras zoomed everywhere at once to capture the riot as it developed. While the faint-hearted took shelter at the back of the hall, a hard core of militant poor launched themselves into the tangle of clowns, fairies, security guards, protestors and police battling it out. In the centre stood Danny blowing his bagpipes fit to burst. By now, most of the rich had abandoned the dining table, leaving behind a few livelier spirits who were gleefully hurling plates, glasses and lobster shells in all directions.

The militant poor seemed determined to make a night of

it, some of them banding together to commandeer the trolleys which they wheeled as near as they dared to the foot of the stage. From behind the safety of this improvised trench-line defence, they mobilized their artillery.

'Rice and rice bowls – Fire!' Water cannon – Fire!'

Cameron McClay caught sight of a clown rushing across no-man's land between the trenches and the stage to secure the short flight of steps. 'Bloody anarchist!' At once he moved to defend the table. Having run out of small-arms, he reached for the carved-ice centerpiece, which was now all that remained intact of the original table setting. He ignored the cameras closing in on him, ignored the people shouting at him to stop before someone got hurt, and lifted up the full weight of the billionaire's yacht. He raised it high above his head. Took aim.

'TERRORIST SCUM!'

The scramble for the exit was becoming a stampede. The Cat had seen enough. Time to get away from this . . . this madness. She pushed her way through the crowd in the direction of the staircase, avoiding as best she could the puddles of water and wine, the crunch of lobster shell and broken glass, the mashed rice slithering underfoot. She was leaving, and couldn't get out fast enough. This time nothing was going to stop her. Waverley, North Berwick, then Melbourne. Solid ground and sanity. And no coming back. Ever.

'Come and get it!' A flush-faced three-piece suit, his trolley pushed in front juggernaut-style, was hurtling himself straight at her. She sidestepped. She was going to need all her nine lives here. A clown – all purple lips and ponytail – stepped into its path, grabbed the handle and brought it to a halt. Pausing only long enough to see him scoop up a double-handful of rice and throw it into the flushed face, shouting, 'Choke on this, you corporate WANKER!', she hurried on.

A serving girl, her face and blonde hair streaked with blood, stumbled into her and apologised – then was pushed aside by another juggernaut. The crowd was denser here. Seeing a sudden look of horror on the faces of the people nearest her, the Cat turned round . . .

. . . . to see Simon, Lucy and several others onstage, man-handling the dining table, dragging it over to the edge. Next, they began upending it.

She took several steps backwards. Continued to watch, hypnotized.

The ten-place dining table was being angled-up to its tipping point. Remaining there for one long-long moment, balanced unsteadily, about to topple its full length . . .

She took another step backwards. And another.

'Timber!'

CRASH! onto the tiled floor. Louder even than the chaos it fell into. Silencing everything in the hall. Bringing the riot to a standstill. Freeze-framing everyone where they stood – the rich, the poor, the police, security guards, clowns, fairies.

Just then the Cat glanced upwards to see floor on floor of men and women in overalls, the office cleaners, at the windows, staring down onto the chaos and destruction. Black, brown and white faces were pressed against the reinforced glass. Alarmed? Amused? Bewildered?

Here was when things could stop. Surely. Whatever current of destructive energy was coursing through everyone and driving them on, had been cut. For a split-second the system had seized up. A long enough pause for its separate parts to disengage, for the men and women to look around and ask themselves: *What the fuck are we doing?*

Or it might have been.

But immediately the current surged back and everyone carried on as before, reinvigorated, refreshed even, by their brief rest. Their energy seemed more vicious, their yelling and screaming much louder, more brutal. Drowning out that embarrassing silence. The thrill of the moment was all – the excitement, the exhilarating high of pitched battle.

DD was helplessly adrift – arms elbows drumming shouting drumming yelling booming loudspeakers booming voices. Trolleys on their sides pools of water wine plastic bowls plastic forks rice. Men women security guards cameras clowns police, pushing her pulling her. Streaming down a man's face – blood? Someone screaming fuck off. Someone grabbing her arm to keep from falling. Stumbles, she stumbles. Legs shoes stamping kicking. She screams fuck off. She screams HELP! FUCK OFF! FUCK OFF! HELP! HELP!

Knocked onto her hands and knees. The hard tiles. Away from the broken glass she nearly fell onto, away from the trampling shoes.

The hem of her dress soaked red – wine? Blood? Hers?

People not seeing her on the floor. She yells! She screams!

Holding onto a jacket, a dress to pull herself up.

A clown's face pressing against hers.

'Let me help . . .'

Knocked aside by arms elbows a fist.

That's blood she can taste?

'Let me . . . Here, take my . . .'

Knocked aside again. FUCK OFF.

Sent sprawling backwards into one of the oases, onto the dirt and sharp stones. Landing on her elbow, twisting her arm. Her hands filthy with earth, wine, blood, mashed rice, only one shoe, her stocking sole torn. Her elbow throbbing. Leaning back against a small bush.

Resting, closing her eyes. Like she's not really here. Sliding into remembered stillness, remembered calmness. Enough tabs and she'd have been floating high above it all, letting the sunlight soak into her, drenching her with its warmth, soothing her as it did whenever she lay stretched full out on the floor of the summerhouse. The shutters wide open, daylight pouring in . . .

Playing a Clementi slow movement or a Bach prelude where the bass figure comes round again and again, its *rightness* taking her to the very centre of the earth, to the absolute peace found there and nowhere else.

The touch of someone's hand. A woman's kindness. Bending down . . . Offering to help her to safety.

'Staying here, thanks . . . Fine . . . Never felt better . . .'

The woman supporting her, getting her onto her feet.

'My arm! It's . . . aaah!' Sudden pain gripping. Then tearing herself free. 'Let me alone.' Staggering away. Away, away. Home. The summerhouse. The sunlight . . .

More and more police had arrived. People desperate to leave found themselves hemmed together, unable to pass through the narrow exit at the top of the staircase. Getting frustrated, angry. Wanting out, and wanting out now.

The Cat went to the side of the stairs to wait till things had eased. Elsewhere in the hall, the drumming had stopped, the pipes were silent, the riot was winding down. Police loudhailers called on everybody to keep calm.

Just along from her, a protester was held pinned against the wall by one of the security guards.

'FASCIST BASTARDS!' Again and again a fairy with torn wings rammed an abandoned trolley full-force at the guard's legs.

He turned round and punched her in the mouth. The fairy was overpowered and forced to the ground. Order was being restored.

Hume shoved his way through the crowd. He had to get to the microphone, had to make some kind of announcement. Something calming, reassuring . . .

*He* was calm? *He* felt reassured? Nearby, an elderly woman was receiving first aid for a bleeding gash on her forehead. A man was being lifted onto a stretcher. Instead of trolley-dollies going through the crowd distributing rice and water, there were ambulance men dishing out first aid and bandages, and police arresting clowns, fairies and other protestors. Rebranding Executive Service? Restoring its rep as a class act? Here was a glimpse into the future, the ES future - his. A shambles. A total and utter fucking disaster. What the hell was he going to—?

His phone vibrated. He glanced down at the screen. Melville. Straight back into his pocket.

Just below the stage, the dining table lay sprawled on its back, four legs up in the air and the other two smashed. It would need to be disposed of, replaced. The owners of the building would want compensation. Suppliers would want paid, staff would want paid. Was he insured against riot?

Fucking protestors, fucking clowns. Fucking London bombers. Fucking Iraq. Fucking Bush and Blair. Fucking everything and everybody and—

His phone again. Melville again. Fucking Melville.

Before he could stop himself, he'd stabbed the answer button.

'Bad day, Mr. Hume? From what I know of the great and good of this fair city, they'll all want their money back. £1,000 a head, was it?'

'What the fuck do you want?'

'Temper, temper, Mr. Hume. I'm offering you a helping hand. To get things tidied up, let's say.'

'I don't need your—'

'That your final word, Mr. Hume?' Pause. 'It's certainly not mine.'

The line went dead.

He had reached the microphone and was about to speak when he felt someone tug at his sleeve. 'Mr. Hume?' The woman was trying to pull him aside. 'Your wife. She's calling for you.'

Enough already! But he stopped himself just in time from saying it out loud.

'I think, she's hurt, Mr. Hume. Wants you to come.'

Without a word he followed her across the hall to where DD sat on the tile floor, just outside the Kitchen Centre conference room. She looked terrible. A woman was dabbing blood from her elbow.

'Your arm, DD. What's—?'

'Just scraped it.'

He crouched down beside her. Managed not to say anything about how she'd fucked things up, managed some words

266

of comfort and concern, managed to repeat them. The words came easier second time round.

'I'll have one of the medics check you over, DD, then get someone to take you home.' He patted her good arm. 'These fucking pills of yours . . .'

Just then the familiar *tic* started up at the side of his eye. Like a wink. Winking, winking like it would never stop.

She reached up and touched his cheek.

Without meaning to, he pulled back. 'You'd better watch your arm. Don't strain—'

'My arm's fine.' She glared up at him. 'I'm fine.'

This time he didn't draw back.

Finally, he helped her to her feet and led her into Kitchen Centre where most of the staff had taken refuge. Having handed her over to one of the maids to take care of and organise a taxi home, he went back out into the hall, heading to the stage and the microphone where he'd do his best to—

'Mr. Hume?' *Sotto voce.* A rentacop was standing beside him. He was big.

'Time you were leaving.' A second rentacop, on his other side. He was very big.

Grabbed by each arm, then frogmarched across the hall, full-speed ahead – sometimes the prow of a ship forcing its passage through crowded sea-lanes, sometimes a battering ram knocking aside anything and anyone in its way. Clowns, suits, trolleys, fairies were scattered and left in its wake.

'Help! Police! Help!' Hume's distress call got louder and more desperate as the main exit came into sight. No one paid any attention, and why should they? – here were two security men bundling away a troublemaker. Arrested, and good riddance.

They arrived at the top of the staircase. A bottleneck of far too many people pushing and shoving to get down the flight of steps and out onto the street. Hume was frantic. His last chance to break free? Make a run for it?

But run where?

Fucking anywhere.

Tensing himself. Ready to kick, elbow, punch, headbutt . . .

'Hume? It *is* Hume, isn't it?'

One of the clowns was calling to him from the edge of the crowd. A woman.

But the ship's prow/battering ram wasn't going to stop for anyone, never mind a clown. Ready to knock her to one side, ready to send her tumbling head-over-heels down the crowded stairs . . .

Left side voice: 'Out the road!'

Right side voice: 'Move it!'

Hume looked closer. Take away the red cheeks, the teardrop eyes, and—

## 3

WITH ITS RAISED chassis, bull bars and tinted windows, the black 4×4 looked like a blinded tank waiting for them outside. The big rentacop zapped the doors open.

The very big rentacop manoeuvred himself into the seat behind the wheel. Hume and the Cat were pushed into the back. St Francis was already there. The big rentacop climbed in. Sitting right up next to them, he too became very big.

'Drive on, my man.' The rentacop took out his mobile.

'Where are we—?' began Hume.

'Shut it.'

The car moved forward. Less than a minute later they had to stop at the Semple Street traffic lights.

'Cat? It really *is* you, isn't—?'

The blow must have split his lip. Hume could feel blood trickling into his mouth.

'Shut it, I said.'

He wiped his lips with the back of his hand, and shut it.

They turned right onto Lothian Road, into traffic that was crawling bumper to bumper towards the lights at Fountainbridge. The whole of Edinburgh seemed to be out enjoying a stroll on this fine July evening - from behind the darkened windows of the slow-moving vehicle, Hume had plenty of time to admire the women in their summer frocks, the men in shirt-sleeves, the skateboarder sway-stitching his carefree path between the pedestrians. The car inched forward, the inside lane took them past Lap Dance/Exotic, an Open Till Late minimarket, a Chinese restaurant called Happy Something. Brought to a stop at the lights next to a brightly lit shoe shop. HUGE REDUCTIONS! A pair of thigh-length red boots taking centre-stage in the window.

'Understood.' The big rentacop put away his mobile. 'Well, Mr. Hume, seems your friend here . . . Frank, isn't it?'

'Francis.'

'*Francis?*' The man savoured the word, didn't seem to like the taste. 'I think I prefer Frank. Well, Frank here has just invited you round.'

'I've – what?' Then seeing the man's raised fist, St Francis fell silent.

'Good man.' The big rentacop smiled. 'Easy rule to re-member, Frank. Like I was saying, Mr. Hume, Frank here has invited you round to help him do some work on his flat. Latest thing, giving the old homestead a makeover. So Frank's having a go now. Problems with the insulation, it appears, like asbestos in the old days. He needs to get rid of it. Right, Frank?'

St Francis's face had taken on a stricken look.

'Don't look so worried, Frankie-boy. Good news is – we'll dispose of it for you, and no charge! Once we've gone, you can turn the flat into the perfect dream-home for you and the missus. Look on it as an opportunity to rethink things, re-decorate, upgrade. Worth checking out IKEA first; bit of a trek following all those stupid arrows and stuff, but they often have great offers on. Some re-plastering, a lick of paint and you'll have the place as good as new. Better even!'

The traffic eased once they'd gone through the main junction at the Tollcross clock, and soon they were picking up speed along Home Street past the King's Theatre, Bennett's Bar, the Barclay Church, the garage, the Taj Mahal carry-out. Then a sharp left into Barclay Terrace.

'This'll do nicely.' The car came to a halt. The engine was switched off. 'Stay here!' The big rentacop got out and walked up and down the pavement, speaking on his phone.

After a few moments the Cat leant across: 'Hume, what on earth have you got yourself—?'

The very big rentacop in the front turned round to face her, raised a warning finger: 'You know the rules.'

They sat in silence. The rentacop outside finished his call.

Their door was opened. 'You want to hear some more good news? That's me and Dougal here on our break. Lucky us!' A big smile. 'Boss is treating us in that Chinese across the road. Is it any good, d'you know?'

Hume remained silent.

'I'm sure it is - he's a good boss is Mr. Melville. Takes care of his staff. But you know him already, Mr. Hume. And seems you'll be getting to know him even better from now on. He's got plans. I won't say any more. Spoils the surprise.'

Everyone was told to get out of the car.

'By the way, this your fancy woman? A wee secret from Mrs. Hume?'

'It's the first time I've seen Cat for—'

'A friend then? An old friend?'

'Not seen her in twenty years and more. You can let her go. She doesn't know anything about . . . anything.'

'An innocent?'

'Yes. She's got nothing to do with—'

'Don't meet many of them, not in my line of work. I'm sure Mr. Melville will be charmed to make her acquaintance. Catherine, is it? You like lemon chicken, Catherine?'

'Do I—?'

'Whatever. They'll have a wide menu. Chinese usually do.' He turned to Hume: 'Here's the thing. Catherine's joining us for dinner.' Another big smile. 'So off up to Frank's, the pair of you. You've got till we've finished our lemon chicken to bring us the insulation. Then you'll be in time for some banana fritters. Sounds good? If you don't come . . .' No big smile this time. 'But you will, won't you?'

St Francis let them in the street door and went on ahead to summon the lift. He needed to tell Hume everything - Megan, the money. He had to tell him *now*. They could make a run for it.

The lift clattered down. The instant the door slid open, Hume stepped in. Still St Francis didn't move, didn't speak.

'Come on, Francis. No time to hang around. Melville's got the Cat, remember.'

Walk away and leave Hume to sort out his own problems? Or - what? The lift was starting to close.

He jammed his foot in the door. 'No point going up. The money's gone.'

'What?'

Out it all came in a rush - *Megan . . . the gutted flat . . . the banknotes . . .*

'Jesus! She's taken *all* of it?'

'Don't know. A couple of bags. She—'

'She's stolen it! Why didn't you stop her? Where's she gone?'

'Not far. She said—'

'Fuck's sake, Francis, phone her! Tell her to get her ass here. I'll go up and grab whatever's she missed.'

'Okay.' But it wouldn't be okay. He knew that already. Took out his mobile. 'No signal in here. I'll need to go outside. Be right back.'

The phone call was brief.

Hume didn't waste time looking around. The place had been well and truly trashed. Gaping holes in the walls, smashed-up flooring . . .

The money. Should be a lot more than two bags' worth. The skirting and the fireplace hadn't been touched. Good. Get what he'd stashed there, add it to what Megan would bring in the taxi. Pay off Melville. Deal with the fallout from the Billionaires' Banquet fuck up . . .

Skirting boards first.

A hammer was lying next to some broken-off lengths of floorboard. Down on his hands and knees, he began working his way along the wall, forcing the claw end as far behind the skirting as he could for maximum leverage, then wrenching it till the wood splintered and a section broke off. Moving along a few more feet, more wrenching, and more skirting came away.

He reached his hand in as far as he could beneath the old lathes, felt around. Loose flakes of plaster, dirt, bits of wood. But no money. Nothing. He moved further along. More feeling around. And . . . yes! Something solid. His fingers scrabbled to get a better grip. Under the layer of dirt he could feel smooth plastic. And . . . yes! Getting a good hold of the nearest corner, he gradually pulled the packet clear and lifted out a folded-up supermarket bag sealed with duct tape. He sat on the floor. Wiped off the worst of the dirt and dust. No time to unpick the tape and so he ripped the bag open. Checked it. Bundles of tens. Be lucky if there was 10k . . . Fuck.

Reached into the wall again. Another bag. Twenties. Better. Which made it Say 40k, max. But there had to be more, lots more.

Back onto his hands and knees. A different wall, hammer-clawing at another skirting board, then pounding another hole in the plaster. Over the years he'd made several trips here when St Francis and Megan were away on holiday, to stash his undeclared cash as it accumulated. For a rainy day, he'd said. Well today was a fucking monsoon. Time was when he'd pictured making a special treat of getting the money out, bringing DD along, having a picnic-cum-treasure hunt complete with his X-marks-the-spot map of concealed hidey-holes. Relaxed and fun. Not this mad panic when he could hardly think straight, let alone having to hack around blindly without an X sight. With both hands, he ripped away the rest of the skirting.

Nothing.

Megan must have been at it for hours. She'd been thorough, he'd give her that. He wasted several minutes feeling around under the most accessible floorboards. Not a thing. And under the floorboards was where he'd stuck most of it. Fuck! Fuck! Melville would . . . Jesus, it didn't bear thinking about.

Next stop, the back of the fireplace. Untouched, thank fuck. Throwing aside the vase of dried flowers that decorated the hearth, he took the hammer to the back panel. *Thwack! Thwack!* Making the painted hardboard crack. *Thwack!* Then splitting it. *Thwack! Thwack! Thwack!* Big enough hole to get the claw in for some heavy-duty wrenching, then his hand.

God, he was hot. Sweat was pouring down his face and back. His hands were sticky and slick from the plaster, grime and soot. He stopped, threw aside his butler jacket, ripped off the wing collar and tie, undid the cuffs and rolled up his sleeves. He was about to give the panel one final mega-batter when he stopped, his arm raised to full height, hammer paused in mid-air.

Where the hell was St Francis?

4

MEGAN PUT DOWN her mobile and stretched herself across the kingsize bed. So many clean-and-sweet-smelling pillows of sinking-into-softness cotton, piled one on top of the other. Pressing her head back deep-deep-deep. She was in heaven, a hotel suite in heaven, like she'd died and gone there. The foaming-pink-soothing-warm bath, the 30-inch 100-channel TV, the room service steak. A half-empty bottle of Beaujolais relaxing within easy reach. She'd tipped the waiter a tenner. And another, just to see the look on his face. Then put the room service Champagne into the minibar fridge, to keep it chilled for Francis. That is, if Francis ever—

And if not—?

Before getting to heaven she'd stopped near the foot of Lothian Road, round the corner from the hotel. Stopped to stand in front of a mud-crusted beanie, hollowed-out face, hanks of grease-straggled hair, matchstick arms. Drugs, definitely drugs. A KFC cup with small glitters of silver down among the copper. Too young, too old - eighteen going on eighty, and too elsewhere to notice her right there in front of him. Head down, beard mess tangled on his chest. Probably asleep. Taking a tenner from her bag to drop into his KFC for old times' sake, when his head rolled back and he was squinting up at her out of those still too-elsewhere eyes: 'The fuck're you wanting?'

Which was?

Washed up back then on the long-ago cement shore was when she knew nothing. Not even how she'd got there. Only the cold, only the wet, the wind. She knew them, lived them. The never-ending tide in front, the stone-hard tenement behind. The skip, the garage, the crazies. Always day, always night.

Wanting what? Rain-Eyes who'd turned the street and the city into the kindness of his warm room and had made their day-and-night togetherness into twenty years.

Wanting what? At least she knew now. Taking that hammer to their house in the sky. That's when she really knew.

So she'd flicked the tenner in the beggar's face, and said nothing. Not staying to see if he snatched it in time from the wind, she'd walked off.

She'd stood for a moment in front of the hotel entrance – its revolving doors, its rank of taxis lined up waiting for fares, its uniformed doorman in his authority of epaulettes, silver buttons and braided top hat.

Everything had begun with Francis, his Rain-Eyes looking down at her. Francis, asking her name. That was the first time she'd woken from the endlessness of dreams mangled within dreams – a children's home, other streets, other places, other men, other women. Always, always others.

It was all she'd had back then, her name. And she'd given it to him. To Francis, and from then on the always-others began to disappear.

*The fuck're you wanting?* Well, she knew now. Knew big time.

She pressed the TV mute button – the same wrecked bus as before, the same broken-apart streets, the same damaged and dying. One thing was for sure – wherever she went tomorrow, it wasn't going to be London.

Just then her mobile rang. Francis.

The Cat made no response when wonton soup was suggested. Ditto to the offer of lemon chicken. Not raising her eyes even when the food was served.

'You no like?' asked the elderly waitress.

Still not raising her eyes, not answering.

The large table was covered with dishes and bottles – char su, duck, pancakes and plum sauce, fried noodles, stir-fry vegetables, lemon chicken, drunken chicken, rice, spare ribs, chop suey, soy sauce, wine. Melville and his men ate with forks and knives.

'One of the oldest Chinese in the city, Catherine, and the best. Others come and go, but the Lee On's been here forty years and more. Ma Lee sees to the front while Keung Lee does the cooking downstairs. Deserves a medal the man does. He could blow away any of these poncey TV chefs.' Melville was feeding himself in stereo – a chicken leg in one hand, a forkful of stir-fry in the other. 'Come on now, don't let it get cold.'

She lifted her eyes at last. Close to, the man was even more massive than she'd first thought when she'd been told to sit down at his table. Such a swollen, wrap-around swathe of flesh and fat that he could hardly bend forward, his hands working a rota system to deliver alternate left and right mouthfuls, and to keep them coming. She looked him full in the face. And was met with a smile.

'That's a girl! Leave Hume to do the hard graft, and we four can sit here and enjoy a pleasant meal together. Plenty for all and plenty to spare. Thing is, the world being the mess it is, what with politicians, terrorists, global warming and all that shite, you can always rely on food, rely on it one hundred percent. Set the likes of our friend Hume against that standard of reliability, and he's nowhere. Needs a caution, he does. For his own good.'

'But . . . what's he done?' she asked. 'I've not seen Hume since I was a student. I don't believe he could get involved in anything that was really . . .'

There was sudden focus and sharpness in the fat man's eyes as he continued:

'Your friend robs the exchequer, that's his business. Everybody does it, everybody and his tax adviser. But when he robs me, that's personal. Mind you, I couldn't believe it when he asked my advice about what to do with his undeclared cash. So I told him, and he did what I said, word for word!' Melville laughed, sucked on a spare rib, and then discarded it. 'He's got brains but no sense, not about what matters.' Another rib – suck-suck-suck. 'Though it's only a sideline of mine, a hobby you might say, the flat at Barclay Towers makes ten times what Executive Service ever could. Thinking he could keep his hands clean, our Mister Hume up there in posh and proper Grange, thinking it was only spreadsheets and some tax-free cash on the side. Well, he thought wrong.' He took a big double-swallow of wine, belched, then wiped his lips. 'Executive Service, may it rest in peace, was just a front, same as how he's always going on about governments being nothing but empty yak-yak-yak while it's big business telling them what to do and ruling the country. Right enough, I've no doubt. But when it's closer to home, when it's him that's the empty yak-yak-yak, he just can't see it. Like I say, the man needs a lesson. Gentle hand of guidance, we'll call it. Boys'll sort him out though, won't you, lads?'

'You're the boss,' chorused the two rentacops.

As St Francis entered the flat he could hear the sounds of splintering wood and Hume swearing. A grey-black cloud of soot hung in the air.

Megan was never coming back, nor was the money. Why hadn't he just phoned Hume from downstairs, and told him he and Megan were getting the hell out? Told him he was on his own, wished him good luck and goodbye? Then gone. He'd wanted to, but just couldn't. And now, seeing the torn clothes, the filth, the panic and Hume's rear end sticking out of the fireplace like he was an overgrown kid trying to make a desperate grab for Santa – he felt sorry for him. But angry too. Wanted to bounce Hume's head off the fireplace like had been done to him in the lift. Bounce some sense into him.

'Here's more.' Another grey-black cloud billowed into the room. Hume emerged soot-smeared, coughing and spitting. Eased himself down on the hearthstone, his back against the fireplace. He struggled to catch his breath while ripping open the Tesco bag. 'This one's fifties, thank fuck. Which I'm guessing makes about 90k so far.' He stuffed all the loose notes into one bag. 'And Megan?'

St Francis reached forward to help him to his feet. 'We have to disappear. Phone DD, meet her somewhere. Then take off.'

'What the fuck, Francis? Stop pulling me.' More coughs. 'I can't just walk away from . . . away from everything.' More spitting. 'And what about Megan? I'm saying. What about the money she's—?'

St Francis headed towards the door. 'Your lawyer'll sell

Grange for you, refund everyone their Billionaires' Banquet money.'

'And the business?'

'ES? After tonight? You must be—'

Hume's mobile rang. He reached into his pocket. 'And there's the Cat, too, remember? If we don't show up—'

᠁

Pushing aside her untouched plate of lemon chicken, the Cat leant forward: 'Listen, Mr. Melville, I don't know what Hume's done . . .'

'Well, Catherine, for a start he owes me—'

'. . . and I don't want to know. But if he owes you money, I'm sure he'll pay you. A selfish dickhead, but he's honest. He'll—'

'His honesty's nothing to me, Catherine. It's his cash I'm interested in. *My* cash, I should say. That's how this works. Sometimes a machine needs seeing to, a firm tap to get it up and running again.'

'You don't mean you'd—'

His lips and cheeks folded themselves into a smile. 'Despite appearances, Catherine, I'm only a tiny cog in the big machine. But not harmless, and the machine's not harmless. Never has been. Nothing new under the sun - pirating and pillaging under Liz the First, banks and big business under Liz Two. They knighted Drake and Morgan. They'll be knighting me next!' His whole body shook as it produced a gulp of laughter. 'But harmless? No, none of it's ever harmless. If nothing else, getting Hume sorted will be great PR, send a message to those who need to hear it.'

'Getting him—?'

'Come on, Catherine, you're letting good food go cold. To put your mind at rest, I'll just give the lad a ring, see how he's progressing.'

❧

Hume pressed to answer. 'Yes?'

'Well, Mr. Hume, how's the makeover coming along? 150 plus interest. Call it a nice round 200.'

'But you said—'

'He said, she said . . . When you hear a ring at the doorbell it'll be my lads to help you down with it. Come down without it and you'll be coming down a lot faster. Understand? It'll be a courtesy ring, mind. They've got a key.'

'Even if I can't find it all just now, you'll get it. In full. Like I said, there's the downstairs flat at Barclay Towers and the house in the Grange must be worth over a million and—'

'Don't talk to me about property, Mr. Hume. Mortgages, community tax, paperwork, agents, tenants, utility bills, insurance, repairs, blocked drains, leaking roofs, all that shite. Anyway, it takes too long. I've commitments of my own.'

The line went dead.

Hume slid the mobile into his pocket.

St Francis: 'Well?'

'Like I said, 90k max. That's nearly half. We'll tell him he'll get the rest in a couple of hours, or first thing tomorrow at the latest. We'll go see Megan and—'

'I don't know where she is.'

'What!'

A ring at the doorbell.

As the two of them scrambled up the ladder and out onto the roof, Hume heard the rentacops letting themselves into the downstairs flat. Then he heard his name being called.

The trapdoor dropped shut. There was no lock on this side so he and St Francis sat down on it to keep it closed, the Tesco bag for life stuffed with cash at their feet. After a day that had been non-stop frantic from the start, before accelerating into full-blown mayhem, here at last was a moment of calm. Neither of them spoke. Around them, the clarity of the summer evening's light silhouetted the nearby chimney stacks and aerials, while across the dips and gulleys of slate the curved roof and clustered steeples of the Barclay church reared up like the sails and masts of a ship becalmed. A slight breeze carried the distant rumble of traffic. From far below on Bruntsfield Links, Hume heard a man call to his dog. The Stones boomed out through an open window – a party was getting started somewhere along the street.

Suddenly the trapdoor was pushed up from beneath, a firm push that made it rise a good couple of inches before their pressed-down weight forced it shut again. There was definitely no lock. Would they have to sit on it forever?

⚜

Melville wiped his fingers on the tablecloth, then reached for his mobile. 'So you're up on the roof, Mr. Hume.' It was a statement, not a question. 'Catherine here's getting worried. Dangerous places, roofs.' He cut the connection.

For several seconds he gazed slowly round the table,

inspecting the various dishes before selecting a particularly plump and grease-glistening spare rib. 'Best in town these. Their own special sauce, you know. Tried getting Keung to tell me the recipe, but no chance. Offered cash. A few other incentives, too, but he's still saying no. I respect that, mind you. A real professional, an artist, don't you think?'

The Cat made no reply.

'Let's be clear about one thing, Catherine. I've nothing against you. But now you know what's happening, you know what's likely to happen. Means you're involved.'

⁂

Several more attempts had been made to push up the trapdoor lid. So far, they'd managed to force it back down each time. But then St Francis had a terrible thought:

'What if they're armed and one of them fires his gun up through it?'

⁂

DD stumbled out of the taxi and into the sudden and slowed-down familiarity of her own street, her own front gate and her house.

Reaching the bottom step leading up to the front door, steadying it to let her sit down and catch her breath, let her gather herself.

No rush now. She can relax, take her time. The paved path at her feet, each slab slotted into its place like the hours slotted into the day. No gaps to fall through except when a brief moment isn't quite able to take her weight . . .

When the moment feels good and solid and when she feels ready, she'll get to her feet and climb the remaining steps up to the door, and let herself in. She'll be ready soon, won't she? She'll be able to deal with crossing the hall? And the staircase that pitches so relentlessly upwards? The unpredictable weather waiting to greet her in every corridor and room?

She must have stood up, for now she's walking round the side of the house instead and into the garden, hobbling more like, one shoe off and one shoe on. Kick off the good shoe? Keep it on? Off/on/off/on, down the path. One shoe's better than none . . . No? Yes? Zigzagging her way across the lawn. Past the koi pond. No reflection on the water's surface. Has she become invisible?

If only.

At least she's no longer carrying the bowl of lottery slips out in front of her like an offering. No longer feeling Hume's rage.

But even if she had known what was going to happen, she'd have continued to walk across the stage towards him. Because that's who she is, and that's what she does. Walk-walk-walk towards Hume, one shoe off and one shoe on. Like always.

The door of the summerhouse. Her piano, her sofa. Her framed diploma on the wall.

Sitting down at the keyboard.

Forgiveness – here?

But she has *herself*, remember. She's not alone. There's the path she's come down. The trees, the flowers, the nymph with her urn pouring water that's now only the barest trickle. They, too, have helped bring her here. The whole world has helped bring her here. Helped bring her and dump her in the here and now. As it always does.

But it's not her world. Never her world. Her world stops at her fingertips, stops when they touch the keys . . . touch the sounds. Her sounds. Her.

Her world never slips from her hands.

*How many pills?/How many pills?*

Enough.

❧

'Nice view, eh Dougal. Quite a panorama. No wonder the tourists flock here. Getting to be the whole year round near enough, considering the wall-to-wall festivals we've got. See, there's the Castle all lit up for them, and St Giles.'

'That dark lump'll be Arthur's Seat.'

'Right. Was a volcano once upon a time, did you know that? Makes you proud of our city. Auld Reekie. Athens of the North. Historic, the Enlightenment, culture, the works. Oh, and look over there – I spy a couple of its prominent citizens loitering behind yon chimneystack.'

❧

Melville picked up his phone.

'Had a bit of a day, haven't you, Mr. Hume? Your business down the tubes, your flat trashed, and now here's the pair of you stuck on the roof with Dave and Dougal. Nice enough lads in their way, but . . . Well, your luck's about to change.

'Your friend Catherine and I have been chatting. Pleasant girl, not a big eater though. Anyway, in an attempt to move things along in as friendly a manner as possible, she's just volunteered to help out. She'll collect the money from you and bring it here . . .

'Don't interrupt me, Mr. Hume. I'm guessing it's not the full amount. So, depending on how much there is – meaning, more precisely, how much there isn't – we'll come to an agreement, you and I, about some sort of penalty. Call it a sliding scale of compensation, to be paid in kind. If everything's hunky-dory, more or less, there'll be no need for the two of you to take that wee tumble. Not all the way down, anyroad.'

Despite the late hour there was a constant stream of traffic on Bruntsfield Place and the Cat had to wait at the pedestrian crossing.

When she'd left the restaurant, Melville hadn't even glanced up from his trough. More spare ribs to gnaw, more duck to pack away. When the time came to tell his men about taking care of Hume, his jaws would hardly pause long enough to pass sentence before continuing to grind away at whatever was in his mouth. A belch at most, and he'd be ready for the next forkload.

A taxi was coming down from Bruntsfield. Its FOR HIRE light beckoned, inviting her to climb aboard and get driven straight to Waverley. *Why not leave Hume to whatever mess he's got himself into?* it seemed to urge.

Why not indeed? What was to stop her?

In fact, what the fuck was she doing helping him out anyway? Hume and St Francis were history, and ancient history at that.

*Go! Go! GO! Flag it down, get yourself as far away from Barclay Towers as you can . . .*

The lights changed. She crossed the road, strode quickly past the garage, an Indian carry-out, then into the familiar stair. A lift! She stepped inside. The first sign of genuine progress she'd seen in the city all day but came, it seemed, with the faintest hint of rotten eggs.

When she climbed out the trapdoor onto the roof, one of the rentacops stepped forward offering to help her. She ignored him.

Hume had called it a rooftop Garden of Eden. But there was no love and hash-cakes now, no teenage tease having the time of her young life to a Heavy Metal chorus of 'Hey, Big Spender!'

In the failing light she could see where the downward rush of slates began. This was no Garden of Eden and never had been.

A sudden gust of wind rattled a length of loose aerial cable trailing from a nearby chimneystack. She'd need to watch, no getting yanked off her feet this time. She crossed the stretch of flat roof to where Hume stood, blackened face and his clothes all a mess like he'd been in an explosion, and clutching a bulky supermarket bag in one hand.

He spoke in a low whisper: 'There's about 100k here, Cat. And when Megan brings the—'

'He's expecting 200. Wants 200 *now* . . .' The Cat whispered back.

'But—'

'Get a move on,' one of the rentacops yelled across. 'Boss is waiting for his money.'

'. . . and you're to stay up here, with *them*.' With a nod of her head she indicated the two rentacops keeping guard beside the trapdoor, the only exit.

'What for?'

Then he understood. 'But . . . but . . . he'll get his money. He will. He knows he will.'

'The money, Hume.' She held out both hands.

'You're on Melville's side now, that it?'

Rentacop: 'Hurry it up or we'll come and hurry you!'

Hume took out his mobile. 'I'll explain. Tell him that Megan—'

Next instant, the Cat had snatched the phone out of his hand and tossed it aside. It rattled and skittered down the slates, coming to rest in the gutter.

'What the fuck, Cat? Melville will—'

There was no time for any of this. She grabbed the plastic sack from him and started back towards the trapdoor.

The big rentacop was coming across to meet her: 'Need to check it first.'

Check it? The instant they glanced inside they'd see there wasn't 200k or anything like it. They'd call Melville and get their instructions. Hume was already falling off the roof.

And her? She was *involved*.

Hume and St Francis were close behind her: 'You bitch, Cat! Fucking, fucking bitch! Getting a cut, are you? These bastards are going to . . .'

She came to a halt. Time had stopped, and she had stopped it.

Once again she was standing in the middle of Princes Street, expecting to be clubbed by riot police.

Once again she was staring up at that Marchmont window on the way back from yet another stranger's bed, and feeling fragments of broken glass cutting into her.

Once again she was crouched in the darkness under the hearthrug, hope-hope-hoping that this time Kirsty would . . .

She'd come to where the past and future awaited her, as they always had. And now she was determined to get things right.

The big rentacop was only yards away: 'Give it here!'

Hume: 'No, Cat. No. They'll—'

Rentacop: 'Chrissake, you bitch! The money!'

She felt something shift inside her, give way.

'Christ?' She reached into the bag. 'I'll give you God Himself!' Flourishing a fistful of notes and as though addressing the entire roof and the city beyond, she cried out: 'Father, Son and . . .'

Hume: 'What the hell are you doing, Cat? That money's for . . . Fuck!'

'. . . Holy Ghost!' She threw it into the rentacop's face.

The man didn't move as the £50 notes fluttered down around him. 'That's Melville's money. He'll kill you.'

She turned and ran.

'Father, Son and Holy Ghost! Father, Son and Holy Ghost!' she yelled at the top of her voice, tossing out fistful after fistful of notes.

The rentacop was coming after her: 'You get the cash, Dougal. I'll grab this bitch.'

'Get moving!' she shouted to Hume and St Francis as she passed them. She reached the end of the flat part of the roof, and with each scattered fistful, as if sowing the sky with money, she felt herself grow lighter and surer. She felt good. She felt wonderful, like she could soar into the air and fly. Next moment, she'd stepped down onto the incline of slates.

The rentacop had come to a stop directly above her: 'You're fucking mad!'

Out of the corner of her eye, she saw that Hume and St Francis had made it over to the open trapdoor. Like some demented Jack-in-the-box, Hume was frantically waving to her, gesturing her to hurry across.

She hurled another blizzard of notes up at the rentacop. He ignored it and took a first step down the steep incline.

One hand on the slates to steady herself, she began edging sideways along the slope.

'Fucking crazy woman!'

Ahead was a chimneystack sticking out the slant of roof. It bristled with TV aerials and had a satellite dish. Two more steps, and she was there.

Gripping a corner of the brickwork, she managed to stand up straight. The top of the incline was a few metres away. At the far end of the roof she saw the very big rentacop still chasing from side to side, grabbing at notes . . .

The big rentacop was coming after her, slip-sliding over the slates. 'Don't fucking move, you bitch, or you'll be taking a dive.'

'Grab hold of this, Cat.' St Francis was at the top of the slates, jiggling a cable that ran down to one of the aerials fixed to the chimneystack. 'I'll help pull you up.'

The big rentacop had almost reached her. Bared teeth, stubble, spittle: 'Fucking stay there!'

She backed away.

'The cable, Cat!'

Next moment she was being helped back onto the flat roof, St Francis and Hume taking an arm each.

'You're dead, the lot of you!' The rentacop yelled up at them. He, too, had grabbed the cable and was starting to haul himself up the slope.

'No, Hume, no!' She saw him flick the cable like a whip.

The rentacop lost his balance, slipped, steadied himself. Then began sliding . . .

'Come on, Cat!'

They turned and ran.

Seconds later she pulled the trapdoor cover down behind her, and locked it.

Once in the lift, Hume couldn't seem to stop: 'That was fabulous, Cat. Really great! A masterstroke! If you hadn't—'

She cut him short. The rentacop? Did he manage to—?

Yes, the rentacop was fine. St Francis had seen him clinging to the chimneystack.

Melville would be getting them *sorted*. It would be permanent. The Cat passed Hume the bag, still well over half-full. 'Take this and leave town.'

'But Melville's a businessman. He'll want to—'

'Fuck's sake, Hume!' St Francis screamed at him as the small lift bumped to a standstill on the ground floor. 'You're finished. Game over, Melville's cashing you in . . .'

Out on the pavement there was no time for lingering farewells. Not that any of the respectable Edinburgh citizens would have paid the least attention if their quick hug-and-kiss goodbyes had turned into a full-scale orgy – Barclay Terrace was a rampage of men and women grabbing at banknotes that had tumbled down from the sky. The ever-growing crowd rushed this way and that as the wind shifted; they shouted and yelled; they snatched at the good times so suddenly within their grasp. Hume caught a £50 note drifting past and was about to offer it to the Cat as a souvenir when he realized she'd hailed a taxi and was already halfway across the main road.

'Bye,' she called back, giving him a big smile. Even when he had known her all those years ago he had never seen her look so happy. Then she was gone.

St Francis, too, was rushing across to the cab. 'Bye, Hume! I'll email.'

Hume tucked the supermarket bag under his arm. By now, the rentacops would have called Melville and he might appear round the corner at any moment. Time to move and move fast.

He quick-marched himself in the opposite direction, full-speed up Whitehouse Loan, and had reached the end of Warrender Park Road when he came to a taxi parked at the side of the Links. The driver had his window down and was eating a roll.

Hume leant in and threw the £50 note onto the man's lap: 'A tip in advance. Another at the airport. Fast as you can. We're picking up my wife en route.'

He climbed in and gave the address. Ham roll tossed out the window, they were off.

DD would need to empty the safe, grab their passports, bank cards and laptops. She'd need to be ready and waiting for him outside in the street. He reached for his mobile. Then remembered. Fuck!

'Step on it, man. We're in a *real* hurry.'

# *Epilogue*

A S USUAL THESE days, Hume has been woken by the touch of warm sunlight on his face. For several minutes he lies and listens to the cries of seabirds, to the surf breaking on the nearby beach. Finally he slips out of bed. Having pulled on his t-shirt and swimming trunks, he pads barefoot across the tiled floor and out onto the terrace.

Another glorious morning. Assuming no terrorists show up to massacre him and whoever else happens be around, he can look forward to a day of blue skies and hot sun. His breakfast swim will be followed by breakfast coffee and croissants; later on, the grilled seafood, chorizo, the vino and ice-cold beer of Mallorcan-British beach life. His small seafront bar gives him a modest living. Some expats, but mostly tourists here for a good time.

It was eleven years ago, almost to the day, that he dashed into the house in the Grange and grabbed everything he'd need for his new life. DD he found slumped over the piano, hands splayed on the silent keys, her forehead resting on an unopened score. He helped her to her feet, then half-carried, half-dragged her out the summerhouse, across the lawn and down the path to the waiting taxi.

After leaving Edinburgh, he contacted the Cat on Facebook, and in return she sent him a smiley. Like the Cheshire Cat itself, the smiley slowly disappeared from the screen and he never heard from her again. St Francis's occasional emails are always short on detail, but invariably sign off with the offer of financial help, if it's ever needed. Megan, it seems, has made excellent use of the money she stole.

The sound of running water. The shower.

His two-room bungalow stands on a low hillside above one of the C-list beaches – if it rains hard enough, the stretch of stony shore looks and feels very Scottish. Out in the bay he can see a few holiday sails and swimmers making the most of the uncrowded waters. Just beyond the horizon, however, there will be refugees crammed together by the leaky boatload, drifting helplessly. And further away still, in distant capitals, arms dealers will be stirring the global pot.

When he read on the internet that Melville, 'the well-known Edinburgh businessman', had died choking on a piece of steak, he'd thought of returning to Scotland. But hadn't. Then came the independence referendum, followed by the landslide SNP election victory. Again he thought of returning. He packed, and then unpacked. Then came Brexit. And then last night's atrocity in Nice, a mere hop-skip-and-jump across the water . . .

After more than sixty years, Hume has given up trying to understand the world. Thinking is over-rated, he tells his customers. Kant's concept of *Perpetual Peace*? Not a chance. All it takes is the profits of perpetual war. All it takes is hatred, a state of mind so very, very easy to manufacture. From time to time he dreams of lining arms dealers up against the wall, any wall. It would be a start.

The shower has stopped running. In a few moments DD will come through the doorway to help him wrest the day ahead from the global chaos gathering around them. Together, they will do their best to enjoy one more day on this sun-drenched beach, one more day shared. Whatever happens.

# Acknowledgements

THE AUTHOR WOULD like to thank Product (Scotland), *1001 Nights* (Australia) and *Variations* (Switzerland), where short sections of this novel, in very early versions, were first published. Also, he would like to thank his ever-resourceful editor Nick Royle and his wife Regi for her never-failing enthusiasm and always-constructive criticism.

This book has been typeset by
SALT PUBLISHING LIMITED
using Neacademia, a font designed by Sergei Egorov
for the Rosetta Type Foundry in the Czech Republic.
It is manufactured using Creamy 70gsm, a Forest
Stewardship Council™ certified paper from Stora Enso's
Anjala Mill in Finland. It was printed and bound by
Clays Limited in Bungay, Suffolk, Great Britain.

LONDON
GREAT BRITAIN
MMXVII